The Reaper

Mark D. DiRienzo

This book is a work of fiction. Names, characters, places are the product of the author's imagination or are used fictitiously. Any resemblance to actual events, locales, or persons, living or dead, is coincidental.

ISBN:-13978-0615923932
ISBN-10:0615923933

DEDICATION

To my son, Jackson DiRienzo: You're the greatest kid anyone could ever hope to have. This is the 2nd book featuring Rick Stevens. This is OFFICIALLY considered a SERIES now! ☺ Get to reading! I love you son!

Foreword

… For me it would always be a fight between what I know to be true and what I think really happens when justice is served. Taxiing down the runway to the rest of my days, I could see her dancing, silently smiling back at me in the shadow of what is my reality.

I had been in the business of killing most of my life. It was one of the few things at which I excelled. It was one of the few times I was able to block out the misery I carried around within me. One of the very few times I didn't have to concentrate on my loss.

I felt like it was finally time to walk away. It was finally time to lay down my guns and misery and move on. I realized too late that I failed to separate the inner me from the outer professional killer. The things I did and saw in my lifetime scarred me, eliminated my faith in everything, weakened my idealism and left me feeling more lost than I ever have. I knew the time had come.

I knew I couldn't undo all of the evil things I had done. I wasn't sure I even wanted to. I was still hurt, still angry, and still wanted answers. I recognized the futility of the mission to which I had dedicated myself. For the first time in 15 years, I realized that nothing had changed or would ever change. All of the killing, all of the hurt, all of the misery, didn't change the fact that they were still gone. It didn't even lesson the pain. Nothing ever would.

Saying good bye is the hardest thing we do. We're never prepared to let the ones we love leave. It was time to end this chapter in my life. It was time to say good-bye and let go. It was time to walk away. It was time to walk away, but how do you walk away from yourself?

CHAPTER #1

Dallas Texas is a total mess in August. With the temperature hovering around 101 degrees and everything covered in cooked earth and dust, it was hard to imagine why people lived here. Every day during the summer months seemed the same, just a hot mess.

I didn't live here, although I did have an apartment here. I was hoping for a quick in and out trip for work. Six months ago, this job started in Buffalo, NY. Western New York in February and Eastern Texas in August: if I could, I would fire my boss and my travel agent. Unfortunately, I was both those people, so I would have to grind it out.

I'm a professional killer. I work for underworld organizations and kill people for money. I didn't always do this. In addition to being a skilled assassin, I was an ex-pastor, an ex-Army Ranger, and a widowed husband and father that still grieved for the loss of my wife and daughter. Right after seminary school, my wife and I were married. We were given the opportunity to move to a large church in Tennessee or a smaller church in Western NY. After much deliberation and praying, I felt that God wanted us to take the smaller church in NY.

Before my wife and daughter were taken from me, we had the perfect life. Our small house was always filled with laughter and love. It was the best life for which I could have ever hoped. That life ended one evening when a drunk driver passed my wife's vehicle on a double yellow line and ran her car into a telephone pole. It is still unknown to me today if my wife and daughter died on impact or if they burned to death in the fire that resulted from the crash.

There isn't a day that goes by that I don't miss my family.

I don't think there ever will be either. There also isn't a day that goes by that I haven't forgiven God for taking them from me. I don't think there ever will be either.

Last February in Buffalo, I killed a low-life hustler and half of his crew over some money he wasn't paying my close friend and head of the Accardo Crime Family Salvatore DiFlippo. The next day, Sal sent me to Dallas to kill a guy as a favor for the Irish Mafia based in NYC, the Westsiders.

While I was there scouting my target, Sal's then underboss, Dominick Mazzio, was planning on killing both Sal and I and taking over the family. There were a few close calls, I was even shot, but Sal and I came out on top.

I needed some help while I was in Dallas last time and Sal had a guy that was responsible for his Dallas interests. He put me in contact with him. Langston Bramwell, I know, he's not Italian, neither am I, proved to be a huge help to me in getting my Texas job done and getting back to NY to help Sal.

When the dust had cleared, Bramwell was brought into NY to be Sal's new underboss and I owed him a favor. After I healed from my gunshot wounds, I disappeared for a while to a sandy beach in South America. I've always been the most comfortable around water. If I had spoken to a Navy recruiter before the Army recruiter, I would have ended up a Navy Seal instead of an Army Ranger.

I was back in Dallas to repay the favor I owed. After this, I was taking a break for a while. Maybe permanently. My old mentor and friend from Seminary School, Bill Jenkins, has been trying to get me to come and stay with him at his home in North Carolina. He doesn't know the work I do now; all he knows is there is a huge rift between what my beliefs are now and what they used to be. He's been trying to get me to come back to the "Side of the Angels" as he calls it.

I haven't seen Bill in almost 15 years, but we stay in contact through e-mail and phone calls. I figured Bill was getting up there in age and didn't have that many years left. The least I could do was visit him and say good-bye.

The rumor on the streets of NY was that I was dead. I had died from my gunshot wounds six months ago. Sal did nothing to dissuade the rumors. I think he may have been the person that originally started them. Sal told me I should get out of the business we were in. I could if I wanted to. I had enough money put away in various banks around the world.

As tempting as the idea was, I knew I never would retire. It's not that I get a perverse pleasure from killing people. I really don't. It's just a job I do and it's something I am very, very good at. One of the best in the world actually.

I was driven by a different desire. I was angry. I figured every soul I sent to heaven was a reminder to the Big Guy upstairs that I was still here, still pissed off at him, and I would keep him busy until it was finally our time to meet. I wanted answers as to why he took my family from me and until I got them, I would continue down the road I was on. I will admit that late at night, after a few glasses of whiskey, Sal's recommendation of leaving the life was tempting.

Bramwell got his start in Sal's organization as a cleaner. It was his responsibility to go to a scene where a murder had taken place and 'clean it' to make it look like a crime had never occurred. Cleaners typically would remove and dispose of the body, eliminate all evidence, and make any repairs that were needed.

When Bramwell started in the business, he was an apprentice. He worked his way up like in any corporation and eventually he had his own apprentice. Bramwell taught his apprentice, Michael Collucci, how to be an effective cleaner.

Bramwell and Collucci parted ways and went on to live separate lives. That was until about a year ago. Collucci had been hired to clean the scene of a murder. It was supposed to be an easy job. Two guys were buying drugs from two other guys. The sellers were supposed to eliminate the buyers and keep the drugs and the money. Unknown to the sellers, the buyers were both undercover federal agents.

Cleaners are generally in position long before an operation takes place. This operation was taking place on an abandoned farm in Western New York. There was only one structure located there: an old garage. The garage backed up to Lake Ontario and was surrounded by absolutely nothing. Just plain, barren fields for as far as the eye could see.

A smart cleaner (a cleaner who wasn't lazy and just going through the motions) would have either rented a boat and came from the lake after the job was done or he would have parked far away and walked in.

Collucci did neither. He planned on hiding himself inside the abandoned garage. This was unfortunate, because the FBI was in position long before Collucci got there. In addition to having a boat in Lake Ontario, the FBI also had one of their SWAT teams inside the garage. Collucci was immediately taken into custody. Once the operation was over, one of the drug sellers talked, as all criminals do, and explained why Collucci was there.

The thought of spending his remaining days in a federal penitentiary was enough for Collucci to cut a deal. The FBI now had an informant that had worked for all the major crime families in New York and literally knew where all the bodies were buried.

Over the previous 10 months, bodies that were literally little more than bones were being unearthed and mafia bosses and their people were getting nervous as the FBI prepared indictments. No one was really sure what evidence, if any, they left behind. Remember, the majority of these killings were over 10 years old, long before shows like CSI became popular. The key to the government's investigation and indictments hinged on the word of Michael Collucci.

Collucci voluntarily agreed to go into the witness protection program in return for his testimony. Every mafia boss on the East Coast had a contract out for Collucci's life. Everyone except for Sal. Sal had never used Collucci, so he wasn't worried.

Bramwell was worried. He was worried that Collucci had talked about how he got into cleaning. Although Collucci didn't know Bramwell's real name, Bramwell was still worried about being identified. Bramwell is six feet five inches tall, with a shaved head, and a long, thick, dyed blond goatee. He weighs well over 300 pounds and has flaming black skull tattoos on each of his large forearms. In his younger days, Bramwell went inside on a stolen car charge.

It wouldn't take a genius to connect the dots from the description Collucci gave the feds to matching it to Bramwell. Instead of waiting for that to happen, Bramwell had Sal's computer hacker, Geoff, crack into the FBI's computers and find out Collucci's new identity and where he was currently living.

Geoff could do amazing things with a computer and was eternally grateful to both Sal and I for saving his life when the owner of an on-line poker website had put a contract out on him. I got a lot of the fake ID's and credit cards I used from Geoff. He also supplied me with different programs for whatever cell phone I was using that would enable me to encrypt the call and to render the GPS chip located in it useless.

Geoff liked to boast that he could crack any system, computer or data base in the world. So far, there wasn't one favor that I asked him for that he hadn't come through on. Geoff got the new identity for Collucci and gave it to Bramwell.

Bramwell gave it to me and here I was, back in Dallas Texas. Collucci was now going by the name of Thomas Hills and living in the booming metropolis of Spearman, Texas: population 3,368. Well, I guess it would be 3,369 now with Collucci living there.

Dallas was seven and a half hours away from Spearman. I could have flown into Amarillo and saved myself six hours of drive time, but my Dallas safe house was the closest place where I knew I could get a reliable weapon.

The plan was simple. Fly into Dallas, rent a car with a false identity, drive to Spearman, kill Collucci, drive on up to Guymon OK, leave the rent-a-car in long-term parking, change my appearance, rent a new car using a new ID, and drive to Oklahoma City where I would fly to North Carolina and spend some time with my old friend Bill.

As far as plans went, it was pretty good. It wasn't complicated, there wasn't a lot involved and everything about it was linear in motion. I like straight lines and moving in one direction, forward. A plan this straightforward and simple couldn't fail. So, of course, I was shocked when the whole thing went to hell.

CHAPTER #2

Salvatore DiFlippo had been in the mafia his entire life. DiFlippo's father, Armando, was a close advisor to Stefano Maggadino. Maggadino was the longest tenured boss in the history of the mafia. Through DiFlippo's long and prosperous career, he made a lot of friends. He also made a lot of enemies.

DiFlippo worked his way up through the ranks. He was never a big guy, not like his father, who was built like a fire plug. He had the long, lanky frame of a kid who never grew into his height. He had his mother's genius level intelligence. Also like his mother, people misunderstood his kindness for weakness. Make no mistake though, he was as ruthless as his father was, if not more so. People very quickly realized and understood not to cross Salvatore DiFlippo. When he was coming up in the organization, he earned the nickname "Icepick".

Nobody knows for sure the number of people he killed, but everyone knows it is a lot. Nobody ever expected the tall, quiet, shy, thin guy sitting next to them at the bar was the last person they would ever see or talk to. He would be talking to his target at a bar or restaurant, or on a bus or subway, and he would talk in an almost inaudible whisper. The person he was talking with would lean in closer to DiFlippo so they could hear him better. When they were leaning in, that's when DiFlippo would reach around their head and drive an icepick into their opposite ear.

On that warm August morning, while he was reading the paper and enjoying his espresso on the sidewalk café of his favorite local coffee shop, the last thing on his mind was a sin from the past coming back to haunt him.

Angiola Gallo was a successful business woman. In addition to owning a very successful accounting firm, she was married and had a beautiful daughter that was on the dean's list at the University of Miami. Her husband, Anthony, owned a very successful restaurant on Ocean Drive in Miami.

They both worked hard and they both earned their success. Just as their daughter, Speranza, was doing in college. Hard work was a tradition in their family. Gallo was Angiola's married name. Her maiden name was DiFlippo. Salvatore was her father.

She knew what her father did for a living. Maybe not exactly, and certainly not any of the details, but she knew he was the head of a criminal organization. She didn't harbor any ill will or bad feelings against her father for what he did. She knew her father, and knew he was a good man with a good heart. She never imagined, not in a million years, that the sins her father committed would come back on her and her family.

So I flew into Dallas and stopped at my safe house. Since this was a straight up hit and not something where I had to make it look like an accident or make the body disappear, I picked up a Whalter P22. It's a small and easily concealed 22 caliber pistol that has a 10 round detachable box magazine. I screwed on a Gem Tech sound suppressor and was ready to go. I also picked up a Glock 23. The Glock 23 is the compact version of their 40 caliber pistol. If things went bad, I wanted to have more fire power than just a 22.

I packed a few other supplies I take with me when I do jobs and I hit the road. I had a long, seven and a half hour drive in front of me. I started it by listening to one of my favorite bands, The Eels. I figured if I listened to their trilogy, Hombre Lobo, End Times and Tomorrow Morning twice, I would be in Spearman, Texas.

DiFlippo was reading about the Buffalo Bills and how well they were doing, and didn't notice the white delivery truck that pulled to a stop across the street from where he was sitting. He normally wasn't aware of his surroundings. He always traveled with at least four body guards and they were the ones that paid attention to his surroundings.

The first two shots startled DiFlippo, but didn't shock him. After all, he was a vehement man, baptized in a life of violence. He was surprised to see two of his body guard's drop to the sidewalk. By the time he put his paper down, his other two body guards were also gunned down.

DiFlippo held no false illusions about his life, or how it would end. Violent men died violent deaths. He smartly folded the paper he was reading and gazed evenly at the two ski-masked men that were crossing the street, pistols held in front of them, towards him.

Anthony Gallo heard the back door buzzer to his restaurant ringing and was surprised. He wasn't expecting a delivery, but sometimes local fisherman from the docks rang his back buzzer and offered up their catch for the day.

Gallo would often purchase the fish, but never serve it in his restaurant; as it violated too many health and safety codes. He would usually never refuse the fish, unless it was old or spoiled. All of the seafood he purchased he gave to his chefs to prepare for the staff.

So he opened the door, expecting to see a guy with a bucket full of fish. Instead, he was face to face with the business end of a semi-automatic. His last thought in this world was where did a guy get a black ski-mask in Miami?

Speranza Gallo lived in a town home off campus near West Church Street. She had one roommate that also went to the University of Miami. She was fortunate enough that her parents helped support her that she didn't have to work a full or part time job. All she had to concentrate on was her school work. And her boyfriend, Troy. He was the most thoughtful person she had ever dated. She would occasionally receive cards or flowers from him just because he was thinking about her.

She was not suspicious when the doorbell to the townhouse she rented rang. She looked through the peephole and saw a man standing there with a bouquet of flowers.

Angiola Gallo was getting into her brand new BMW 760Li sedan to head to a lunch meeting with a potential client. She hated working on Sundays, but this person was talking about sending a lot of business her way and wanted to meet for lunch and today was one of the few days he would be in Miami all month.

She had to stop by the office to pick up some paperwork and a contract that he specifically requested. She could make the sacrifice and if she landed this client, she could take off early on Friday. She was not aware that she was a widow yet. As she was putting her car in reverse, she was surprised by a security guard tapping on her driver's side window.

She braked and put the car in park. The security guard made a cranking motion with his hands, indicating she should roll her window down. She rolled her window down.

I made excellent time getting into Spearman. I am very careful and meticulous about my safety and not getting caught. When I am on a job, I like to work within my own timeline. I don't like to be rushed. When you rush, you make mistakes. When you make mistakes, you leave evidence behind. When you leave evidence behind, you go to jail. I've been killing people for close to 16 years all over the United States and I have never once been named a suspect or even a person of interest in any one of those deaths.

This job would be a little different. With a little over 3,000 people constituting the entire population, it was safe to assume anyone that wasn't a resident would be noticed almost immediately and remembered. Especially after a murder had taken place.

I figured I would have less than an hour to locate my target, kill him and get out of the town before too many people noticed and remembered me. Possibly 90 minutes, and that was really pushing things. My goal was to locate my target, finish the job and be on my way out of town all within the first 20 minutes.

My hair had grown out from the last time I got it cut. It was dyed a rusty red color and I hadn't shaved in about six months. I also had a matching, thick, NFL defensive lineman, rust colored beard. I was wearing a pair of wranglers that had the Skol tin ringed in the left hand back pocket, a used pair of cowboy boots I had picked up at a Good Will Store several years ago, a dark blue Troy Aikman Dallas Cowboy's jersey, and a matching Cowboy's blue ball cap.

I liked wearing big, baggy shirts that were not supposed to be tucked into your pants when I was going on a job. You can easily conceal all kinds of things that could be used to kill other people and no one would ever suspect anything was there.

Instead of following my target for days and learning his patterns, I had Geoff follow him electronically to see if he could find a discernable pattern I could exploit a weakness in. Geoff had all of the targets info from the FBI database, so he was able to track the target's credit and debit card purchases.

There was one glaring pattern that I could easily exploit.

Every Monday through Friday, between 12:55pm and 1:10pm, my targets credit card was charged $10-$15 at a place called Butler's Smoke House BBQ.

As the two men were approaching DiFlippo with their guns expertly trained on him, the one on the right was shouting instructions. DiFlippo found this interesting. This wasn't a hit. If it was, he would already be dead. This was something else. DiFlippo had something one of these men wanted.

This was a kidnapping. They were here to take him someplace else, someplace quiet, where they could question him, and torture him until they got what they wanted. DiFlippo knew about kidnappings and torture. He had been involved in several of each over his lifetime. He knew that once the kidnappers got you to that quiet place, few ever returned.

DiFlippo knew the highest chance he had for surviving the day would be to act right now, during the actual kidnapping.

When Speranza opened the door, she had a big smile on her face. The man with the flowers smiled at her, "Hi, you must be Speranza Gallo? Did I say that right?" he asked.

"Yes, you did. Nobody ever says my first name right! I go by Spree."

"Well Spree, someone must think you're very special, these are for you." And he smiled as he handed her the flowers. Before she could thank the delivery man, he sprayed her right in the face with liquid chloroform. He caught her before she could fall to the floor. He quickly brought her inside the townhouse and closed the front door.

His delivery van was already backed up to the garage in her driveway. He calmly walked through the house and opened the garage door. He opened the back doors to his van. He scanned the street and felt confident that anyone either walking or driving by would not be able to see him as he carried Spree from the house to the back of his van.

Angiola rolled her window down. "Yes?" she asked
"Mrs. Gallo?"

"Yes, that's me. What is it?" Without replying, the security guard raised his right hand that had been hidden from Angiola's view and fired two rounds from the Ruger LCP .380 Ultra Compact Pistol he was carrying directly into Angiola's face, killing her instantly.

I had just finished eating a very good pulled pork sandwich with a side of "Bobby's Almost Famous Beans", that really are good enough to be famous, when I recognized my target walking in. I had asked for my bill at the start of the meal so I could leave when my target arrived. I left enough money on the table to cover the bill with enough left over for a 20% tip. I walked outside to my rental car.

I found the vehicle my target was driving and backed into the spot next to the driver side. I set my rearview mirror so I could keep an eye on the front door. It was looking like I wouldn't even have to get out of my car to complete this job.

The parking lot had people coming and going but it wasn't real busy. I had my ball cap pulled low and was wearing mirrored sunglasses. I put on a pair of black Hatch neoprene gloves and waited. I kept a watch on my surroundings, and quieted my mind.

As I was scanning the parking lot, I noticed two other vehicles that each had one person waiting in them. They both arrived within minutes of each other. One was at each end of the parking lot. Our cars were in the middle of the lot.

Interesting. It was like I was boxed in. Who were these guys? Other hitters? Had someone else found the target and sent a team to kill him? Possible, but not probable. The chances of another team getting the same information that I had and being in the same place as me at the same time to kill the same person were astronomical. Kind of like winning the lottery while being attacked by a shark at the same time as being struck by lightning.

I knew I wasn't followed. This wasn't like the last job. No one was here to kill me. Everyone already thought I was dead. This was just an odd coincidence, and I don't believe in coincidences These guys were cops. The FBI keeping watch on their golden goose? I picked up my phone and speed dialed Geoff. As soon as he said hello, I jumped in. "Geoff, it's me. I need a favor. When you got the info on my latest job, was there anything else that pointed towards the FBI keeping this guy under surveillance? Any logs, or reports, or anything?"

"There was nothing. I dug through the entire case, front to back, and there was nothing. No other surveillance logs, or daily activity reports, nothing. No one knows who or where this guy is."

I could feel a headache coming on. "Well, someone knows something because there are two people watching me watch the restaurant. What about time sheets or pay logs? Is there anything like that? If the FBI has people out here, they have to be getting paid. Can you look into it and I need an answer in the next 5 minutes or so, because we'll be in that 15 minute time frame when he usually leaves."

"I'm already looking. I am cross referencing the case number, the internal file number, Collucci's personal identification number within the witness protection program and pulling everything by date. There is a ton of stuff early on, but other than the once a week meeting with a contact person, there isn't anything. I'm scanning the reports now, no, nothing. I don't know who those guys are but I can tell you without a doubt, they're not FBI."

"What about US Marshals?" I asked.

"I don't know, you told me this was an FBI operation, so I haven't checked the Marshals. I thought they just moved them and the FBI protected the asset?" Geoff replied.

I was definitely feeling a headache coming on. As much as Geoff helped me on jobs, he wasn't 'in the life'. I had never specifically asked him to monitor the US Marshals so he didn't. I was angry but not at Geoff. I was angry at myself for making such an amateurish mistake.

I thanked Geoff and hung up on him. I pulled out both of my guns. I did not like to kill bystanders when I was on a job. Especially police officers or federal police officers. They have a hard enough job for what little they get paid. Also, if you kill a cop, you'll be hunted forever, and rightfully so. Even though I work on the other side of the line from law enforcement, I have nothing but respect for everyone that carries a badge.

Just because the two people watching me weren't FBI, didn't mean they weren't police officers of some sort. My money was on them being Marshals. How they reacted to my target when he left the restaurant would tell me everything I needed to know.

Both cars started moving at the same time. One headed towards the front of the restaurant and the other drove directly towards my car. Shit! This was going to get messy. So much for my simple and easy plan. Time to improvise.

I tucked my guns beneath my shirt and popped the hood on my car, got out and lifted it up. By the time I had the hood support rod in place, I heard from behind me

"U.S. Marshal's service! Get on the ground! Right now! Do it immediately or I will shoot you! Do it now!"

It was one of the few times I hated being right.

DiFlippo still held his newspaper as the men approached. He stared evenly into his attacker's eyes, refusing to let them see the fear he was starting to feel. The man on the right, the one that appeared to be in charge, stopped a few feet away from DiFlippo and kept his gun centered on DiFlippo's chest.

DiFlippo recognized the smartness of this, as opposed to having the gun pointing at DiFlippo's head. The body was the bigger target and would take a lot longer to move out of a bullets range than the human head would.

The second man kept his gun trained on DiFlippo's head and walked right up to DiFlippo and grabbed him by his left arm, the one not holding the newspaper, and started to yank him to his feet.

"Get up old man, you're coming with…" Before the man could finish, DiFlippo let go of the newspaper and used the straight razor he was holding to slice his throat, from ear to ear.. The straight razor was a forgotten item from a forgotten time. DiFlippo's father had given it to him when he was just a boy, and it was something he loved and cherished his entire life.

DiFlippo knew he delivered a killing slice as blood spurted from the kidnapper's neck. He had definitely sliced the carotid artery. DiFlippo was turning to face the second kidnapper, fully expecting to feel the bullet enter him before his mind recognized the familiar sound of gunfire, when he felt a sudden jolt to the side of his head and everything went black.

In the span of half a second, my mind did several things

simultaneously. The first thing I thought was how to not get killed or arrested by the Marshal? The second thing I thought was two marshals on site here means there are at least two more within a mile of this restaurant. The third thing I thought was how very bad the situation I was in was and the fourth thing I thought was that it was time to move.

My guns were safely tucked into the front of my pants, hidden by my Cowboys jersey. I slowly raised my hands away from my body as I started kneeling down. Half way through my kneel down, I tucked my shoulder and rolled in between my car and the target's car. I was now out of the marshal's line of fire.

This was good because he was serious about shooting me. Not that I had doubted him before, but after the two rounds from his weapon struck the car I was using for cover, any lingering doubts were eliminated. I continued through my roll and popped up in a standing shooter's position with both my guns drawn.

The Glock had seventeen total shots in it. From the distance that separated the Marshal and I, I figured I could cross it in about 7 or 8 seconds. If I could keep the Marshal from firing back at me, I could then restrain him as opposed to killing him. Figure eight seconds, just under 20 feet, two shots a second, when I made contact with the Marshal I would still have one round left in the Glock and my 22 would still be full.

I ducked behind the car again as the Marshal fired two more shots to the spot I was just standing in a second ago. The marshal was using his car for cover, and using his radio. Things were going to get a lot worse in another minute or so.

As I started to come from behind my car to advance on the Marshal's vehicle, I raised the Glock and started firing. Just briefly, I thought about the second marshal, who was somewhere behind me. I'd deal with him next, assuming I survived the 20 foot rush.

The Marshal stayed hidden behind the back of his car, waiting for my firing to stop before he looked up to fire back at me. I rounded the car he was hiding behind with my gun trained on him, and the look of shock and surprise on his face was complete. He wasn't in a position to bring his gun up in time to shoot me, not with my gun already pointed at his face, but he tried anyway.

He never made it. Instead of shooting the Marshal in the head, I kicked him very hard in the center of his face. I felt his nose break and the viciousness of the kick snapped his head back and bounced it off of his car.

I wasn't sure if he was completely unconsciousness or not, but I kicked his weapon away and used his own handcuffs to secure him. I dropped the almost empty magazine from my Glock and inserted a new one. I figured I had another 30 seconds to eliminate my target while avoiding the second Marshal. I started heading towards the front of the restaurant.

CHAPTER #3

Kate Riley was born in Syracuse, New York and lived there until she was seven years old. Riley was the youngest of four children. She had two older sisters, and one older brother. Her father, Rob Riley, was an ex-Army Military Police Officer who also served in the Syracuse Police Department.

A close friend of his from his Army days was elected Sheriff of Madison County Alabama, and had reached out to Rob and asked if he would serve under him as a Captain. The Riley's left Syracuse, NY and landed in Huntsville, Alabama. Eventually, the Army friend retired and Rob Riley was elected Sheriff.

Rob stressed the importance of education and required all four of his children to attend college. He also required all of his children to work part-time in the Madison County Detention facility while they were in college. Rob was sure at least one of his children would be bitten by the law enforcement bug like he was and follow in his footsteps. The only child that really enjoyed the challenge of working in law enforcement was young Kate. Everyone said she was exactly like her father: honest, firm, focused, and stubborn.

Kate excelled in her studies at Calhoun Community College and was accepted to Alabama State University so she could pursue her criminal justice degree. Rob called the Sheriff in Montgomery County, who was another old friend, and Kate was able to work at their detention center while she was studying.

Kate nearly broke her father's heart when after she graduated, she decided she wanted to work in Federal Law Enforcement. With her schooling and her background, she was quickly accepted as a recruit for the Federal Bureau of

Investigation. She breezed through the academy and quickly worked her way up within the organization.

She was half way through her sixth year and currently assigned to the Buffalo, New York field office. She was writing up her final report on another case she had just cleared when the Agent in Charge, Tom Phillips, called her into his office.

Everything was working out according to plan. This payback was a long time coming. It wasn't often that everything lined up perfectly, so when it did, when opportunity knocked, you had to be ready to answer. That's exactly what Marcello Moretti had done.

There were five major crime families in New York State. The largest, The Russo Crime Family was headed by Antonio Ricci. Ricci had worked his way up through the family and spent a lot of years as the Underboss to Joseph "Lil Joe" Prisco. He learned from the old legend and now ran the largest criminal enterprise in New York State.

The second largest family in New York is the Cosimo Crime Family, and that was the family that Moretti was the head of. Like Ricci, he was an Underboss for a lot of years serving beneath one of the most brutal mafia bosses in history, James "Jimmy the Fix" Polizzi. Polizzi was known for his quick temper and violent outbursts. He once shot a man to death in a grocery store parking lot because the guy was taking too long to back out of a parking spot.

The third largest family in New York is the Camarillo Crime Family. Vince Augostino is the head of that family. Augostino was promoted to the top spot when his predecessor, Anthony "Tony the Butcher" DeMayo, was convicted on an arm's length long list of federal RICO charges (Racketeer Influenced and Corrupt Organizations Act). Tony the Butcher never did get to see the inside of a federal prison cell. Shortly after he was arrested and formally charged, someone had burned him to death with a molotov cocktail while he was locked in his cell in the secure housing unit of Rikers Island.

Mario Costa is the head of the 4th largest family in New York, the Marion Crime Family. Costa came to power the old fashioned way: by taking it. He and his Underboss, Santo "Silk" Silvino, murdered Nick "Needles" Scarfo in a horrible blood bath that ended with over 30 people dead. It is still talked about in mafia circles today.

Finally, Salvatore DiFlippo is the head of the Accardo Crime Family. He came to power when then acting boss, Peter "Petey Mass" Massino decided to retire and 'crowned' him the new king. Massino is one of a handful of mafia bosses that actually retired from the mafia and didn't die in a prison cell or was assassinated.

Moretti had respected the things DiFlippo had accomplished, but he never respected DiFlippo personally. He didn't agree with DiFlippo's soft spoken way. He didn't like the way DiFlippo ran his family. When news broke last winter that someone had attempted to kill DiFlippo, Moretti was disappointed the attempt failed.

He did learn that DiFlippo's Underboss, Dominick Mazzio, had been killed along with the best hitter in mafia history, Rick Stevens. Steven's was known in the underworld as The Reaper, but that name was only whispered, and never said aloud. All five of the families had access to Stevens, but he was only loyal to DiFlippo. DiFlippo's enemies and detractors, the few that he had, quickly, and quietly, disappeared.

Though it was never spoken, everyone knew that DiFlippo's place at the big five table was always secure as long as he had Stevens. The rumor was that while defending

DiFlippo and killing Mazzio, Steven's was shot and later died. No one knew the truth, not for certain, but Moretti had it on very good authority that Stevens was no longer amongst the living. If someone was going to make a move against DiFlippo, now was the time to do it.

Fortune smiled on Moretti a second time when he discovered two people that truly hated DiFlippo's guts and thought of nothing else for the past 20 years other than getting their revenge on him. Technically, the two he was referring to belonged to another family. Moretti had no issues with arranging to buy their freedom. He didn't want them associated with his family in case the thing he had planned went South.

It cost him a lot of money, but he had a lot of money and knew that in order to make money, you had to sometimes spend money. The initial meeting was very positive and Moretti's Underboss, Bruno Conti, laid out the plan and the new free agents were thrilled at the opportunity that was presented to them.

Very soon, DiFlippo would be out of the picture and there would only be four families left to run New York State.

As exciting as the news was that Phillips was telling Riley, she didn't understand why he was telling her. She didn't work in organized crime. She worked primarily bank robberies, and a few white collar embezzlement cases.

"Riley, you just wrapped up the bank case you were working on, right?"

"Yes. I was finishing the final report when you called me in here."

"Excellent. I want you to assist local law enforcement on this. See what's happening. Our organized crime people have been trying to get DiFlippo forever. There has been a lot of chatter and rumors the past six months regarding him. If he really was kidnapped, and is still alive, this could be a huge opportunity for the Bureau…And you."

"Sir, you said it yourself. Our organized crime people have been after DiFlippo forever. I've never worked organized crime…"

"Exactly! I think they need a pair of fresh eyes on this! Listen Riley, I know you're the best investigator this office has. This could turn out to be something huge!"

"It sounds like it could turn out to be a huge pain in the ass is what it sounds like."

"Kate. We don't even know what it is yet. Give it a day or two. Maybe three. See what the locals have. See if this looks like something we should be involved in. If it's not, you're out. I promise."

"Tom, I'll make some phone calls. I'll talk to a few cops I know. If something else breaks in the meantime, if another bank gets hit, I go back to what I'm good at. Deal?"

"That's more than fair. Thank you. You know Kate, sometimes I wonder who the agent in charge of this office is, you or I?" He said smiling at her. She smiled right back and replied

"Tom, you already know the answer to that." Then she gave him a wink and left his office.

CHAPTER #4

In a lot of places, if there were gun shots fired outside a restaurant in a parking lot, people would panic, hit the floor and call 911. In Texas, they all seemed to wander over to the windows and a few even came outside. I ran towards the restaurant, a gun in my right hand, a badge, the Marshal's I had taken off him, was held high in my left hand. I kept shouting "Federal officer! Everybody get back inside! NOW!"

The entire time I was scanning the front of the restaurant looking for the real federal officer. His car was parked half on and half off the curb, but I didn't see him anywhere. I had to finish off my target before the place was swarming with more federal officers. I knew the clock was against me and time was running out.

I figured the other marshal would go in and secure the target, but this didn't feel right to me. I was a few strides away from crashing into the front doors of the restaurant when the other marshal popped up from behind his car and fired at me three times.

Thankfully, all three shots missed me, but the third one was very close. I felt and heard it whistle by my face. An object in motion is harder to hit than a stationary target so I continued on my course and some Good Samaritan held open the door as I made it inside before shots number four and five missed me by shattering the glass in the door. I stumbled going through the door and fell very hard on my right side. Ever graceful was I.

People in the restaurant were starting to get nervous and everyone was staring at me. I held the badge up and said, "I'm a federal officer. There were two men out there trying to kill me. I took out one of them. The second one is behind that white Ford parked on the curb. What I'd like to do is sneak out the back door and circle around the restaurant so I can arrest him. If he comes into the restaurant after me, everyone get down on the floor and do what he says. I think he is pretending to be a police officer. If everyone remains calm, we'll all get out of this safely."

Three older gentlemen were still sitting in the booth that they had been in when I ate my lunch there earlier. One was still drinking coffee as if gun fights were an everyday occurrence. They spoke quietly for a few seconds between themselves then they all shook their heads and stood up.

One of them said to me "Do what he says? I don't think so. Son, if he comes in this restaurant, we'll take care of him. How 'bout we don't give him the chance of coming in? How 'bout we send some lead of our own down range? Think that would help some?"

"Excellent idea! If you've got a firearm on you, please shoot at the white Ford on the side walk out front. If you do not have a weapon or are not comfortable doing this, please get down on the floor of the restaurant. But please, try not to hit the man out there. We only want to pin him down so I can arrest him. I need him alive. He has very important information."

After that, things moved quickly. The three older gentleman and two other people in the restaurant, all drew concealed pistols from their pants and approached the front windows. I think the marshal was content to wait for reinforcements. Five guys lined up in a firing line in front of the window and all started to pull the triggers at once.

My target was in the back, on the floor, watching the men firing their guns through the front window. I walked by him, extended the 22 pistol with the silencer and pulled the trigger twice. Both bullets penetrated his head and tore his brain to pieces. I didn't even break my stride as I continued through the restaurant and out the back door.

The first thing he noticed when he regained consciousness was that he was naked. He recognized this even before he felt the cold, hard, wooden chair he was bound too. He also had a very bad headache and tasted blood in his mouth. What brought him completely back to a conscious state was the hard slap across his face, followed by the freezing cold ice water that was dumped over him.

"SALVATORE DIFLIPPO!" yelled his attacker, "It's time to wake up! Your afternoon nap is over!"

He wasn't wearing his glasses, but he could still see. He was in the finished basement of a house. He recognized the layout of the room, a basement bar on one wall, two closed doors. One would lead to a bathroom; the other would lead to where the furnace was. The walls and ceiling were complete, and there was a very nice plush carpet on the floor.

Sal noticed that the expensive carpeting beneath him was not protected by plastic or a tarp. This meant his abductor didn't care if the carpet was destroyed. It was more bad news. For a moment, Sal remembered lots of other basements, exactly like this one, where he had taken people on their final journey.

His kidnapper stood near him, smiling. He no longer wore the ski mask. His kidnapper was over six and a half feet tall and built solidly. He had very thick arms and a large, muscular chest. The kind of thickness that can only be achieved by many hours on a weight bench with a set of barbells. The type of thickness that a man puts on while he is in prison with nothing but time. Sal put on his hardest look. This was a look that had made some men urinate right in their pants. He directed this look at kidnapper and spoke quietly, "You're probably wondering why I called this meeting…" The kidnapper smiled wider and laughed.

"Oh, Salvatore! You always had that dry sense of humor. You were known for it! People didn't know if you were ever joking or not. I'm glad to see you've still got it. I'm going to be interested to see how long you keep it."

The more the man spoke, the more familiar he became. Sal didn't exactly recognize him, or his voice but it was something else that was familiar. The way the man moved or the cadence in the way he spoke. His mind was racing as he tried to figure out why he was here and a way to get out. Sal was about to ask him what he wanted, and started to, but a memory made him change his question. "Wait, I know you, don't I? Where do I know you from?"

"You hurt my feelings. Come on, you're the mighty Salvatore DiFlippo! Head of the Accardo Family in Buffalo, NY! You're all-seeing, all- knowing. Give it a minute old man. Take your time. I'm sure it will come to you."

His kidnapper continued to pace around the area in front of him. With every step he took, he became more agitated and angrier. Sal tried to think of a way to use that agitation, that anger to his benefit. That thought process sent a whirl of activity in DiFlippo's mind and he suddenly realized how much trouble he was in.

"Primo Patrizio." Sal said it as a statement, not a question.

"Winner! Winner! Give the man a cigar! Everybody just calls me Rock now old man. It's been a lot of years. I've been waiting for this. I've been dreaming about this." He smiled, clenched his fists, and walked towards where Sal was tied to the chair.

Patrick "Bull" Patrizio was hoping his older brother,

Primo, was having as much luck in NY as he was down in Florida. Bull wanted to stick together in Buffalo to take out DiFlippo and send the other two guys in their crew to take care of the Florida business. Rock refused. He said it would be better if they split up, to make sure everything went according to plan. So Bull sent Roman Russo to take care of DiFlippo's son-in-law and daughter, while he handled the delicate situation of abducting DiFlippo's grand-daughter.

He knew his brother Bull and Vito Tommaso would take care of grabbing DiFlippo in NY. He wanted to be there to extract some revenge on DiFlippo too but he eventually agreed with his brother (He always did) and went to Florida.

Russo was driving the van and Bull was sitting on the floor in the back, next to the bound, gagged and still passed out Speranza, or what had she called herself? That's right, Spree. The van was a typical white Dodge windowless panel van. They would take turns driving and sleeping. Stopping only to get gas, food or use the restroom. Spree had been fitted with a pair of adult diapers and she would have to make them last the entire 22 hour ride.

I went out the back door of the restaurant and kept going. I couldn't leave the car I rented in the lot. I was remembering the CD's I had been listening to. The CD's I had inserted into the car's radio without wearing gloves. I was angry at myself for not thinking of this beforehand. I knew the car had been shot a few times by the Marshal, and I could only hope it was in a drivable condition. Leaving the rental car behind was not an option. I was pretty sure the make and model had already been broadcasted to the other officers that were certain to be already en route to the location.

I circled the restaurant, making sure I stayed clear of the front doors and gunfire. I stayed low and made my way quickly to my car. The hood was still up. I noticed a shattered window and flat tire. I knew I didn't have time to change a flat tire.

I got back to the car and squatted next to the side of the vehicle. I took off the jersey I was wearing and removed my t-shirt. I put the jersey back on and tore the t-shirt to pieces. I opened the gas tank door and tucked one of the roiled up pieces of t-shirt into the tank. I pulled it out and repeated the process three more times. The last time, I left the tee-shirt stuck in the tank. I lit the shirt on fire. I had just created a 3,000 pound molotov cocktail.

I lit the other three pieces of t-shirt and threw them in the car. Two in the front seat, and one in the back seat. I continued through the parking lot and across the street to a home improvement store. By the time the first police cars were entering the lot, the fire in the car was raging.

I was now thankful this was Texas in August. There were several cars that had their windows down to moderate the stifling Texas heat. I walked up to an older Honda Accord and reached through the window and unlocked the door. I got in, cracked the steering column and got the car started.

I drove calmly out of the parking lot as several more police cars and undercover vehicles sped past me towards the restaurant. I heard an explosion. That would be my rental car going up in flames, eliminating all evidence that could tie the hit to me. Twenty-minutes later, I was in Perryton, Texas. I left the Honda and grabbed a new vehicle. I switched from the 15 to the 83 and headed into Oklahoma. I was still on time to make my flight to North Carolina.

I reached into my pocket and grabbed my cell phone. I wanted to call Bramwell to let him know that the job was done, so he could rest easy. The screen of the phone was cracked in half. It must have gotten broke during my fall coming into the restaurant.

If there was time, I would reach out from the airport. If not, I could reach him once I landed in North Carolina. By then, I was sure he would see the news reports and figure out he was in the clear.

It didn't go as smooth as my jobs normally do, it definitely wasn't pretty, but it was complete and it served its purpose. It quickly dawned on me, that this might be the last job I ever do. I might not ever do another hit again. I wasn't sure what I would do next. My plans went as far as getting to North Carolina and seeing Bill. After that, who knew?

"Old man, you must have been hell on wheels in your day, no doubt" Rock said. As if the physical torment wasn't enough DiFlippo thought to himself, he had to listen to this idiot verbally assault him as well.

DiFlippo could tell Rock wasn't hitting him with all his might. He was pulling his punches. Again, a man with no false illusions, he knew if he hit him one time with just half of his strength, it would probably kill him.

So far, DiFlippo had only been beaten. He hadn't been asked anything. DiFlippo knew why he was being beaten. He understood that point very clearly. He had all but forgotten about the Patrizio brothers. It had been so long ago, so far in his past. Over 20 years? He wasn't sure, but it sounded about right.

"Hey Primo, let me know when your hands get too sore from punching me. Then we can talk about what you want, or how much you want. What happened to your brother, what was his name…Patty, no, Patrick. He never made it out of prison? I figured it would be too hard for him." The big man didn't answer. He let a solid shot go that ended up breaking DiFlippo's jaw, and several of his teeth. DiFlippo was on the verge of losing consciousness, when he was hit with another bucket of ice water.

"Your problem, old man, is you forget what respect is. Remember when you were a child? You were not to speak until spoken to. You've been the top dog too long. You forget the most basic lessons. That's ok. I'll teach them to you. My brother sends his best. He apologizes he couldn't be here himself to show you how much he missed you, but he had another pressing engagement. In Miami. At your daughter's house. Then after that old man, at your granddaughter's house. What, no jokes? Nothing to say now old man?"

CHAPTER #5

Kate hated to admit it, but the case surrounding Salvatore DiFlippo was interesting. It wasn't every day that a mafia boss was kidnapped and five bodies were left behind. After talking to a captain she knew in the Buffalo PD, she decided she would take a drive out to the crime scene. On her way out, she let Phillips know she was heading there and asked he call the local cops to notify them.

She got into her two year old black Jeep Grand Cherokee and started the short drive across the city. She started to think about the case. Why would someone want to kidnap DiFlippo instead of just killing him? She did not believe there would be a ransom demand made for DiFlippo. She believed that whoever had taken him did so for personal, rather than monetary reasons.

Maybe he had some information that was critical to someone else. Maybe they would make him transfer all of his money from his bank accounts to theirs. Maybe they *had* taken him for monetary reasons. Monetary or personal, either way, she was certain they would never see Salvatore DiFlippo alive again. She doubted they would ever find his body either.

Langston Bramwell was not a man that panicked easily. Like everyone else he worked with, he had been accustomed to violence at a young age and had certain immunity to it.

However, when he received word that DiFlippo's body guards had been killed along with someone else, and DiFlippo was nowhere to be found, he was scared.

Without knowing what happened, and having never been in a position with so much authority and power before, he wasn't sure what to do.

He tried calling Steven's cell but the number was just

going directly to voicemail. He had sent him an e-mail when he first heard, but Stevens had yet to get a hold of him. He also left a message for a Buffalo Police LT that was on DiFlippo's payroll.

Bramwell then called several of his families assets in Florida that were loyal to DiFlippo and requested they secure DiFlippo's daughter. He didn't want a local cop telling her that her father was missing. He also wasn't certain what was going on and wanted to make sure she was protected. He was waiting for a call from Florida to let him know when they were safe.

Hell, he was waiting for Stevens to call, the Buffalo PD to call, waiting for a call from Florida, and waiting for a call from the kidnapers. Waiting for someone, anyone to call! Bramwell was good at a lot of things, but waiting was not one of them.

Finally! The phone was ringing…

After badging her way onto the crime scene, Riley approached where DiFlippo's body guards were still lying dead. She imagined where DiFlippo must have been sitting and where the bodyguards were standing when they were shot. She lined up the shooters sight lines, first in her head, and then she visualized them on the street.

The bodyguards were careless she thought. In her mind's eye, she could see the vehicle pull up on the opposite street corner. With four bodyguards killed without even pulling their weapons, she knew there were at least two attackers, if not more. That, and the fact that one of the attackers was still here at the crime scene with his throat slit.

No, she felt confident there were only two shooters.

There might have been one other person, a driver that maybe stayed with the vehicle? Which way did the vehicle arrive from, and more importantly, which way did it leave by? As she was piecing it together, her thoughts were interrupted by Brian Davis and his partner, Eric Wilson, the two FBI lead investigators that worked the Organized Crime (OC) desk for Buffalo, NY.

"Hey Riley, what are you doing here?" asked Wilson.

"Hey Wilson, Davis. Phillips sent me down. He's thinking this might turn into something big and he might create a task force. I've never worked OC before so tell me what you guys think."

"I think someone finally took out Salvatore DiFlippo. There was word on the street about six months ago that his underboss, Dominick Mazzio, was going to take him out and claim the family for himself" said Davis.

"Just a rumor? What happened?"

"No one really knows. One night, all the rumors just stopped. Coincidently, since that same night, no one has seen or heard from Dominick Mazzio."

"Yeah, that was also tied into the Richard Lazlo slaying on Chippewa Street, you remember that?" asked Wilson.

"Yeah, I remember something about it. I thought it was a drug deal or something. So, we think Mazzio disappeared for a while and came back and, what, kidnapped DiFlippo?" Riley asked.

"No, we think DiFlippo had Mazzio killed. We'll never find his body or hear from him again. Whoever Mazzio was working with, we think they were involved…"

"Yeah, but we just don't know who that is. We thought it might be someone from the Camarillo Family, but DiFlippo and Augostino go way back and there doesn't appear to be any bad blood between them."

"So walk me through the scene guys, what do you think happened here today?" Riley wanted to see if what she thought happened matched what the Organized Crime Investigators thought.

Davis started "DiFlippo is here reading his paper and drinking an espresso.."

"Cappuccino. All these Guiney's drink cappuccino's now.."

"Wilson, please, let your partner finish. If you disagree on how it went down, we'll talk about it at the end. Davis, go on." Riley knew she hurt Wilson's feelings, but she didn't care. The back and forth between the two of them always drove her crazy! She always thought better when she was alone or listening to music. She hated to bounce her theories or ideas off of anyone until she was nearly certain she had it figured out.

"Ok, DiFlippo's here drinking his coffee and reading the Sunday paper. His bodyguards are standing around him. From the positions of their bodies, we figure two were standing behind where he was sitting and two were standing in front of where he was sitting..." So far, she agreed with Davis. "So a car pulls up..." She interrupted him

"Why a car?"

"What? Oh, I don't know. Maybe not a car. Maybe a truck..."

"Could be a SUV or a van too...". said Wilson, trying to sound helpful.

Riley interrupted "Ok, let's just call it a vehicle for now. A vehicle pulls up, then what?"

"Then we figure, two guys exit the vehicle, cross the street, shoot the four body guards, only four shots were fired, so they knew how to handle their weapons. Then, one of them goes to grab DiFlippo and he gets his throat cut, then the other shooter, and we're assuming a kidnapping here because there isn't a body, incapacitates DiFlippo and takes him back to the vehicle and they leave."

"Wilson, you have anything to add or change?" She asked

"No, I think that's how it went down. I agree with Davis."

"Ok, here are my questions. What kind of vehicle were they using? If it was a car, they would have to pop the trunk, probably before they hit the body guards, and that would raise some suspicion with the body guards. I don't see it being a car, right? I am not seeing it being a pick-up truck either. It's not a practical vehicle to use during a kidnapping. Even if it had a cab or hard back they would still need to secure DiFlippo in the back. If not, he would be rolling around back there, getting beat to hell. A man his age could end up dead. That would go against kidnapping him. If they were going to kill him, he would be on the street next to his body guards, right? So right now, I say a truck is a long shot."

She continued, really just thinking out loud at this point. "An SUV is possible, but you run into the same issues. Securing DiFlippo in the back of the SUV, then what if you get stopped by a cop or someone sees him struggling in there? No, I don't like the SUV idea either. It's better than a car or truck, but a van is better yet."

"With a windowless van, they could pop the back doors or side sliding door but not have them opened all the way. Once they had DiFlippo, they could toss him in the back, secure him, and even hide him if they had to. Yeah a van feels right...Or almost right..." She stopped talking. There was something that was bothering her...She was close...

"What is it?" Wilson said

"Eric please. Just be quiet. Let me think..." It was gone. *Damn it!* Her concentration was gone. It was right there! Just something was off. She started walking through it again in her mind. The bodyguards. Why didn't they draw their guns when the van or vehicle pulled up across the street? She agreed with Davis's assessment on where they were standing, so they would have seen the vehicle pull up and yet, not one of them had drawn a weapon.

Riley examined the way the dead shooter was dressed but didn't see anything that was out of the ordinary. He was wearing jeans, black boots, a short sleeve blue polo-style shirt and a light blue zip up windbreaker. Other than the black ski-mask, everything else about the would-be kidnapper was normal.

"Eric, Brian, why didn't the bodyguards react when the vehicle pulled up across the street? All four of them should have seen it. If two suspicious guys got out, wouldn't at least one of the guards have pulled a weapon?"

"Good point Riley. I was thinking the same thing, maybe they had some kind of uniforms on or something, but, the way this guy is dressed, he just looks like a regular guy." Wilson said. All of a sudden, she had it!

"What do you think Riley? You have this look…"

"It wasn't how they were dressed! It's what they were driving! The body guards see a vehicle pull up. They dismiss it as a non-threat, why? Because it fits in with the area, with one of the businesses. Check the businesses on this block. What makes sense for a Sunday morning?" They looked around the block. There was the restaurant, next to the restaurant was a closed shipping and receiving store, and on the other side of the restaurant, there was an alley and then a hotel.

Across the street, there was a strip mall that had a health food store, a high end liquor store, a store that sold gourmet dog treats and a ladies clothing store. There was only one place it could be.

"It's got to be the hotel. They pull up in a truck, a delivery truck or something. They start crossing the street to the alley; it looks like they are heading to the hotel…"

Wilson interrupted her thought process "Maybe they were wheeling a handcart or carrying a box or something. The guards don't mark them as a threat; the first two get popped and go down. Before the next two can react, they're taken out as well."

"Exactly!" Riley continued "So we're looking for a delivery truck of some sort. Could be a van, something along those lines. Maybe a produce truck, or a food truck or…"

"A laundry truck!" Davis said.

"Yes. A laundry truck would be perfect! It would fit in, the way the shooter is dressed would make sense and it would be the perfect vehicle to kidnap someone in. We need to get video. Get the Buffalo PD to canvass the entire block. I want video from every store in an eight block radius. Call the city. I want the video from all the traffic lights at all the intersections. Check all the stores, private businesses. Anywhere there is an ATM, there's probably video. Make sure we get those."

"There's a bank two blocks up with a drive up ATM in front of the building. It's Sunday though, the banks not open. We might have to wait until tomorrow."

"No we don't. I have a list of every bank and bank manager's home phone number. I'll make some calls. Let's put this together. The clock is ticking."

Back at DiFlippo's estate, Bramwell was wishing he never answered the phone.

"Manny, slow down, tell me one more time. In English this time! All of it in English! I don't understand a word of Spanish!" Manny Rios was in charge of DiFlippo's business interests in Miami. He was the Florida version of Bramwell, before Bramwell was brought back to Buffalo and promoted.

Manny Rios was born in Cuba and immigrated to the United States in 1959 with his parents, Eusebio and Blanca, after the Cuban Revolution and Castro taking power. Manny's father worked as a fisherman in southern Florida. Often times, Manny helped his father out on the charters he ran. It was on one of these charters that Manny and Eusebio met DiFlippo.

Manny and Eusebio impressed DiFlippo with their hard work and attention to detail. He went out of his way to get to know them on a personal level over his three day charter. At the end of the trip, Eusebio and DiFlippo were friends. Where other people would have only seen an immigrant and his son scraping by, DiFlippo saw an opportunity where he could help enrich the life of a new friend.

DiFlippo steered business to Eusebio. So much business, that he had to buy another boat. Then shortly after that, a third boat. Blanca went from making cooler lunches for fisherman, to running a very successful catering company. Eusebio and DiFlippo remained friends until Eusebio passed away. Manny recognized what DiFlippo had done for his family. He didn't give them a handout, but provided them with an opportunity because he believed in them. Manny never forgot that and he was fiercely loyal to DiFlippo because of it.

That's why Bramwell was having such a hard time understanding Manny. Not only was Manny speaking in half English and half Spanish, he couldn't control the tears that were streaming from his eyes because of the feeling of having failed DiFlippo.

"I'm sorry, man, you know? This is hard. I failed man! *Me gustaría estar muerta!*"

"Damn it Manny! English! Say it in English!"

"Sorry Bramwell. Angiola and Anthony, they're both

dead! DEAD!" Bramwell was speechless. Literally speechless. Without conscious thought, he pulled the receiver away from his face and just stared at it for a few seconds. In times of distress, it was often the man that was able to think and make decisions that succeeded. He had learned that from DiFlippo.

"Manny, tell me what happened." In half English and half Spanish, through cries of anguish and tears, Manny told Bramwell what had occurred in Florida. He finished by saying he could not locate Speranza. The police were also looking for her, but no one could locate her. Bramwell filled Manny in on the situation with DiFlippo.

"Listen, I'll keep doing everything I can to find DiFlippo. You do everything you can to find Speranza and Manny, reach out to everyone you know. I don't care if you have to threaten them, buy them, whatever. Someone is going to know something. Find out what it is. You need anything, I don't care what it is, you tell me. You need a crew? I'll have one there in hours. You need a cleaner? I'll have one there before the body is cold. You need cash? Name the price. You get where I'm coming from here Manny? Oh, and Manny? I need you. You're my guy down there. I need you on your game. We can feel bad after we get Sal and Speranza back. But right now, right this very second, I need you handling this, the way Sal would expect you to. Got it?"

CHAPTER #6

The flight into North Carolina was quiet and uneventful. I was pressed for time and didn't have a chance to call Bramwell. After we landed, I used a pay phone. His phone didn't even ring; it just went to voice mail. I told him the job was complete and I would be in touch with him and Sal in a few days.

I rented a car and stopped at a drug store to buy a few toiletries. I never check bags on a plane, so I always pick up what I need when I arrive at my destination. As I was at the car rental counter, for just a second I considered renting the car in my real name. I wondered what it would feel like to travel and rent a car in my real name. Would I ever feel comfortable doing that? Could I really just walk away from the past 15 years?

Once I got to the hotel, I took a long, scalding shower. I rinsed all the hair color out of my hair and shaved off the beard. When the mirror became un-fogged, I barely recognized the person staring back at me.

I had new scars from my recent gunshot wounds. My black hair was starting to grey at the temples. If I had not put color in my beard, it would also have been mostly grey. Time was catching up with me. I got dressed and headed to the hotel's bar for a cold beer and a burger before bed. Maybe a little whiskey as well. Hopefully they would have Buffalo Trace, but if not, Old Number 7 would do just nicely.

Spree woke up very groggy. She didn't know where she was and couldn't remember what happened to her. Her arms and shoulders burned and she couldn't see. She was also having trouble breathing. Where the hell was she?

Slowly it started to come back to her. Her boyfriend sent

her flowers…No, the delivery guy did something to her. As she become more awake, fear and panic started to take hold. She started to remember what happened and she wished she didn't. Her arms and shoulders burned because of lactic acid build up. Her hands were cuffed behind her back and she couldn't move them. She had a hood or something over her face. It was hot and humid and she had to pee.

"Hey, I think sleeping beauty is finally awake" Russo said. Bull was driving the van. Even though Spree had a pulse, he was starting to worry that he had sprayed her with too much chloroform. He was wondering if she was ever going to wake up. He felt relieved when he heard her try to scream for help. The duct tape covering her mouth would prevent that from happening.

"Hey sleeping beauty, we've got a long trip a head of us. If you have to use the bathroom, you'll go in your pants. You're wearing an adult diaper. You're not going to eat anything or drink anything until we get to where we're going. Once we get there, we'll see. Just so you know what's going to happen. We're going to torture and rape you. Repeatedly. It's going to be horrible for you. We're going to have a bunch of other people rape you as well. It will be painful, degrading and you'll wish you were dead. Don't worry, when we've used you up, that's exactly what you'll be. Dead."

The kidnappers no longer wore masks. They didn't care if Spree saw their faces. She would never have the opportunity to identify them to the police. Their orders were clear. Threaten the victim, create and cause as much physiological damage as they could but they were not allowed to rape or disfigure her in anyway. At least, not until after they got everything they needed from DiFlippo. After that, all bets were off. After that, they could do anything they wanted.

I got up early, had a big breakfast wiped the hotel room down. Then I drove to Bill's house. I had called him late the night before from the bar and told him I was going to be in town for a day or two and would love to see him.

I had never been to Bill's house before. That was a shame, because it really was a beautiful place. He had a ranch style farm house that sat on a hill. The ground behind his house sloped down to reveal a large barn and beyond that, a pond. After the pond, the forest started and across the valley, I could see the rise of the mountains.

I couldn't help but think back to an earlier time when I stood at a crossroads. I had a choice. I could get on a plane and come here to stay with Bill. The second option was to get into a car and have lunch with Sal. I had chosen to go see Sal instead of coming here to see Bill. That lunch meeting changed my life. That lunch started me down the path I was on.

It was hard not to imagine what kind of life I would be having right now if I had chosen to come here instead. Maybe it wouldn't have been different at all. Maybe after leaving here and going back to Buffalo, Sal would still meet me for lunch and still give me the identity of the person responsible for killing my family. Maybe I would still kill that person and end up working for Sal.

My thoughts were interrupted by the front door opening. My old friend and mentor, Bill Jenkins, walked out the front door wearing an ear-to-ear smile. "My goodness, I am so happy to see you!"

Even though we talked occasionally and stayed in contact through e-mail, I was still surprised to see how old my friend looked. I had only seen him one other time in the past 15 years. I was in North Carolina doing a job and after the job was over, we met for dinner before I jumped on a plane. I couldn't help smile back at him.

"Hi Bill, you look great! I am happy to see you too!" And I was. I truly was.

Bill and I spent the entire day sitting on his back deck, overlooking the valley and catching up. We drank homemade sweet tea and talked for hours. It was the first time in 15 years I can remember doing something so simple, so normal.

After several general answers, and steering the conversation in different directions, Bill finally said "I'm going into the house to get some steaks for the grill. I picked up some fresh potato salad and I have some corn on the cob I got from a farmer friend. I'll roast it on the grill with the steaks. We'll have a great dinner and, when we're finished, you'll tell me about what you've been doing for the past 10-15 years."

A few hours later, after a great dinner, I helped Bill clean up and put the dishes away. He opened the cabinet above his fridge and pulled out a bottle of whiskey. He poured us each a few fingers over ice in crystal glasses and we went back out to the back porch.

The sun was down, the valley was dark and there was a slight, intermittent breeze. I sipped my whiskey, looked up into the night sky and started talking. I started at the beginning; from the minute he left me a plane ticket in Buffalo to come see him. I told him everything. I told him how I felt betrayed by God; I told him I had killed literally hundreds of people.

I told him I was paid by different mafia families to do the killing but would have done it for free. I told him it was a way I was getting back at God. He had taken my family from me and I was angry. I killed people and sent their souls to judgment as a reminder that I was still here and I was still hurt. As I was speaking to him, he never questioned me. The more I talked, the easier it was.

I talked for over an hour straight. It was the longest conversation I had had in over 15 years. Bill refilled our glasses several times throughout that hour. I ended by saying, "So that's what I've been doing for the past 10-15 years. Bill, I'm still angry, I'm still hurt, but I'm tired now too. The best thing for me these days is when I am asleep. At least there, I can dream of them, still have them, hold them, in some way."

"Rick, I'm sorry. I'm so sorry."

"Sorry? Why? Bill…"

He held up a hand to stop me. "I'm sorry because I wasn't there for you when you needed me most. I knew I never should have left Buffalo without you back then. I prayed for you. I prayed for the Lord to carry you through the sorrow and darkness you were experiencing. I'm sorry I didn't do more to help you back then."

"You did enough. You did more than anyone else did to help me. I know that, knew it back then. Julie and Faith were my reason for existing. They kept me grounded; they were my tether to the world. When they were taken from me, I was just lost. You were there you remember…"

"Rick, it wasn't your fault. They weren't taken from you because of anything you did in the Army. God works in mysterious ways, but he doesn't work like that."

"How do you know? How can you be so sure?"

"My faith, the scriptures and my personal relationship with Christ. We serve a kind, loving God. He doesn't want anyone of us to suffer…"

"And yet Bill, he allows it. He allows people that have harmed no one to suffer horrible things. How is that kind or loving?"

"We live in a world that has lost sight of what is truly important. We have taken our eyes off of God and the world is corrupt and full of sin…"

"So he's turned his back on the world? Lost interest in this little science experiment?"

"Rick, please. Hear me out. You know God has a plan for everyone. You know we don't know His plan, understand his time-line or get to see how the story ends. That's where faith comes in."

"I've lost my faith Bill. I lost it years ago." Bill's reaction to my statement surprised me. He smiled and chuckled a little bit. I asked him what he thought was funny.

"You haven't lost your faith Rick. You still believe. You said so yourself. You're angry and in pain so to remind God you're still mad you kill people to send Him their souls. Rick, if you lost faith, you wouldn't be angry at God. You wouldn't be killing people to remind him you're still here."

I was about to argue the point with him, but I didn't. Maybe he was right. I needed to think about what he said. The five, no wait, six glasses of whiskey I had weren't helping me concentrate. He continued, "It's late. I've had more whiskey tonight than I have in the past six years put together. The guest bedroom is made up for you. You'll stay here tonight and we'll talk again tomorrow. I'll pray for you tonight Rick." With that, he got up and went into the house. I finished my whiskey and went in after him.

Bull, Russo and Spree made excellent time and arrived at their destination in under 22 hours. A house was rented in Bella Vista Arkansas. Bella Vista is in Northwest Arkansas, in Benton County, and is located between Bentonville and the Missouri state line. There are approximately 24,000 residents in the community, which covers roughly 65 square miles.

Bella Vista is primarily a retirement community and has eight lakes and lots of hills and forests. The house Bull pulled up to was at the end of a private road, on top of a hill. The house had one story and a walkout basement.

After making sure the house was empty, Bull and Russo carried a struggling Spree down into the basement. They each took turns urinating on her and then left her lying on the floor.

Bull sent Russo into Missouri to stock the house full of groceries. While Russo was out shopping, he called his brother. It was the first chance they had to talk other than to give status updates. They were both happy and excited with each other's progress. All Bull had to do was wait. Rock had a little more work to do with DiFlippo and then they were home free. Once Rock executed the next part of their plan, he would leave New York and head down to Arkansas. He figured he would be on the road within 48 hours.

After a fitful night of sleep, I was up early and hung-over. I put on a pair of warm-up pants and a t-shirt and went for a long run through Bill's property. I needed to clear my mind and think about our conversation from the night before. I ran for 45 minutes before returning to Bill's house. I estimated the distance I traveled just over five miles.

When I got back to Bill's, I took a shower and got dressed. When I left my bedroom, Bill was in the kitchen cooking us breakfast. He had fresh eggs scrambling from his chickens, and bacon cooking in the oven from a hog he slaughtered a few months ago. Everything smelled wonderful. I poured myself a cup of strong coffee and sat down to eat.

After breakfast, we cleaned the kitchen again and were on the back porch with fresh squeezed lemonade. Like yesterday, Bill started the conversation off.

"Our conversation troubled me last night Rick. I thought about it all night. I prayed about it."

"I knew you would be disappointed Bill. I know. I'm

sorry for letting you down. I'm…"

"Rick stop. Let me finish. I can't justify what you did. I don't even think I fully understand your reasoning behind it. It doesn't matter though. What matters now is what you do next."

"That's the thing. I don't know what to do next. I've been doing this for a long time Bill. I'm not sure I can do anything else. I've got enough money that I don't ever have to work again but I just don't see sitting on a beach somewhere until I die as a realistic option."

"Travel the world, see the sights, and fall in love…"

"I did that when I was in the Army and I fell in love with Julie. That was my chance. It's over now."

"So that's it? You'll never love again? Since she's been gone, you've never been interested in another woman or interested in meeting someone else?"

"No. Not even close. There's not a day that goes by that I don't miss my family. I'm not over them now and I'll never be."

"I'm going to ask you a question. I don't mean it in any offensive way, and if you are offended, please forgive me, but I need to ask it. What if it had been you that was taken in the car accident, rather than Julie? Do you think she would go the rest of her life without loving again?"

I was not offended, not really, I don't think, but I was worked up. Bill's question did bother me, but I didn't exactly know why. I had never thought of this before, at least not in the simple way Bill had put the question.

I stared out into the valley from Bill's back porch and sipped my lemonade and gave Bill my honest answer. "I don't know."

"I'm going to push it a little further now. Remember Rick,

I knew Julie too. Not as well as you, but I knew her. I know how wonderful and special she was. I'm going to ask this, and I don't want an answer. I want you to think about it and answer it to yourself. I'm going to ask this and then I have to lie down for a little while. Would Julie want you to go through the rest of your life without loving again? Would you want her going through the rest of her life without loving again if the situation was reversed?" Then true to his word, Bill got up and went into the house and took a nap.

I sat there, alone, and thought about his questions. I looked to my glass of lemonade and decided that wasn't nearly strong enough to face the answers to Bill's questions. I went inside the house and pulled the bottle of whiskey out and added a healthy dose to my lemonade. I recognized that I was stalling and trying not to answer the questions. We can lie to anyone else, except ourselves. I went back outside and sat down.

The answers were simple. Of course I would want Julie to fall in love again. Of course I would want her to be happy, that's all I ever wanted for her. That's all she ever wanted for me too. I finished my drink and wept.

Bill took me to a great place for BBQ. We had a great lunch and talked about everything except our earlier conversations. It's rare to find a friend that you've seen once in the past 15 years and when you do see him you tell him you've worked for the mafia as a murderer for hire and he doesn't judge you.

We spent the rest of the afternoon and early evening driving around the town where Bill lived. He showed me the church he was still pastoring at. He asked if I wanted to go inside, but I respectfully declined his offer. He just smiled, chuckled, and said "baby steps" and we drove off.

We grilled chicken and ate more potato salad and corn on the cob. After dinner and clean up, we retired to the back porch with more whiskey. Our conversation was subdued. There were moments of long silence between us, but it wasn't uncomfortable. I knew we weren't done talking yet.

"I just feel like if I found someone else, I would feel, I don't know, unfaithful to Julie and Faith or something. Over time, I fear that the memories I cherish would fade away. Does that make sense?"

"It does, and it's an understandable fear, but it's not correct. We were created to be social. We were created to love and be loved. The memories of Julie and Faith will never fade Rick; they will never lessen or be tarnished because you are making new memories with someone else."

"I just don't know how to let them go…" I said this with tears in my eyes.

"Rick, you don't have to let them go. Don't you see that? They'll always be there. They'll always be a part of you. They're gone from here, but they still exist, in Heaven and in your heart. They'll always exist in both places."

We talked for a few more hours. We drank more whiskey. We both laughed and we both cried. When I finally went to bed that night, when I closed my eyes, I thought of Julie and Faith like I do every night, but it was different. I can't explain it, I don't understand it myself. I didn't feel ashamed, or maybe, I didn't feel like Julie was looking down from Heaven and feeling ashamed of me.

CHAPTER #7

Using the different video images from various businesses, Kate was able to track the delivery truck until it got onto the I-90 (New York State Thruway). Before she started calling to request video for every traffic light for every exit the way the truck was traveling, Davis got a report from the New York State Troopers that the truck was found under an overpass, empty. It was on the way to the FBI crime lab to be processed.

They were on the right track though. The truck was a stolen laundry truck that serviced the hotel next to the restaurant where DiFlippo was abducted. Wilson and Davis were working the phones and their criminal informants (C.I.'s) trying to get a lead on what happened. They were waiting for something to happen: a CI to give up some information, the crime lab to come up with a new lead for them to run down, contact from the kidnappers, something.

Kate had all of the video that they had of the truck from where it was stolen until it got on the I-90 burned onto one computer's hard drive. She was going through the video, frame by frame, to see if there were any helpful clues when Phillips called her into his office. Kate went in and sat down. Phillips was just finishing up on a phone call.

"Ok, Mayor, no problem. Thank you." He hung up the phone and addressed Kate, "Do you know who that was Riley?"

"The Mayor?"

"Huh? Oh, yeah. Sorry. Yeah, it was the Mayor. He wants to know what happened to DiFlippo and what we're doing to get him back!"

"The Mayor does? Is he dirty Tom?"

"I didn't think so, Kate, but he sounds pretty tight with

DiFlippo. We're putting together a task force. I'm going to run it and you're going to be my number 2."

"Tom, we're barely into this thing 24 hours and we're already at a dead end. Why are we putting a task force together for an old Mafia guy?"

"Because it's not just about DiFlippo anymore. His daughter and son in law that live in Miami were killed yesterday and, are you ready for this Kate? His granddaughter is missing!"

"Kidnapped?"

"We don't know, not for sure, but that's the assumption we're going with. We're putting together a duel task force with the Miami office and we're going to run a parallel investigation with them on this! They just e-mailed all the info they have on their end to us and I did the same. I need you to start going through it right now. I just sent it to your in-box."

"Tom, this is huge. This is going to be a mess. There is no way this is going to end well."

"I know Kate, that's why we're going to run it and push it to the end. Between you and I, I don't give a shit about DiFlippo, but his granddaughter is what we need to concentrate on. That's who we have to save. I'm going to call an all staff meeting in 20 minutes and announce the task force. What are Davis and Wilson doing?"

"Working the phones, trying to dig up a lead."

"Ok, after our meeting, get with them and get a list of who's who in DiFlippo's organization and I need you to get out there and start interviewing them. See what you think, see if they have anything helpful."

"Let me go through the Florida file first and then I'll see if I can find someone who will talk to me."

"Fine, fine. Kate, this is a huge opportunity for both of

us. You realize that, right?"

"Tom, I work all my cases the same. I don't just put effort into the cases that might help my career."

"I know that Kate, that's not what I'm saying. If we can crack this, get the girl back safely and maybe shut down DiFlippo's organization, this is my ticket to D.C. This will be your ticket to running your own office Kate!"

The next morning I was awoken by a knock at my bedroom door. I looked at the clock and was surprised to see it was just after 6:00am.

"Rick? I'm sorry to wake you" Bill said through the bedroom door, "But I need to talk to you. It's important."

"I'm up. I'll be out in a minute." I got out of bed and walked to the door. As soon as I opened the door and saw the look on Bill's face, I knew something was wrong. I knew something terrible had happened.

"What is it Bill. Just tell me."

"I caught the end of a news report on Fox when I got up. The FBI had a press conference. From what I can understand, Salvatore DiFlippo is missing." Bill knew Sal and I were friends and after the past two days, he knew how close Sal and I were.

I went out into the living room and surfed the news channels until I found the report. As I stood there watching the news report, I felt like throwing up. I was also very angry. "Bill, I need to use your phone."

I called Bramwell. I got his voice mail. I hung up and called Geoff on his private line. He didn't answer. I was frustrated and wanted to throw the phone across the room. "Bill, I need to use your computer."

I shot an e-mail to Geoff and Bramwell telling them what number I could be reached at. I told Geoff he had exactly 5 minutes to call me or I would be very angry with him.

Approximately 18 seconds after I sent the e-mail, Bill's phone started ringing. "It's for me" I told Bill and I answered it "Hey!"

"Rick, man, I'm sorry, I didn't recognize the number, and when I did a phone search I didn't recognize the name…"

"Geoff, forget it. Listen, I'm calling from an unsecure landline. I need you to get in touch with Bramwell and tell him to answer his damn phone! I also need a ticket on the next plane to Buffalo. I need to get there ASAP. I have one ID left. So you'll have to…" Geoff interrupted me.

"I just booked you a private flight that will be ready to leave when you get there. You won't need to show any identification. Tell them your name is Mr. Jones. You'll be good to go. It's already paid. For an additional 'pre-screening security fee' you won't have to show ID or need a ticket. You'll be leaving from a private airfield that is within 10 miles from the location where you called me from. What else can I do?"

"I'll be picking up a pre-paid cell phone, after I get it I'll…" Geoff interrupted me again.

"Done. On the way to the airfield is a Wireless Hut. A phone will be waiting for you, already activated and paid for. I'll text you the program, just download it. I let the store know you were pressed for time and would have less than a minute to spend their or else you would miss a very important flight. Go to the main counter and ask for Mike. Tell him you're Mr. Jackson and he'll hand you the phone."

"Geoff, thank you. I'll be in touch." I turned around and Bill was standing there.

"Bill, I…"

"It's ok Rick. You have to go. I understand."

"I've got to go back to Buffalo and see what's happening with Sal. If I can, if I'm not too late, I have to help him."

"I know you do. I wouldn't expect anything else." Then he smiled the saddest smile I had ever seen. We embraced.

"Bill, thank you again. For everything. I can't thank you enough."

"If you want to thank me Rick, then come back when you can."

"Deal. I'll be back Bill. Whenever this is over, I'll be back. I promise." I went into my room, got dressed and packed my stuff. Five minutes later, I was out the door and heading to the Wireless Hut to get my new phone. In a few hours I would be back in Buffalo.

DiFlippo was in bad shape. Rock had gone to work on him, hard. He knew he had broken bones and possibly internal bleeding. He knew he was very close to dying. Without medical assistance he would perish.

He would gladly accept death at this point. The thought of what Patrick, or Bull as he was now called, was doing to his granddaughter made DiFlippo wish for death. Not to mention what had been done to his daughter and son-in-law. Today would be DiFlippo's last day on earth. He would die a horrible, painful death. He was sure because he planned on instigating Primo and sending him into a killing rage.

The basement door opened and Primo walked in carrying a hammer and a bucket of water.

"Good morning Sal. Glad to see you're awake and conscious. I'll set the water aside. I'm sure I'll need it later. We've got a lot to do today old man. A lot to do…"

I picked up the phone without any issues. As soon as I got back into my car, I downloaded the file Geoff had texted me. This was the file that would 'cloak' my cell phone. The NSA would not be able to listen in on any of my calls or use the GPS chip to find where I was located. I called Bramwell, and he picked up on the first ring. Geoff was three for three today.

"Bramwell, it's Rick…"

"RICK! I've been trying to get a hold of you…"

"I know, I'm sorry, I went off the grid for a few days. Bring me up to speed." Bramwell did. He told me everything he knew about the Sal's kidnapping. He also told me about what happened in Florida. It looked like a double kidnapping occurred after Sal's daughter and son-in-law were murdered.

48 hours. I kept thinking all of this happened in the last 48 hours because everyone thought I was dead. No one would have even thought of doing this if they knew I was alive. This was my fault. Sal was missing and his remaining family was dead because I wanted to walk away. He was suffering because I wasn't strong enough to continue on the course that I chose.

"I'll be in Buffalo this afternoon. I'm supposed to be on the ground 90 minutes after we take off." I told Bramwell what private airfield I was flying into and he said he would send a car to pick me up. "I'll see you soon Bramwell. We'll take care of this. I promise."

Bramwell had just hung up the phone with Stevens. He felt better that Stevens would be here by the afternoon. He always thought it was a mistake for Sal to let people think Stevens was dead, but he had just been promoted to the #2 spot and didn't feel comfortable voicing his concerns. People were going to be shocked when they found out Stevens was alive.

He was about to call Rios in Florida for an update when he was buzzed.

"Mr. Bramwell?"

"Yeah, hey, listen Maria, it's just Bramwell. Mr. Bramwell

was my father." His secretary or assistant or whatever the hell she was insisted on calling him Mr. all the time. It made him feel old and damn uncomfortable.

"Yes sir, sorry. The FBI is here to see you."

"What?"

"Yes sir, the FBI is at the front gate to see you. The lady said she wanted to talk about Mr. DiFlippo. What should I tell her?"

"Tell her she's shit out of luck. Tell her I'm not here. Set an appointment with her and then call Rosenberg and get his ass over here. If the FBI wants to talk, we'll have the family lawyer present for that."

"Yes sir, I'll tell her."

The FBI? It made sense. A high profile kidnapping like Sal would constitute the FBI getting involved. Bramwell was sure they knew about the problems in Florida and Sal's missing granddaughter. Before he talked to the FBI, he wanted to talk to the lawyer and Stevens. He picked up the phone and dialed Rios's cell phone number.

Money. No matter what it was, it all boiled down to one of two things: Money or sex. With the Patrizio brothers it was about money. They wanted to be compensated. If Sal wasn't dying, he would almost think this was funny.

"The way I figure it, you still owe us our cut from the job. That would be $25,000 each, so $50,000. Add on another $25,000 in interest for the past 20 years and we're at $75,000. Now, we're going to add in another $25,000 just because you're tied to a fucking chair and I say so, so we're at $100,000 for the job. $100,000 each, that is."

Sal didn't want to tell him his math was off and that he already added his brother's take in on the front end to get to $50,000. So they wanted $200,000, big deal. Sal could have that amount here in minutes, seconds.

"Now, let's talk about a silence fee. After that, we'll talk about a yearly salary, for my brother and I, for 20 years, plus hazard pay, and missed holidays..."

" Gimmie-r-tuttle" *Give me your total.* It was hard for Sal to talk with a broken jaw and missing teeth.

"I didn't catch that old man. Let me finish." Sal was now wishing he would die because this uneducated half-wit liked to hear himself speak. Sal's mistake was forgetting about the Patrizio brothers. He should have reached out and had them killed while they were in prison.

"...So, if my math is correct.." No chance of that DiFlippo thought "You owe Bull and I, five million dollars." Five million dollars DiFlippo thought? Five million dollars? Now he thought he was going to die because of an aneurism. Now DiFlippo was really angry. Five million dollars? DiFlippo made more than that every year in his legitimate business dealings! He wouldn't even have to call Geoff to arrange the transfer of five million dollars! His regular banker could do that!

"Drun"

"Did you say 'done' old man?" DiFlippo shook his head yes. "Oh, I meant, 7, no, 8 million dollars. Yeah, 8 million dollars." DiFlippo recognized his mistake. If he wasn't close to falling into unconsciousness, he wouldn't have made the mistake he made. If he agreed again, Rock would want more money. DiFlippo's family was already gone, he was dying, and he had nothing to lose.

"Huck roff"

"What?"

DiFlippo took his time. "Fuck off"

"Salvatore! Respect please! I could easily kill you! Or

torture you more. We're just two business men discussing business now." DiFlippo never wanted to kill anyone more than he wanted to kill Primo. He concentrated and took his time and pronounced the words the best he could.

"Srix ril rr krell mre. Sero." *Six mill or kill me. Zero* |

"Maybe I take the six million and kill you anyways?"

CHAPTER #8

Now Kate was pissed off. Set an appointment? Really?

"Ma'am, this is a federal investigation I'm running. I asked to be nice, but I'm done being nice now. Open the gate." After almost a minute of silence, the intercom came to life again.

"I'm sorry, but I'm the only one here right now. The estate is empty at the moment."

"Fine. Open the gate and you and I will talk. In person." Another minute of silence.

"What was your name again Agent?"

"Special Agent Riley, ma'am and in case you forgot, I'm with the Federal Bureau of Investigation." She was trying hard to get into the compound. After September 11th, everyone went out of their way to appease the FBI. Talking to DiFlippo's secretary without anyone else present could be gold mine!

"I'll open the gate Agent, but first, just hold your warrant up to the camera so I can verify you have a legal reason to enter the property. I mean, if you're *really* with the FBI, then I'm sure you would have a warrant."

Now Kate was really pissed off. "Ma'am, I'll be back this afternoon with a warrant. I was hoping not to have to go that route. I am here trying to help gather important, time sensitive information that might just save Mr. DiFlippo's life. If you want to play games and he dies, that's on you. I will be back this afternoon and rest assured, you and I, we're going to talk. In person."

Kate turned around and drove to the end of the street. She called her boss and let him know the situation. He said he would find a friendly judge and call her back. It was a touchy situation because they weren't questioning people because they were suspects in a crime, and they did not have any evidence, so getting a warrant was probably unlikely. He would talk to the FBI lawyers and then call a judge.

In the meantime, she would wait outside the compound for 60 minutes or until Tom called her back. If anyone showed up to enter the compound, she would piggy back her way in behind them. Fifteen minutes later, her patience was rewarded.

Moretti had just received the latest status update and was very happy. Everything was going exactly as he had planned. He opened a bottle of Johnny Walker Double Black Label and fired up a Cuban Hoyo De Monterrey Churchill cigar.

It was time to activate phase II of his plan. He buzzed his secretary and had his underboss, Bruno Conti, summoned to his office. Conti had been with Moretti since the beginning. He was tough, brutal, loyal, and most importantly, lacking in ambition. He never wanted to be boss of the family. He was very happy with where he currently was.

"Maria said you wanted to see me? What's up?"

"That thing is going exactly as we hoped it would go."

"That's great news boss. Never had a doubt."

"It's time to start on phase II. I need you to reach out, talk to the others, get word going we need to have a meet. We need to discuss the DiFlippo thing, and the current state of his family. The commission will be expecting this, but no one wants to be the first guy to make the call for fear of looking guilty. Fuck that! It's time to do what should have happened six months ago...Hell six years ago..."

"What's that boss?"

"Time to wipe DiFlippo's organization off the map. I have a plan for the commission where we all can split his area, evenly, according to the size of our families now. Everyone will go with it because DiFlippo's gone, and everyone likes more money."

"I'll make some calls right now. I'll let you know when the meet is." With that, Conti left the room. Moretti sat back and enjoyed his drink and cigar.

Fifteen minutes into her wait, a Lincoln town car with blacked out windows left DiFlippo's compound. Kate couldn't tell if anyone was in the backseat or not. Now, she was super pissed off. Whoever that secretary was, had lied to her. Kate hated being lied to. She sat there fuming for another ten minutes.

Just as she was really getting herself worked up, the same Lincoln town car sped by her heading towards DiFlippo's compound. The front gate was already opening for the car. Not this time, she thought as she started her vehicle and followed the Lincoln into the estate.

She was putting her car in park right behind the Lincoln when the back door opened and out stepped a man. He was a little over six feet tall, and weighed around 200 lbs. He had short black hair, but she couldn't see his eyes because of the sunglasses he wore. Even though he was wearing a suit and button down shirt, without the tie, she could tell he was in very good shape and worked out regularly. She wouldn't call him handsome exactly...

She immediately noticed how he carried himself and how he checked out his surroundings. He had some type of training. She recognized it. After he got out of the car, he just stood there for 10 seconds, then turned and looked at her. Then he did something that was odd, that was the last thing she expected. He smiled at her.

The private flight was great. It was fast, efficient, quiet and comfortable. Everything commercial flying is not. Geoff had even gone as far as having a bottle of Buffalo Trace Whiskey on board. I hesitated before having a glass. I never drink when I am on a job and I felt like I was on a job. Since it was my favorite whiskey and I had more than an hour of flight time, I decided to enjoy a glass. As usual, it was fantastic.

When we landed, Bramwell was with the car waiting for me. He approached me and for a second I thought he was going to embrace me, but he didn't. I was in operator mode, and putting out a bad vibe. I think he was in tune with that.

We got into the car. "Anything new?" I asked.

"Nothing. Nothing at all. The FBI is camped outside the front gate wanting to talk."

"You call Rosenberg?"

"First thing I did. He said to wait until he got there before we talked to them. Without a lawyer present, he said they would go beyond what they would normally ask us in a situation like this. You know."

"When will he be available to sit with you?"

"Late tonight or tomorrow. He's in New York City."

"Not good Bramwell. You don't want the FBI getting a hard-on for you when they should be looking for Sal."

"I know Rick, I know. I wasn't sure what to do, you know? This is all new to me."

"You're doing fine Bramwell. Calm down. Sal brought you in for a reason. He has confidence in you and so do I. I'll talk to the FBI. They might have something that can help us."

"What about Rosenberg?"

"Fuck Rosenberg. If he has a problem with it, he should have been here. He's getting paid enough to be here, he should be here. As a matter of fact, when we get back to Sal's, call him again. Let him know that I'm a little pissed off that I have to meet with the FBI without him being there because he's too busy to get back to Western New York. Let's see how fast he moves his ass then. Since he's not here, I now have to waste time dealing with the FBI when I should be trying to find who has Sal. I am not very happy Bramwell, and I doubt Sal has the time I am going to waste this afternoon."

The rest of the ride was quiet. Bramwell left me to my thoughts. I couldn't help but feel guilty about this whole mess. My earlier conversations with Bill about walking away were just a distant memory.

Moretti was excited. The commission agreed to have a meeting in three days to discuss DiFlippo's organization and what should happen next. They were still working out the details for the meeting. The meeting would occur in Ricci's lawyer's office located on 5th Avenue in Manhattan. The building was perfect for a meeting. It backed up against Central Park and offered a great view. There was a secure, underground parking area with a second, even more secure private parking area and a private elevator that would lead up to the top floor. The meeting would take place there in the conference room.

The details they were working out were the logistics: how many men each boss would be allowed to bring, were they allowed to be armed, the exact arrival times of each boss and most importantly, who was going to cater the event.

Moretti wasn't pleased when Ricci's suggested they invite Bramwell from DiFlippo's organization. He was even less pleased when Mario Costa agreed with Ricci. It was a small speed bump in the road. Moretti was still confident that he would be able to obtain everything he wanted, even with DiFlippo's man there. It might actually be easier with him there. They could offer him a cash settlement and have him go away quietly.

Bramwell was right. The FBI was camped outside Sal's front gate. As we were pulling into the driveway, the government issued car followed us right in. "Bramwell, I'll talk to the FBI as soon as I get out of the car. Eventually, they'll want to move the meeting inside, and I'll bring them in. Let's be up front about Sal's disappearance and what we know. Let's also try to find out what info they have that we don't."

The car stopped and I opened the back door and got out. This was the first time I had been back to Sal's estate since I left after recovering from my gunshot wounds. I always loved his property. It had a calming presence on me. I scanned the area as soon as I stepped from the vehicle and noticed the FBI agent was alone. I took a few extra seconds to gather myself then I turned towards where the FBI agent was parked.

The first thing I noticed was the FBI agent was female. Almost as soon as I noticed that, I noticed that she was beautiful. Strikingly so. As she was getting out of the car, I thought she was about 5'4", maybe 5'5". Her hair was shoulder length, and was a medium brown, but it had lighter streaks in it. It was almost like she had natural highlights. She was wearing a pair of flat shoes, grey pants and a button down top tucked in. Just by looking at her, I could tell she was in great shape. I also couldn't help notice how incredibly sexy she was. The third thing I noticed almost immediately was how angry she was. In spite of myself and the circumstances that brought me back here, I couldn't help it, but I smiled right then.

She was out of the car and barely able to contain her rage. Why was this asshole just smiling at her?

"FBI. Who are you?" The smile didn't even falter. He extended his hand.

"Rick Stevens. I'm sorry, what did you say your name was?" Instead of shaking my hand, she extended her FBI credentials towards me.

"I said FBI. I have some questions to ask about Salvatore DiFlippo. What is your relation to him?"

"Wait. Come inside. We'll talk inside." Without waiting for her response, I turned around and started walking towards the front door. "Can I get you something to drink? Coffee or water?"

"What you can do Mr. Stevens.." I held up my hand to stop her.

"Rick. Please call me Rick."

"As I was saying, what you can do, Mr. Stevens, is start answering my questions." We were in the foyer of the house now. Kate noticed how beautiful and lavish it was and how comfortable Stevens was navigating through the house. Kate followed him as he led her to a sitting room off the main living room area.

"Agent, I will answer all of your questions. I promise you I will..."

"Is that before or after your lawyer gets here Mr. Stevens?" Kate gave him her best, don't bullshit me stare.

"Rick. My name is Rick. I don't have a lawyer. I don't need a lawyer. Why are you mad at me?" I leveled my gaze into her eyes. My smile was gone, and I was all business now. I noticed how her eyes were green, but depending on what color her outfit was, or the lighting, her eyes could easily look light blue or even gray. Those are eyes I can get lost in I thought... What? What the hell was that? What was I thinking?

"Mr. Steven's, I'm not mad at you. I'm just upset about trying to help y'all out by finding Salvatore DiFlippo and getting the run around. I've been waiting outside for over 30 minutes. In kidnappings, time is the most important thing and to be completely honest with you, we're running way far behind. And frankly Mr. Stevens…"

"Rick. Please."

"Frankly Mr. Stevens, I don't like being jerked around by anyone, especially people I'm trying to help."

"I understand. That's fair. You asked my relation to Sal earlier. He's one of my closest friends. I'm going to do whatever I can to help." She pulled out a voice recorder.

"I'm going to record this conversation and take notes." After giving her name (Special Agent Kate Riley), and the date, she started asking her questions.

She was very thorough. I could tell she was a skilled interrogator. She had a comfortable rhythm in her questioning. She would get you agreeing with her and saying yes, and then she would ask a tough question. Just as you were starting to get a line on what she was asking, she would ask a completely different question heading in another direction.

I could tell at certain times during her questioning that she was becoming frustrated with me and how I was answering her questions. Every time she made an allegation to Sal's ties to organized crime, I refuted her claim and asked for evidence. She finally gave up. After she put her note pad away and turned her recorder off she said, "Thank you, Mr. Stevens, for wasting my time here today. How do you expect me to do my job if you refuse to tell me anything?"

"Kate…"

"Agent Riley, Mr. Stevens"

"It's Rick. Agent Riley, I told you everything I know. I've been traveling and I literally haven't set foot inside this house or this entire city in the past six months."

"Traveling for work or pleasure Mr. Stevens?"

"I keep telling you, my name is Rick. It was a little bit of both. A business trip that I took a little extra time on."

"And what kind of business are you in, Mr. Stevens?" Wow, she was good. I walked right into this one. She wanted to know what type of work I did and by her asking if I was gone on business or pleasure was brilliant on her part. If I said business, she would have asked what type of business I was in. If I would have said pleasure, she would have asked what type of business allows me off for half a year at a time.

Sal has me listed on the board of directors for a company he owns here in Buffalo. My official job title within the company is Director of Strategic Solutions and I get paid a healthy annual salary without having to actually do any work. This allows me to keep my real identity 'clean' and useful. For times like these.

"I'm a Director for Empire State Developers Group."

"I'm not really familiar with them. What do you do?" She asked it innocently enough, but I knew everything I said would be remembered, cataloged, and checked by her.

"I'm over the Strategic Solutions Department. I'm a problem solver…"

"Like a leg-breaker, Mr. Stevens, that kind of problem solver?"

"It's Rick, Kate, my name is Rick and I…"

"Agent Riley. My name is Agent Riley. I was just joking with you Mr. Stevens. I have a lot of work to do. Who else is here that I can interview?"

"I'll introduce you to Mr. Bramwell before I leave. I'll be right back, let me go get him." I got up and started walking towards the door to leave the room.

"Rick?" I was surprised to hear her use my first name. I actually kind of liked hearing her say my name.

"Yes, Agent Riley?" I turned and smiled at her.

"Can we cut the bullshit here? I mean, you've just wasted

almost 45 minutes of my time by telling me absolutely nothing and now you're going to pass me off to someone else that is going to do the same thing. Let's just talk about the big white elephant in the room for a minute so I can get out of here and get back to working this case. Can we do that?"

"Are we going off the record here Kate?" I asked her.

"It's Agent Riley and Mr. Stevens, I'm not a reporter, and I *never* go off the record. However, in certain situations and on certain cases, sometimes, certain things get left out of the official report. Assuming they do not have any relevance to the final outcome."

"Agent Riley, let me ask you this: are you a woman of honor?" I was looking right into her eyes. I was looking for a tell, something that would give away the fact that she was about to be untruthful to me. I knew if she called me by my first name again, it would be to butter me up. I more than expected it.

"Mr. Stevens, I work for the Federal Government. Now, setting that fact aside, yes, I am a woman of honor. Why do you ask?"

"I want to know who I'm dealing with is all. I have my own reasons for asking."

"Are you a man of honor?" That was an interesting question and one I was not sure how to answer. It was a question I never looked at too closely because I was afraid of what I would discover. I decided to answer her question honestly.

"That's debatable. Am I a man of my word? Absolutely. No question, no doubt. Kate, ask me the question you came here to ask."

"Is DiFlippo's disappearance connected to his ties in organized crime? Was this a hit or something?"

"I don't know, not yet. But I will find out. If I had to guess, I would say that this ties in with Sal's business dealings. Notice I did not say organized crime, I just said business dealings. So in your report on this interview, don't say I confirmed your suspicions on Sal's involvement on anything illegal. Is that clear?"

"Crystal clear. So you *think* this is tied into some of Sal's business dealings..." When she said business dealings, she made quotes in the air with her fingers. She was very good. Anytime I was around her I would have to be conscious of every single thing I said. She continued " You don't know who is behind this, but you will find out? I have to tell you, Mr. Stevens, stepping all over a FBI case is a quick way to get thrown in jail."

"Kate, let's cut the shit here. You don't have any leads and by coming here, you're grasping at straws. Not only do I know the world Sal operates in, but I have connections there as well. I can find out more in the next 6-8 hours than you have since Sal was kidnapped yesterday. We can be friends and work together or we can be enemies and work against each other. There are a lot of places I can go that you can't. Just as there are a lot of doors your badge will open up that I can't get into. You say you're a woman of honor, and I'm a man of his word. Assuming we both want the same thing here, Sal being found, we're on the same side and can help each other. Make no mistake Kate, with or without your help, I'll find out who did this. I will find Sal. The only question is, will that be with or without your help. Which is it?"

CHAPTER #9

Sal knew that once the money, now up to eight million dollars, was transferred he was a dead man. Overall, he had a great life. He didn't have any complaints. He was stalling on making all the transfers not because he was afraid of death, but because he was trying to get some sort of assurance that once they had the money, they would let his granddaughter go free.

Sal was in a lot of pain, and was in and out of consciousness. Primo had really gone to work on him again, breaking more bones. The way Sal was making the transfers; he knew that Geoff or even the FBI would be able to easily track the money. Assuming they were looking for that already.

"Old man, you're starting to piss me off. I'm thinking you're dragging your feet on this on purpose. Just so you know, if you die before I get the entire eight million dollars transferred, your granddaughter's death will be the most horrible, painful thing I can imagine. And trust me, I can imagine some pretty messed up things. So finish this up."

Sal composed his thoughts and concentrated on being understood when he talked through his broken jaw. "Tru mnrrr ours" *Two more hours.*

"Ok old man. Two more hours. You better not die before then."

I was surprised when FBI Special Agent Kate (Not Kathryn) Riley agreed to my terms. She would work her end of the investigation and I would work my end and we would update each other as we went. I figured I would test her right out of the gate by asking her if I could see the video of the attack and kidnapping.

I was even more surprised when she agreed. She said she would burn me a copy of the disc and get it to me later around dinner time. We exchanged contact information and she left. I went into one of the spare offices in Sal's house and picked up the phone.

"This is Geoff."

"Geoff, it's Rick. What can you tell me? What have you found out so far?" When I was on my private flight back to Buffalo, I called Geoff using a phone in the airplane. I told him to start digging. He asked me where, and I told him everywhere. Check the other four crime families in NY. Check their bank records. If one of them did this, money would be involved and if they were sloppy, we might be able to figure out which one.

"I started with Augostino. I already knew where most of his money was so he was easy. I went back 24 months and analyzed his banking records. His accounts get weekly deposits, but the deposit amounts vary. Sometimes vary by as much as $7,000."

"Shit. That's no good."

"I don't know if it means anything, but starting about four months ago, five of his accounts have seen an average increase of almost $2,500 a month. After four months, from what I can tell, they returned to what is more or less a normal deposit structure."

"I don't know Geoff. Seems weak. It could be anything, gambling winnings or something…" Geoff cut me off.

"I don't know Rick. Do the math. $2,500 a month, spread over five accounts is $12,500. Multiply that by four months and you get $50,000. That's a nice, round, even number. I am digging through the other family's financials now trying to see if I can find someone paying out $50,000 but it's taking a lot of time."

"Ok, it's better than nothing. Keep at it."

"Rick, I also flagged the bank accounts that I helped Mr. DiFlippo set up."

"What does that mean?"

"Someone took Mr. DiFlippo so they want something from him. I assume it's his money. If large amounts of cash are being moved from his accounts, it might help us figure out where he is or who's behind this."

"Good idea Geoff. Keep at it and if anything breaks, anything at all, find me. Oh, and Geoff, if you have time, I need one other favor..." Geoff said he would check into what I asked and get back to me.

Head of the Camarillo Crime Family, Vincent Augostino was who I initially suspected was behind this. Six months ago, it was one of his captains that teamed up with Sal's underboss in a failed coup attempt. I had dealt with the captain, but Sal worked something out with Vince and he was allowed to live.

Now this. With Sal gone, Bramwell was essentially the head of the family. I needed to meet with him to let him know what I was going to do. Not to seek his permission, but to warn him that war was coming.

Kate was interested to see if Stevens could deliver on his promise of an even information exchange. The first thing she did when she got back to the office was pull everything she could on him. She was very surprised at the results.

His credit score was perfect. He had not paid a bill late...Ever. His tax records were spotless. He had a job making $150,000 a year and owned a condo and an old Ford Bronco. There was absolutely nothing in his criminal background. He was spotless.

She saw that when he was younger he served in the Army and was honorably discharged and served as an Army Ranger. That would explain the way he carried himself and the way he surveyed his surroundings when he got out of the vehicle earlier that afternoon. She was surprised to see that after the Army he graduated from a bible college. It didn't fit the profile she had in her mind for him.

She kept digging. She discovered he was married. She dug further and discovered why he wasn't married anymore. It wasn't too long after his wife and daughter's death that he started working for Empire State Developers Group. She sent another agent in the office an e-mail asking him to run down the company. She wanted to find out if it was a legit company or a front for something else. Stevens' background was spotless. Too spotless. Something about him wasn't right.

Geoff had just finished running down the favor that Rick asked him for. After compiling all the information into an e-mail, he sent it to Rick. He also sent him a text letting him know it was there, waiting for him. He felt better that he was able to get something done that Rick wanted. He did not want Rick to be unhappy with him.

He went back to work digging through the records of the other three New York Crime families. He was trying to find the link from the $50,000. He was sure it was out there, somewhere, he just needed to be smart enough to see it.

For a minute, he thought about Vince Augostino. A shiver ran up his spine and he physically shook. He knew the information he discovered and passed on to Rick sealed Augostino's death warrant. He wanted to feel bad about it, or even guilty, but he didn't.

He kept digging through the financial records, the bank statements, the deposits and withdrawals, the off-shore accounts, looking for and finding patterns, identifying the anomalies, trying to make the numbers work and add up to $50,000.

He was running one of his programs he designed on a rather lengthy checking account based out of a Swiss bank located in Toronto, Canada and he decided to go into a few of Sal's other accounts. He had a pretty good idea of what companies Sal owned or was involved in and had a working list. He was going to crack into their financials and see if anything looked out of the ordinary. Maybe he would get lucky?

"Hello?"

"Mr. Stevens?"

"Hello, Kate, please, call me Rick…"

"It's Agent Riley Mr. Stevens. I have your video ready for you. I'm tied up at the office, you know, working this case so you're going to have to stop on down here to pick it up. That won't be a problem, will it?"

"Agent Riley, stopping by your office will not be a problem." It seemed like it was some sort of power move on her part. I was thinking she wanted to get me on her turf and go at me with her questions again. It would be a time waster and unproductive. "Where is your office located?"

"We're located at One FBI Plaza. Are you familiar with where we're at?"

"Over on Elmwood and Niagara?"

"That's the one Mr. Stevens. The big FBI building. You can't miss it."

"I know exactly where it is." I decided to take a chance. "Agent Riley, have you had dinner yet?"

"Dinner?" She sounded surprised.

"Yes, dinner. You know, the meal after lunch, the one that comes before the next morning's breakfast. Dinner."

"I know what dinner is. Why do you want to know if I've eaten dinner yet?"

"I haven't eaten dinner yet. Since I have to drive all the way into downtown Buffalo, I was thinking of which fabulous restaurant I was going to eat at. One of my favorites is Della Terra, over in the Embassy Suites on Huron and Delaware. If you haven't eaten dinner yet, I was going to see if you would like to join me."

"Mr. Stevens, are you asking me on a dinner date?"

"What?" I was actually embarrassed. I tried to recover with a little dignity. "Kate. No. Like I said, since I was going to be down there anyway, and you and I have to meet up so I can get the video, I thought we could do like a business dinner or something." Pathetic. What the hell was I doing? Was I really asking her for a dinner date or was it just a business dinner? I was confused myself.

"You sure know how to make a girl feel special Mr. Stevens, I can tell you that. No, I haven't eaten dinner yet. I'll bring the video with me and meet you there in an hour. Bring whatever new information you have with you as well, ok?"

It was a long shot, but it was all he had left. Sal had another $150,000 he was going to transfer and then the process would be complete. All eight million dollars would be in Primo's hands. Primo may have been in prison for the past twenty-years, but he knew a lot about banking and financial institutions.

The first thing he did was make Sal lay out all his accounts, business and personal. He wanted sign on information and passwords. He wanted to look at each account and decide where the money would come from.

This posed a problem for DiFlippo. He had over 25 different business accounts and at least that many personal accounts. He had to decide which ones he would show Primo and which ones he would keep private. He didn't want to show

Primo an account that had in excess of two or three million dollars in it.

He gave Primo eight business accounts he had access to that all together totaled almost twelve million dollars. He also gave Primo three of his personal accounts. The first account had almost $300,000 in it. The second account had a little over one million in it and the third account had about $275,000 in it.

After looking through the accounts, Primo wrote down several different account numbers and amounts next to them. He told DiFlippo to start making the transfers. Primo had selected all eight of the business accounts but had left the personal accounts alone.

It was a smart move. DiFlippo would have done the same thing on the assumption that someone in Sal's organization was watching his personal accounts waiting for money to be removed. They would then follow the cash. The business accounts were different. Money was always flowing in and coming out of those accounts, like the tide at the ocean.

Another sign that Primo knew what he was doing was when he was having DiFlippo making the transfers. It was late on Monday afternoon. The money would be moved out of the accounts tonight, but no one would be notified about it until Tuesday morning. By then, internal alarms at the banks would be sounding off but it would be too late to help Sal.

Primo had Sal explain to him, in step by step detail, what he was going to do to transfer the money. He even took notes. Sal was trying to think of something he could do to send a warning out when he was transferring the money. He suspected that Primo wasn't as ignorant on the transfer process as he led on. Sal decided that trying to deceive Primo about how to do the transfers would be a very bad idea.

Sal was right. As soon as he transferred the first million

dollars to the account Primo gave him, Primo went to work on his own computer and bounced the money through four other banks, breaking it down into four equal deposits of $250,000 each. After that, he split all the balances in half again and sent it through several other banks. Then Primo ended up transferring the money from those banks all back into one account.

Sal was sure he was bouncing his money through the banks as a way to hide it from the US Federal Government. Sal didn't see all the banks, but he saw enough to know that they were located in several different countries. Tracking the money and finding out where it finally ended up would be nearly impossible. Well, assuming you went about it in the legal way. There were just too many different countries involved that would not respond to a United States subpoena for information. If you knew a world class computer hacker, anything electronic was possible.

Primo was watching Sal work and also moving money from his computer. Sal signed into the last account under Primo's watchful eye. He went through the required steps and set up the transfer. Primo wanted to approve all of the transfers that took place before Sal made them. He gestured towards Primo that he was ready.

Primo put his computer down and viewed Sal's screen. It was the moment of truth. "It looks good old man. Real good. This is the last transfer. Our time together is almost at its end. Complete the transfer." Sal typed in the password and hit the required button that would send the final payment of the eight million dollars into one of Primo's numerous bank accounts. Then he looked at Primo and through his broken jaw and cracked teeth, he smiled.

Holy Shit! Geoff thought to himself! The last two business accounts of Sal's he looked at had rather large wire transfers taking place. He was excited but he wasn't sure this was what he was looking for. He wasn't familiar enough with these accounts to know if the $100,000 transactions were odd or regular occurrences.

He started looking backwards into the company's financial transactions. There were a lot of high dollar money transfers in the first account but not any in the second account. Geoff quickly modified an existing program he had created and set it to work on all of the other business accounts Sal had.

He would have his answer within a few minutes. In the meantime, he would get another Mountain Dew and something to snack on from his kitchen while his programs did all the heavy lifting for him.

A few minutes later, he was standing on his back deck that overlooked the Pacific Ocean and a beautiful beach drinking his high caffeinated soda and snacking on a homemade shrimp taco he had put together in his spacious 1,200 foot kitchen. He was trying to catch the eye of the beautiful blond or her friend, another beautiful blond that were strolling down the beach.

How he loved thong bikinis! He was wearing a pair of vibrant blue swim trunks, Ray Ban Sunglasses, and had a towel draped around his neck. His medium length dirty blond hair was in that stage between being slightly combed and slightly messed up that drove girls crazy.

Geoff knew he was good looking in a male model way and had a great body. He had a large chest and matching biceps. His body fat percentage was in the low single digits. Sure he spent half his time plugged into the on-line world and drank a lot of high calorie, high caffeinated energy drinks, but he spent the other half of his time exercising on the beach in the beautiful California sun. He was a man in perfect balance.

Finally, one of the blonds noticed him and gave him a smile. He smiled back and wandered off his deck to introduce himself.

I was almost 20 minutes early getting to the restaurant. So I was surprised to see that Kate was already there, seated in the dining room and looking over the menu. She was also facing the entrance to the restaurant. She was wearing the same clothes I had seen her in earlier, but I still thought she was the best looking woman in the room.

Anytime I am meeting someone, I like to get to the meeting place first. It's a safety thing for me. I never know if someone is setting a hit up on me. I also like to sit with my back to a wall and facing the entrances and exits of where I'm at.

I had changed since our earlier meeting. I was now wearing a black Ralph Lauren Black Label Anthony Wool Gabardine Suit and a matching black button down shirt. I wasn't sure where the night would take me after my dinner meeting with Kate. I knew I would be on the move. I couldn't sit idle anymore. I felt like a shark: I had to keep moving or I would die.

I walked up to the table and without looking up from her menu, Kate said "Mr. Stevens, you're early."

"Yeah, Traffic wasn't as heavy as I thought it would be. I made great time." I said. I was still standing. She looked up from her menu and smiled. It was the first time I had seen her smile and it had an effect on me. It lit up her face, especially her eyes. I couldn't help but smile back.

"Why aren't you sitting down?" She asked me.

"I was going to ask if you would like to trade seats with me. I have a weird thing about not being able to see the front door when I am in a restaurant. Sorry, I know it's odd but I would appreciate it."

"It's not weird at all. I have the same weird thing. Don't worry Mr. Stevens, I'm armed, I'll protect you." She said it, while still smiling, "Please don't make a thing out of this and sit down." I didn't like it, but I sat down. As soon as I sat down, a waiter appeared and took our drink order. She ordered a sweet tea and I ordered an unsweet tea.

"How do you know I'm not armed as well?" I asked her. I wanted to see how far she had gotten into my background.

"If you are, you're committing a felony. I did a pretty thorough background check on you, standard operating procedure for an investigation like this and discovered you do not have a valid concealed carriers permit for the state of New York." Kate didn't know that I often commit felonies on what is sometimes an hourly basis. Carrying a weapon concealed without a permit was the least of my worries.

I was armed. I was carrying a black polymer Springfield XD 3" sub-compact pistol. The model I had was the 40 caliber and I had the 16 round high capacity magazine with the grip extension. It was tucked into an inside the pants concealed holster on my right side. My suit jacket covered it.

"What else did you discover about me?"

"Everything Mr. Stevens. You were born and grew up in Pittsburgh, Pennsylvania. I know your parents were taken from you when you were younger and you went to live with an Aunt and Uncle. After graduation, you joined the Army, finished as a Ranger. After that, you went to a bible college and worked as a pastor for a while. That's how you ended up here in Buffalo. I know you're widowed and shortly after that, you started working where you work now. How am I doing so far?"

"That's pretty good Kate…" She was about to correct

me, so I held up my hand "Agent Riley. Pretty good. You have the broad strokes. Impressive." I took a sip of my tea. "My turn now. Kate Riley, born in Syracuse New York. You're the youngest of four. You moved when you were still a kid to Alabama. Your father was a cop in NY and ran a sheriff's department in Alabama. At the age of eighteen, while attending community college, you went to work for the same department your father was in charge of, in the jail. After that, you went to the big school, Alabama State. Roll tide roll.

You worked for a different Sheriff's department, in the jail again. I'm guessing your father called in a favor? You graduated near the top of your class and the FBI snatched you up shortly after. You work primarily bank robberies, which has me confused as to why you're working this case. How am I doing so far?" This was the other project I had Geoff do for me. I asked him to run a complete background on Kate for me.

She looked surprised and a little angry. "How did you know all that? Do we have a corrupt agent in the office?"

"I don't know if you have a corrupt agent or not. I got the information like you did, out of a computer."

"No, tell me how you got all of that in such a short time."

"Kate, I told you, I did it searching on line. What? You mean to tell me you're angry?"

"Yes I'm angry!"

"Why? Because I did the exact same thing to you that you did to me?" There was no doubt on the color of her eyes now. They were a fiery emerald green. "Why are you so quiet? What are you thinking?"

"I'm thinking about arresting you is what I'm thinking." I couldn't tell if she was kidding or not. She looked like she was serious.

"Arrest me? For what?" This dinner meeting was not going the way I expected it to or wanted to. It dawned on me that I hadn't been on a date, or even shared a meal with another woman other than my wife or Sal's wife in the past 15 years.

"I don't know. I'll think of something…"

"You can't be serious. All because I ran a background check on you? I'm a careful person."

"No bullshit Stevens. I want the truth. Don't you dare try to lie to me either. If I don't like your answers, you're not going home tonight."

Sal knew it wouldn't be long now. He had completed the last transaction almost five minutes ago. Hopefully, his ruse would work. In his greedy excitement, Primo didn't check the account number Sal had signed into. It wasn't the last business account like Primo thought. It was one of Sal's personal accounts. It was an account that Geoff had helped set up for him. Sal knew if Geoff was monitoring his accounts, like he hoped he was, this would be a huge red flag.

Sal wasn't sure, but he hoped if Geoff saw the money transfer, he would be able to figure out where the transaction occurred. He knew he would be dead long before anyone made it to wherever he was to rescue him. He was just hoping that they would get here in time to kill Primo.

As Sal sat there and contemplated the last minutes of his life, a deep sadness overtook him. He felt like a failure. He had failed to prevent the death of his wife. All of the money and power he had accumulated couldn't save her.

Because of all of that money and power, his daughter was killed. Something else he had failed to prevent. He realized he hadn't even wept for the loss of her and his son-in-law. That thought disgusted him. What kind of a monster had he become? He was more concerned with his own life than the passing of his child.

His only granddaughter was kidnapped and suffering because of the person Sal was and what he did. What he chose to do. Were these more punishments from God? Hadn't he taken enough from him already?

He wondered where Rick was and what he was doing. He still worried about Rick. He had lost his way a long time ago. Sal thought that once Rick killed the person that took his family, he would start to heal. Just the opposite had occurred though. It was one of Sal's biggest regrets: giving Rick the name of the person that killed his family.

He thought of Rick as the son he never had. Like any parent, all he wanted for his son was the best. As the years passed, he saw what little goodness that was left in Rick disappearing. This saddened him in ways he couldn't believe. He tried to persuade Rick to leave the business and disappear.

After he was shot and nearly died, Sal thought Rick had finally taken his advice. He had spoken to him a few weeks back and Rick was struggling with a decision. He hoped he made the right one. His thoughts were broken by a loud clap!

"YES! It's complete! The eight million dollars has been deposited into my bank account. It's time for us to part ways old man. It's time for you to finish paying for what you did twenty years ago to my brother and me." Primo set his laptop computer down and stood up. He cracked his neck from side to side and stretched out his shoulders. He approached Sal and reattached his free hand to the chair. "Don't go anywhere. I'll be right back." Primo left the room and thundered up the stairs into the house above.

Sal went back to his thoughts. He had lived a good life. He had few regrets and accomplished much. He did a lot of bad, evil things in his time but he also did a lot of good things too. His body was hurt and broken. He was in a lot of pain and bleeding. He hadn't eaten in almost two days and was sitting strapped to a chair in his own waste. He was afraid. For the first time in a very long time, Sal realized he was afraid and didn't want to die. Not yet, not like this.

He chuckled to himself quietly. So much for going out with guns ablazing and any shred of dignity, he thought. Everyone considered Sal a stand-up guy. He was powerful and ruthless. He had murdered over 20 people personally and sent hundreds of others to their death. He gathered his remaining resolve, and strength. When Primo came back, whatever he had, whatever he did to Sal, he would endure it and not give Primo the pleasure of seeing the fear he felt.

Geoff was walking back into his house from the beach. He was excited because he had gotten one of the blonde's numbers. He didn't exactly remember which one was which, or which one gave him the number, but to him, it didn't matter as they were both beautiful blondes, and interchangeable in his mind.

He stopped at the fridge and grabbed another soda. He went back into his office to check the results of his programs. His screen savers were on. He was gone longer than he had expected to be. He grabbed his wireless mouse and shook it to bring up the icon where he typed in his password and the screen came to life.

HOLY SHIT! He had alerts, alarms, things were flashing all over his screen. He had hit pay-dirt! One of Mr. DiFlippo's personal accounts had been accessed, 23 minutes ago and a large amount of money had been transferred out of it.

Geoff's hands were a blur as he worked the keyboard. Some people could hear a song and play it note for note after listening to it just one time. Some people could paint amazing pictures that took your breath away and made you want to weep. Geoff's calling was surfing the blue nowhere.

If he wasn't the best computer hacker in the world, he was within the top three. He bounced from webpage to webpage, cracking into secure, encrypted websites as fast as his fingers could type. There wasn't anything he couldn't get into. Almost there he thought and then, he had it. He had the address of where the computer was used to transfer the money. The address where Mr. DiFlippo was being held captive at.

Kate wasn't sure if she was kidding or not about arresting Stevens. The guy was a mystery. He was very smooth when he talked and she had trouble telling the difference between the truth and his lies. "What do you do for DiFlippo?"

"I wasn't being entirely dishonest earlier when I said I was a problem solver. I handle difficult situations for Sal. A lot of the work I do is completely legitimate…" A lie for sure, but one he thought he could get away with. I'll go back to that Kate thought, then he continued "…and sometimes, less than legitimate." Finally, we're getting to some truth. How much will he tell me and how much will he try to sell me on?

"What does that mean? Exactly?"

"Ok, say a shipment of something goes missing. I might make a few phone calls, talk to a few people until it gets found. Stuff like that." He said it in his most sincere, convincing voice.

"Rick?" Kate saw the hope blossom in his eyes. He thinks I'm buying his line of crap she thought.

"Yes Kate?"

"You're sitting across from me in a $3,000 suit and you're trying to tell me that you work loss prevention for a mafia kingpin and you can't figure out why I'm so pissed off at you and why I want to arrest you?" Kate could tell her response surprised him. Good. She wanted to keep him off balance. "One more chance Stevens. One." She said icily to him.

She saw a coldness flash into his eyes, it was barely there, but she saw it, and it scared her. In spite of the expensive suit and excellent table manners, she understood she was sitting across the table from a dangerous man. He was about to answer her question, when he held up his hand in the stop sign gesture and removed his cell phone from his pants pocket. Kate noticed he answered without looking at who was calling him.

"Yes?" She could only hear his side of the short conversation but she could tell his anxiety level jumped up 100 notches.

"Just now? I know where that is. I'm on my way, leaving right now from downtown. I should be there in 10 minutes, 15 tops. Text me the address so I don't hit the wrong house." Then he hung up the phone and looked at Kate.

"I'm leaving. I have a line on where DiFlippo is."

"WHAT? I have to call this in, this could be a hostage…" He was already up and moving across the restaurant. "Stevens! RICK!" He didn't even glance back. Kate got up and followed him outside. "Where are you going? What are you going to do?" He kept walking but answered her.

"I'm going to where he might be and if he's there I'm going to get him back."

"I'm going with you." He kept walking, quickly across the parking lot. God, she thought, he is irritating! "Rick, I'm serious, I'm going with you or I'll place you under arrest." He slowed up for a second, and in that second, Kate sensed that her life was in extreme danger, but the second passed and he said "I figured you would go Kate, but you have to move your ass, we're short on time." She ran to catch up and they both got into his truck. She noticed he was driving an older model Ford Bronco, the one she found while running his background. An odd thought occurred to her that his suit probably cost more than his car.

"We can take my car. Will this even start?" She said as she was climbing in. He didn't answer her; he just started the truck up and was moving before she had her door closed.

"You valeted your Jeep and we don't have time for him to get your car. Buckle your seat belt."

"How do you know I used the valet? How do you know what kind of car I drive?" Once again, he didn't answer her. He concentrated on his driving. He was breaking every traffic law but Kate knew if she said anything, he would just ignore her. She wasn't sure if she wanted to arrest him or shoot him.

Primo was gone longer than Sal expected. Maybe 30 minutes, maybe 45. When he finally did come back, he was dressed and had a jacket on. It looked like he was going to be leaving. He was carrying a red, five gallon gas can and he had something else in his other hand. Sal couldn't make out what it was.

"20 years ago old man, you sent me to hell. A living, breathing, physical hell. I endured. I survived. My hatred for you kept me alive. Now, I have eight million dollars, and I get to kill you and send you to Hell."

He set the gas can down and opened his hand to show Sal what he was holding. "I know you recognize this. This is what you were named after, no?" He saw that Primo was holding an ice pick. Sal couldn't help it, but a shiver ran down his spine.

"How many people did you kill with this, huh? I bet it was a lot. I bet you never once thought about what it felt like.

You're going to experience it now old man. Then, I'm going to set you on fire. Not only will you burn in Hell, but you'll also burn here on Earth."

Sal didn't even see Primo move, he was fast. He felt a coldness enter the right side of his chest. He lost his breath and tasted blood. He wasn't sure how many times Primo stabbed him but he felt pain everywhere.

Almost as quickly as it started, it was over. Primo dropped the ice pick on the floor and picked up the gas can. He poured some gas around Sal's chair and left a trail of it heading to the basement stairs. Primo walked around the basement, dumping the gas out onto the carpet.

Sal noticed Primo had a mask or something over his face. The fumes were very strong now and Sal was having trouble breathing. After using the ice pick on him, Primo hadn't looked back at Sal one time. When the gas can was empty, Primo went to the top of the stairs. The last thing Sal remembered was a loud WHOOSH and then intense heat.

I was driving as quickly as I could. Sometimes I hit curbs and sometimes I had to drive on the sidewalk. Red lights and stop signs I passed through flashing my headlights with my hand holding down the horn.

It didn't help my concentration at all that Kate was with me. It really didn't help my concentration that she hadn't stopped talking since we left the restaurant. When she invited herself along, I figured it would take too much time to try to talk her out of going with me. I knew she wouldn't take no for an answer. I would have had to kill her if I didn't want her to come with me. I didn't want to kill her because I think I was starting to like her.

I didn't know what we would find at the address Geoff had given me. All I knew was that if Sal was there, I would get him out and kill everyone inside. This would be hard to do with an FBI agent looking over my shoulder.

I took a hard left turn onto the street where Sal was being kept prisoner. I was about to look at my phone to get the exact address when I heard a small explosion. SHIT! I was too late! The explosion happened at a house where a car had just pulled out of the drive way.

I sped down the street and confirmed my worst fear. The explosion occurred at the house where Sal was being kept. I started to see smoke coming out of some busted out windows from the basement. It was decision time. I could chase down the car and kill the driver, or I could rush into the house on the off chance that Sal was inside and hadn't died in the explosion. There was really no decision at all.

I slammed the brakes on and cut the wheel. My Bronco jumped the curb and came to a stop on the front lawn. I jumped out of my truck, drew my weapon and rushed around to the back of the house. I didn't wait to see what Kate was going to do.

I kicked the back door open and went into the house. I was standing in what is often referred to as a "mud room". This one doubled as a laundry room for the house. There was also a small sink in one corner. Attached to the sink's faucet was an 18 inch rubber hose. I yanked the hose free from the sink. I opened a standing cabinet and saw what I was looking for: a large winter parka stored away until the next snow storm, a scarf, ski goggles and snowmobile gloves.

I put my gun back in my holster and dressed in the winter clothes and put one end of the rubber hose into my mouth. I tucked the other end of the hose into the jacket I was wearing. This was an old fireman's trick I had picked up when I was in the Army.

You don't see them too much anymore, but the old respirators that attached to the Scott Air Packs used to have a large, plastic/rubber hose that was part of the face mask and attached to the air pack. If you were in a fire and got trapped or ran out of air, you could disconnect the hose from the air pack and tuck it into your coat and be able to survive off the air trapped in your coat and around your body. It wouldn't last long, but I wasn't planning on spending a lot of time in the basement.

I put the goggles and gloves on, and wrapped the scarf around my face. I went into the basement and immediately dropped to the floor and started crawling. Smoke rises so I had a pretty good view of the entire basement. There was fire around the perimeter of the room and it was spreading into the center area.

I didn't see Sal anywhere and I was starting to panic. I closed my eyes for a second, took a deep breath, focused my mind, opened my eyes and crawled further into the room. Normally in a situation like this, fireman would stay on the perimeter of the room unless they saw someone that needed to be rescued.

I got as close to the perimeter as I dared and kept moving forward. I noticed the back half of the basement had a bar. I scanned the area and kept my eyes moving. WAIT!

I saw something odd, something that didn't look like it belonged. It was something small, skinny and white. What the hell? Then I realized what it was: it was a leg! I crawled as quickly as I could to the bar. When I got there, I pulled myself behind the back of the bar and found Sal.

Kate didn't know why she kept talking. She knew Stevens wasn't listening to her. It was a nervous habit she had and she couldn't stop herself from doing it. He was driving so recklessly! It would be a miracle if he got them there without killing them first.

As Stevens came around the corner, there was a small explosion from a house on the street. Kate was going to pull her cell phone out and dial 911, but she had to use both hands, one braced on the Bronco's dashboard, and one holding onto the "Oh Shit" handle above the door.

After the explosion, Stevens accelerated and when he came up to the house he jumped on the brakes and came to a sliding stop in the front lawn. Before she could comment, he was out of the truck and had moved down the side of the house towards the back door.

Kate jumped out of her side of the vehicle and dialed 911. She told the dispatcher she was an FBI Agent and was calling in a small explosion and gave the address. After hanging up with 911, she called her boss. She explained where she was and how she got there.

"KATE! This is huge! You can crack this case right now!" Phillips said his voice full of excitement. "I'll get a crime scene crew on the way ASAP! Keep everyone out of there until they get there!"

"Tom, Stevens is already inside and the house is in flames. If the firemen don't get here fast, there won't be a crime scene to investigate." After hanging up with Phillips, Kate started around the side of the house where Stevens had gone. She hadn't gotten very far when the first police car pulled up, lights flashing.

She held up her badge, identified herself and explained the situation as she knew it. By the time she was done, she turned around to head back the way Stevens had went when she saw a man dressed in a winter jacket carrying an elderly, naked man.

I didn't know if he was alive. He looked so small, fragile. He was naked, bleeding and burned. I felt a tremendous sense of loss and pain. I was almost paralyzed by the hurt I felt at seeing my friend in the condition he was in and not knowing if he was alive or dead.

I picked him up; he really weighed nothing, and sprinted across the basement to the stairs. I ran up the stairs and out of the house and into the back yard. I held Sal up with one arm as I ripped the scarf and goggles from my face. I spit the rubber hose out of my mouth and started towards the front of the house.

When I got to the front, Kate was standing there, looking at me with a confused look on her face. There was also a police car and two of Buffalo's finest. "HELP!" I don't remember yelling but Kate and the cops came running over.

One of the officers took Sal from my arms and laid him on the ground. He tilted his head back and checked for a pulse. Kate and the other officer threw me to the ground. At first I didn't understand. I thought they were arresting me.

Then I realized the hood of the jacket I was wearing was on fire. I rolled around until the flames were out. I stood up and tore the jacket from me. By then, the ambulance was there and there were two paramedics working on Sal.

I went over and as much as I wanted to shout and ask how he was, I knew I would be hindering their life saving efforts. There were a lot of lights on in the area now and I realized that Sal's upper body was covered in blood.

One paramedic was hooking up an oxygen tank to Sal's face, while the other one worked quickly to cover the wounds in Sal's chest. As soon as the oxygen was hooked up, he started hooking Sal up to an EKG. That was when Kate pulled me away from the scene. I also noticed how angry she was. Her eyes were a brilliant green. Amazing.

"What the hell were you thinking? You run into a burning house? Are you crazy?" I didn't answer her right away. I couldn't. I was exhausted. I just wanted to sit down. "Rick?"

"Not now Kate. Give me a minute." I walked to my truck and sat in the driver's seat. I pulled out my cell phone and called Bramwell. He was aware of the situation and was on his way with two cars full of people. Geoff had called him after calling me.

I rerouted Bramwell and his crew to the Erie County Medical Center where they would take Sal. I told him to get a hold of Rosenberg and tell him he better be at the hospital by the time I got there. I also made sure to tell Bramwell that I had an FBI agent with me and anyone carrying a firearm into the hospital with them had better have a New York State pistol permit.

I hung up with Bramwell and got out of my truck. Sal and the ambulance were gone, the fire department was there battling the fire, there were more police officers, and detectives in suits. I needed to go. I needed to get home and change. I needed to call Geoff. I needed all the info I could get on this house, its owner, and the car that left. I didn't have a plate number or even a make or model, but I remembered the color. I was hoping the car would have a tie in to the house. I was hoping for a miracle. I needed to get home and shower and change. I needed to get to the hospital.

I knew I wasn't going to be able to do any of that until I answered questions. I didn't want to spend the next several hours in an interrogation room with a few detectives answering the same questions over and over again. I needed to keep moving. Like Newton said, an object in motion and all that.

"Kate, I mean, Agent Riley. Can I talk to you?"

"Agent Riley? What do you want, *Rick*?" She responded with a raised eye brow. This ought to be good she thought. Agent Riley. Obviously he wanted something.

"Listen, we got off on the wrong foot. My fault. I'm sorry. I want to start over again. I'll answer everything you want to know, to a point. I'll tell you how I knew where Sal was. I'll let you know what I'm planning to do next."

"Again, what do you want?"

"I don't want to spend the next four hours in an interrogation room with a bunch of detectives that aren't going to end up handling this case anyway. I want to go home and get a shower and change into some clean clothes. I missed dinner and I am starving, I want to stop at Mighty Taco and pick up a Mighty Pack with a large root beer. I want you to throw your Federal weight around here and get us out of here."

Kate was surprised at Stevens' request. This was the most sincere she had ever seen him. She would get to see where he lived, be inside his house. Maybe poke around while he was taking a shower. She was starving too and she loved Mighty Taco.

"You better get two Mighty Packs because I haven't eaten dinner yet either and I'll need a root beer as well.

CHAPTER #10

Primo heard the explosion as he was driving away. He smiled to himself. He had just stolen 8 million dollars and then killed one of the most powerful men in history. He felt like a God. He was so impressed at the monumental feat he had just pulled off that he failed to notice the Ford Bronco speed up behind him and then suddenly turn into the house he had just left.

He didn't notice because he was looking at the cell phone he was holding and trying to speed dial his brother. He wanted to let his brother know he had completed the important task of extorting 8 million dollars and would soon be on his way to Arkansas to meet up.

"Hey Primo, Roman wants to know if we can, you know, have a little fun with the package here."

"Roman wants to know Rock, or YOU want to know?"

"I'm just saying Primo…."

"Just wait until I get there. I get the first go with her, then you, and then Roman. He's the hired help, there ain't no way he's getting a turn before I do. If he can't wait, tell him to find a sheep or something. Got it?"

They chatted for a few more minutes and then said good-bye. Primo wasn't sure how long he would need to complete the first part of his task, the kidnapping and extortion, so he didn't plan beyond that. He wanted to put some distance between himself and Buffalo. He decided to drive two hours into Erie, Pennsylvania. Once he got there, he figured he would get something to eat, check into a hotel and call an escort. Or two. Then tomorrow, he could get up and head to the airport and find a flight to Arkansas.

Bramwell had three of his best guys standing guard

outside of Sal's ICU Room. There were a few heated moments when those two assholes from the FBI, Davis and Wilson showed up. It got tense, but Bramwell handled it. Eventually, the family's lawyer showed up and that also helped keep things civil between everyone.

Sal had a lot of friends and there was a constant stream of well-wishers trying to stop in to pay their respects. The three guys with Bramwell were armed, but Bramwell wasn't. He hadn't applied for a NY State Pistol Permit and he didn't want to take the chance of being arrested on a weapons charge.

The prognosis for Sal wasn't good. He was alive when he got to the hospital and was immediately rushed into surgery. He had six puncture wounds in his chest and stomach and was badly bleeding internally. He had a multitude of broken bones, and had various 1st, 2nd and 3rd degree burns on different parts of his body.

The pisser was, now that he was out of surgery and recovering in the ICU room, the biggest threat to his health was infection from all the fluids in his stomach seeping into other parts of his body from the stab punctures. He was also in a coma and the surgeon said it would probably not be optimistic to believe he would ever wake up.

It took all three of the bodyguards to pull Bramwell off the shocked surgeon. Apparently, he didn't know who Sal was. Not optimistic he would ever wake up? Bullshit Bramwell thought. Sure Sal was old and his best days were behind him but he was healthy and had always taken good care of himself. He had survived several mob wars and several assassination attempts on his life and always came out on top. Bramwell believed he would again. At least he hoped he would.

He was waiting to touch base with Stevens to see what he knew. He hadn't talked to him since their brief conversation earlier. He had called and left him a message regarding Sal's condition but he hadn't heard back yet.

He wanted to talk to Stevens to see if he thought they should cancel the New York City meeting in two days. They needed to come up with a plan. Bramwell wanted to walk into the meeting and start killing everyone in there until someone confessed to being in on the hit on Sal. He was smart enough to know that was just a fantasy and would never work. He had a few ideas to run by Stevens, if he ever called him back.

Mighty Taco, affectionately referred to as just 'Mighty", is a small chain of fast food Taco Restaurants located in Western New York. It's a guilty pleasure of mine. Anytime I am back in Buffalo I have to hit them up at least once. There have also been a few occasions through the years that I didn't get back to Buffalo and I overpaid to have it shipped to where I was.

The Mighty Pack consists of six Mighty Tacos. A Mighty Taco has taco beef, cheese, lettuce and tomatoes. I always get mine with sour cream and add hot sauce. We hit the drive thru window and headed to my house.

As I was driving there, I was going through a mental check list of what illegal items I had in my house and where they were located. I knew Kate would search my house while I was in the shower but I felt confident she wouldn't find my stash of weapons, fake identifications, credit cards, large amounts of cash, or other items that are often classified as 'burglary tools'.

On the drive back to my place, Bramwell called me but I didn't answer. I wanted to limit the conversations I had in front of Kate. I did have to get Geoff working on identifying the car and was trying to work that out. Kate pretty much talked non-stop the entire way home. I didn't know if her ability to talk constantly was a nervous tick or a con to get me to relax in front of her and slip up and say something I shouldn't. I thought it could go either way.

I listened to my message from Bramwell about Sal's condition. I was frightened and angry all over again. I would find out who was responsible and I would kill them and everyone that got in my way or tried to stop me.

I had to call Geoff and get him tracking the vehicle that left that house. I couldn't believe I didn't get the license plate number. I didn't even look at the plate. Stupid. I let my feelings and emotions for Sal come into play on a job. I just realized I was on a job. I was worn down and tired and making stupid mistakes too early in the game to be effective. I needed to get in my zone.

I pulled out my phone and started dialing Geoff's number. "Kate, I have to make a call. This guy might be able to help us identify who was driving away." His line started to ring. I should have known she would ask me 15 questions from the time I pushed the call button to the time Geoff picked up the phone.

"Allen, It's Rick. I'm going to put you on speaker phone. I have Agent Kate Riley with me from the F.B.I." I get a lot of my fake identities from Geoff. He commented on how cool it was that I got to use different names all the time and it must be fun. I genuinely like Geoff, I really do, but I think that once he hit seventeen years old, he stopped maturing. I asked him if he wanted me to give him a fake identity that he could use when I was on a job and called him. He jumped at the chance. I gave him the name Allen. Allen was the owner of an on-line gambling website that Geoff had hacked into and stolen millions of dollars from. Allen ordered Geoff's hit. Sal got involved but the real Allen refused a more than generous offer and even had the nerve to threaten Sal.

A few hours later, the real Allen was dead, the victim of a stabbing in a night club in the Bahamas. Once I found out he had threatened Sal's life, I killed him and didn't charge Sal anything. Geoff thought I was going to kill him but I calmly explained to him, in front of his elderly mother, that he wasn't dead because of me. We worked out a deal and he's been helping Sal's organization and me out ever since. Allen was a reminder of what he owed me. Everything.

"Agent Riley, this is Allen, Allen this is Agent Riley. Now that we all know each other, here's what I need. I need everything you can find on the address you gave me, I need..."

"I already have it all put together and e-mailed over to you."

"Great, thank you. I need everything on the current owner and previous owners, especially what vehicles they own or owned. When we were pulling up a car pulled out of the driveway. I don't know the make or model. All I have is the color. Kate, you remember anything else?" She shook her head no.

"Give me an approximate time and direction of travel and color of the vehicle and I'll see what I can dig up." I gave him everything I could remember.

I thanked him for his help and was about to hang up when Kate asked "Allen, what exactly do you do?"

Before he could answer her, I said "Allen is a private security contractor. We're old friends. Allen has to get to work now. Say good-bye Allen." Then I disconnected the phone call. I gave Kate a sheepish smile.

"You know, you're not very slick. You couldn't have made it more obvious that you didn't want me talking to him." I didn't respond to her. I just continued driving to my house.

What the hell was he doing driving around with an FBI

Agent Geoff thought to himself? He would ask him about it later. Right now, he had work to do. He started with the owner of the house. She was a 78 year old widowed woman that lived in Florida.

She had a 42 year old son that was still in the area. He hacked into the DMV website to see what he could find. The son had a Dodge pick-up truck and a different mailing address. It appeared that the house was a rental property. Geoff dug deeper and found the son's cell phone number. He called it.

"Hello?"

"Hello, This is Sergeant Cruz with the Buffalo Police Department. I'm trying to reach Randy Horton." Geoff said, using his most officious voice.

"This is Randy. What's going on?" Geoff started by confirming the fact that Horton owned the house. After he established that Horton was the owner and the house was a rental property, he asked for and received the name of the person that was the current tenant.

As Geoff was running the tenant through various websites on the internet, he asked Horton if he had a copy of the renter's driver's license or other photo identification. By the time Horton found the paperwork the tenant filled out, Geoff discovered all the information was false.

"Sir, on that form you have in front of you, did you happen to write down the make and model of his vehicle or maybe even get a license plate number?"

"Yeah, I have that. Let me find it. Ok, here it is, it says the make is a Mazda and the model is the 6. I don't have the year, but I have the color, dark blue, and the plate number." Geoff got the plate number, and quickly found out it was also fake.

"Ok sir, I'm sorry to have to tell you this, but your house was burned in a fire this evening. I don't know how extensive the damage is. We'll have more information in the next few hours if you could keep this line open. Once we get more information, someone from my department will call you back." They spoke for a few more minutes and then Geoff disconnected the call.

Maybe the call wasn't a total bust. The color of the car was the same as Rick had given him. Maybe the make and the model were the same as well. Geoff pulled up the address on Google Earth. He looked at the way the car was traveling away from the house.

He zoomed the screen out a bit. Ok, he would have to make some guesses, and it would take some time, but Geoff thought he would be able to find the vehicle. The first guess Geoff had to make was, where would the driver be going? He didn't need an exact destination to find what he was looking for, just a general idea.

Geoff knew if he just kidnapped and tried to kill a mafia kingpin, he would be trying to get away as fast and as far as he could in as short amount of time as possible. So that meant, he would take the most direct route to get onto the highway. Ok, this was the theory Geoff was going to explore first.

The address was on West Ave, which is a one way street, heading south. At the end of the street was an intersection. The vehicle could continue heading down West Ave, or make a left turn onto Jersey Ave, which was another one way street, this time heading east. This was the complete opposite direction of where the highway was located.

If the driver stayed on West Ave for another block, this would take him to Pennsylvania Avenue, another one way street. This time heading west, towards the highway. Geoff then hacked into the Buffalo traffic camera system to see where there were and weren't cameras.

Assuming the driver is now on Pennsylvania Avenue, the first traffic camera he will encounter will be where Pennsylvania intersects Niagara Street. Geoff found the approximate time he was looking for and started viewing the video from the cameras located at that intersection.

The traffic cameras at this intersection were in color, but it was dark out and the camera shot was a wide angle covering as much as it could. He found two possible dark colored cars in the time frame he was looking for but he couldn't tell if either of them were blue or a Mazda.

To complicate the issue even more, one car turned right and the other car turned left. Either way would bring you to another intersection that led you to the highway. If you went right on Niagara Street, you could take that up one more block to Porter Ave, then hang a left on Porter and that would run you into the I-190 heading North and give you access to take the Peace Bridge into Canada. Leaving the country might be what the kidnapper was thinking.

However, if you took a right on Niagara you could go down four blocks and pick up the I-190 and catch it in either direction, North or South. If the driver went south, he could stay on the I-190 or he could jump on the Buffalo Skyway.

Geoff would concentrate on the first car, the one that turned right. He assumed this was the car the kidnapper was in and he was heading towards Canada. Right or wrong, Geoff knew he had to find the correct car before it got on the highway. If that occurred and he didn't have the plate number, there were just too many variables to consider and finding the correct car at that point would be against the odds.

Kate could eat. She polished off four of the six tacos and her entire extra-large root beer. I ate all six of my tacos and drank all of my root beer. I put the other two tacos in the fridge and told Kate to make herself at home while I showered and changed.

I went into my bedroom and shut the door. I thought about starting the shower but not getting into it to see if I could catch Kate snooping around but decided against it. I was too tired to care. The sooner I got cleaned up, the sooner I could get Kate back to her car and I could get to the hospital to check on Sal.

I left my ruined cloths on the floor in a pile and took a very long, hot shower. I let the scorching water cleanse my body, but it did nothing for my soul. The only lead I had so far, and it was weak, thin, beyond thin even, was Augostino. I would work him for all he was worth. If he knew anything, I would get it from him, of that I had no doubt.

After my shower, I put on a pair of worn, comfortable jeans and a pair of socks. I unlocked the wheels on the bottom of my bedframe and rolled it away from the headboard. Underneath the headboard, I popped the baseboard away from the wall revealing a hidden wall safe. The safe was secured using a biometric locking system that would only unlock when it read my right ring fingerprint.

Inside the safe, I had $25,000 in hundred dollar bills, several sets of fake identities, complete with driver's licenses, passports, credit cards, and library and/or grocery store cards. I kept all of my different identities in wallets so everything was together. The passports were with the wallets.

Also in the safe was a matching pair of Heckler & Koch USP45CT pistols. The USP is the model design, 45 is the caliber, and the CT stands for compact tactical. The USP45CT is a compact .45 caliber handgun developed for U.S. special operations use. Features included an extended threaded O-ring barrel with polygonal bore profile and the ability to function with a variety of sound suppressors.

I took one of the pistols out, double checked to make certain it was loaded(Of course it was because an unloaded pistol is useless), and grabbed two extra magazines. I put everything I had removed from the safe on the bed and put everything back the way it was. I went to my t-shirt drawer and pulled out an UnderTech UnderCover white t-shirt and put it on. The t-shirt is an all-weather compression power shirt that features two identical easy-access holsters sewn in under each arm.

I put the H&K on my left side holster and the spare magazines in the right side holster. Then I put on a short sleeved, button down shirt. I left one or two extra buttons undone in the event I needed to get at my weapon in a hurry. I took a look at myself in the mirror. Perfect. You couldn't tell I was carrying a weapon.

I went out into the living room and found Kate sitting on my couch looking at something on her phone. Before I could ask her what she was looking at she said "Where do you really live? Because it's not here." She then looked at me.

"I do live here. Why do you ask?"

"Rick, I've seen cheap motel rooms that have more personality than this place. I was planning on doing a little snooping around while you were taking a shower but after you opened the fridge and put the left over tacos in there and I saw what else was in there, or actually, what wasn't in there, I realized there is no way you actually live here."

"I was away for a few weeks and just got back into town today. I haven't gone shopping yet."

"Come on Rick, all you have in your fridge is bottled water and a jar of dill pickles. You don't even have any condiments! I bet if I looked through your cabinets, I wouldn't find dishes or pots or pans or anything a normal person would have in their kitchen if they actually lived in a place." I didn't say anything at first because she was right.

"I…I like pickles…Are you about ready to leave? I have to get to the hospital. I'll take you back to pick up your car."

She rolled her eyes, got up off the couch and followed me to the front door. "You remember our deal, right? I have a few questions to ask you on the drive over."

The first car Geoff ended up following, via intersection cameras, ended up being a dark green Honda instead of a dark Blue Mazda. He discovered this when the car pulled into the parking lot of a well-lit convenient store parking lot.

He backed tracked and picked up the second car. He was able to track it all the way down Niagara Street. When the car made the right turn from Niagara Street onto Virginia Avenue, Geoff was able to confirm that car was a dark blue Mazda. He couldn't get the license plate number from any of the camera views.

He did get a partial photo of the driver but it was hard to tell any detail. The driver was holding what appeared to be a cell phone up to his ear and his head was turned towards the right on the video so it was a grainy profile photo. He wasn't sure if it would be helpful or not, but he kept a copy to be printed off later.

Geoff zoomed the Google Earth Map out so he could look at a bigger picture of the area. It was time to make another guess. There was no way the kidnapper would stay in Buffalo. Once he got on the I-190 heading south, where would he go? The I-190 would run into the I-90 and he then could go east or west.

Geoff didn't care which way he went. He only wanted him to stay on the highway long enough to get onto the I-90.

If he did that, Geoff would be able to hack into the NY State Thruway Camera System and get a good photo of the driver and his plate number when he traveled through one of the toll plazas.

CHAPTER #11

True to her word, Kate had questions for me. At first, they were general questions about the structure of Sal's organization. I described it in the most corporate terms with Sal being the owner and CEO, and Bramwell being the next in line. I made certain not to mention anything even remotely illegal, and I knew the stuff I was telling her were things her organized crime partners could have told her.

She didn't work organized crime and didn't understand the structure and the ins and outs of the business. She asked where my place was in the chain of command. I told her I didn't have a position. Her eyes fired that brilliant shade of green warning me that she was getting frustrated but before she could say anything, I told her Sal was a friend and I was more or less an independent contractor for his organization.

She asked me what I was contracted to do, and that's when I said to her, "Kate, what I do has no bearing on the investigation of who took Sal and it won't help us get back his granddaughter."

"I don't care, I want to know. You said you would tell me anything I wanted to know. Well, I want to know this."

"Ok, I did say that. However, I didn't exactly say when I would. When this is over, when we've gotten who is responsible and freed Speranza, if you still want to know, ask me again and I promise you I will tell you. I won't sugar coat it or bullshit you. Deal?"

"I don't know. I kind of feel cheated here, like you're running a game on me. I don't like that feeling. Not at all."

"I don't blame you. I don't like that feeling either. I promise I'll tell you if you ask. In the meantime, I'll call Allen and have him copy you on everything he e-mails me." I replied as we were pulling up to the valet where her Jeep was parked.

She took a business card out, wrote her e-mail address on the back and handed it to me. "I expect to get regular updates from you, Mr. Stevens."

"Absolutely. I expect the same."

"I bet. So far, it feels like I am the only one that's been doing the giving here."

"You're looking at the situation wrong Kate. You cracked this case wide open. You found where Sal was being kept and you even rescued him. You'll get the credit for all that. I'm just a bystander that happened to be in the right place at the right time." This gave her pause. I could see her thinking about what I said. "As a matter of fact, if you keep my name out of your report, I can be even more helpful."

"Rick, I don't care about getting the credit. I care about solving this case and finding the people that did this. I'm not in this for the glory or for a promotion. I like what I do. I like catching bank robbers. I'm good at it." The valet came up to my car. I rolled the window down and gave him Kate's claim check and a $10 bill.

"You like catching bank robbers? I have a hypothetical question for you. There was a bank robbery at the Brockport Federal Credit Union last summer. You familiar with the case?"

I was certain she would be familiar with the case. Brockport is not even a city really, it's actually a village located in the Town of Sweden in Monroe County, New York. The population is under 12,000 people.

The previous summer, on a Wednesday morning, two armed, masked, gunmen entered the Brockport Federal Credit Union at noon and after killing five people, three bank employees and two customers, they exited the bank with a little over $400,000. They were in the bank for almost four and a half minutes.

Time is a funny thing when you think about it. If you look at the average work day of eight hours, four minutes and thirty seconds is not a lot of time. A work phone call or answering one e-mail can eat up that short amount of a time. Compare that to the last four minutes of regulation time of your standard N.B.A. game, and you start to appreciate the difference.

When someone is robbing a bank, they usually go with what is often called the "Two-Minute Rule". What that means is, from the time the robber walks into the bank to the time he walks out of the bank, he has 120 seconds to complete the robbery. For every second over 120, your chances of getting caught sky rocket.

The average take on a bank robbery is just over $4,000, perpetrated by an amateur, usually alone. The North Hollywood Bank Robbery in 1997 is not typical or standard. The average prison sentence for someone getting caught robbing a bank is 16 years, assuming they haven't pulled a weapon. It goes up from there if a weapon is involved.

So how did these two guys spend more than double the amount of time they should have in the bank, execute five people and walk out with 100 times as much as the average robbery AND still get away with it? Simple. They planned for it.

The Brockport Police Department employs eleven full time officers, two part-time officers, and two civilian officers. They have one chief of police, two lieutenants and two sergeants. At 11:30 in the morning, the first explosion went off at the State University of New York at Brockport.

The second explosion, also on campus, went off at 11:35

am. The third explosion went off at 11:40 am. The fourth explosion went off at 11:45 am. The explosions were on opposite ends of the college. After each explosion, the 911 system was jammed with frantic people calling. There were conflicting reports: some people had seen masked, armed gunmen storming the campus, some said it was a terrorist attack. Complete chaos ensued.

At 12:04 pm, the armed, masked gunmen casually strolled out of the bank and got into their car and drove away. The torched hull of the car was recovered 24 hours and approximately 65 miles away in Sodus Point, NY. No evidence was left behind. The FBI had put out a huge reward for any information leading to the arrest of the gunmen but none of the leads panned out. The FBI and the cops were at a dead end.

"Yes, I'm familiar with the case. Everyone is familiar with the case. Why?"

"Remember, this is all hypothetical. What if I could provide you with not only the names of the two men that robbed the bank, but the evidence you would need to convict them? Hypothetically speaking, of course." I was waiting for an outburst of anger from her and was surprised when she calmly answered me.

"See? This is what I'm talking about. I feel like you're running a game on me. You're asking me to falsify an official federal document by leaving your name out of it and acting like I don't know who you are, and in return, you're going to give me the names and evidence of the murdering bastards that robbed a bank? No. Screw you Stevens. I'm not going to fall for it."

"Fall for it? What do you mean *fall for it*?"

"You'll only give me the info *after* I turn in my final

report, right? I see your game here. I'm not dumb you know."

"Kate, not at all. I don't think you're dumb. Far from it. I have my own reasons for not wanting to be named in your report..."

"Of course you do! God forbid you give me the names of some ruthless killers because it's the right damn thing to do! You're such an asshole, you know?" In the dim lighting being projected from the valets' entrance to the hotel, I could see the deepness and depth of her soul in her eyes.

"Let me finish, ok? If you don't like my offer, if you think I'm going to renege on my end of the deal, you can tell me to piss off and you can do what you want, ok?"

"Or I could arrest you under the Patriot Act and site you as a domestic terrorist and watch you disappear until we got what we wanted out of you." Being arrested under the Orwellian Patriot Act was a scary thought. I would have no legal standing, or rights. They could detain me for as long as they wanted, without council. They could make me disappear, forever, if they wanted to. If she tried to arrest me, I would have a decision to make. I took a deep breath.

"By 8:00 am tomorrow morning, you will have a file on your desk, from me, with the details of the Brockport robbery, the names and locations of the people who did the robbery..."

"And murders..."

"Yes, and murders, the evidence you need to convict them and where that evidence can be found. Everything will be neatly wrapped up for you. I'll even give you the key to the entire thing Kate. I'll give you probable cause to stop one of the suspects and have him arrested. From that arrest, and using the info in the e-mail I send you, you'll be able to get a search warrant that will tie this individual to the robbery. If he doesn't flip on his partner, the evidence you collect will be enough for you to bring him in for questioning and obtain a search warrant."

"From there, it's over, case closed. I'm betting he flips though. Earlier tonight, you said you were a woman of honor. I believe you are. I'll give you all of this Kate, before you write your final report. If you think I'm screwing with you, if I haven't delivered everything I've promised, then write your report whatever way you want to. If I give you everything I promised, all that I ask is you leave my name out of the report. I was an innocent bystander, a good Samaritan that disappeared in the night before anyone could get my name. Do we have a deal?"

I had made my best pitch to her. She would either take it or not. Or maybe try to arrest me. Her face was blank, and I couldn't tell which way she would decide. I thought it would be hell playing poker against her.

"If I don't have it by 8:01 am, I'm cutting a warrant for your arrest and leading the hunt." She held me by her stare. The valet pulled up with her Jeep. She turned away and got out of my truck without saying anything else. I thought to myself that she was tough as hell and I would not want her hunting me.

On my way to the hospital, I called Geoff. He said he was working on getting me the rest of the info on the car. He said he would e-mail me everything when it was done. He said he had a few partial photos of Sal's kidnapper from several traffic cameras. He said he wanted to try to clean them up for me before he sent them to me but he hadn't had a chance to yet.

I thanked him for his help and all his hard work. I also told him I needed another favor.

"Rick? Are you sure?"

"Yes, I am. Get it all together and send it to me. I need it all Geoff and I need it ASAP. Once we have a few minutes, I'll explain everything to you. I can assure you now though that I am not under any type of duress nor have I lost my mind." I talked to Geoff for a few more minutes and told him to call me after he sent me all the info I requested. I hung up from him and made another call. I told the person who I was, why I was calling and what I needed. I was assured everything would be ready for me to pick up at the time I requested.

On my way to the hospital, I made the pick-up. Everything went as smoothly as promised. I parked my car in a spot reserved for doctors and walked inside. I knew my way around the hospital and headed straight to the ICU floor. When I stepped off the elevator, I was surprised to see how many people were still there waiting, just to show support for Sal. The waiting room was packed!

I by-passed the waiting room and went into the Unit. I went to the nursing station. I figured the nurses were probably irritated by all the well-wishers trying to get in to see Sal. The call I made after I hung up with Geoff was to the owner of an excellent Italian bakery.

I told him I needed a party tray of his best assorted Italian cookies and pastries. I also requested two of his large, square to go boxes of the best coffee he had. Everything was packed up and ready to go when I got to his bakery. I gave him $500 for his trouble, but he refused to take it at first. He said it was an honor that I thought of him for something like this. He was truly sincere when he said it. I thanked him again, tucked the hundred dollar bills in his apron and left.

I smiled at the two nurses working the desk. "Good evening ladies. I know you've had a rough night. I know it's only going to get harder as the news of who's in your unit gets out to the press." They both eyed me suspiciously.

Still smiling, I pressed on "Sal is a friend of mine. A genuine friend. I love him like a father. I know visiting hours are over, and I'm not here to ask you to break any rules by letting me visit with him. I just want to say 'thank you', I appreciate everything you do, and 'thank you' for helping my friend. As a gesture of my appreciation, I brought you some pastries and coffee."

They both said thank you but still eyed me suspiciously like they were waiting for the other shoe to drop. I carried the desserts and coffee to the ICU nurses break room and left. I made sure I knew each of the nurse's names. I knew in the future, if I needed to get in to see Sal or needed some info, I would find one of these nurses and ask for help. I figured I had a 50/50 shot of them giving me what I needed. After leaving the desserts in the break room, I found Bramwell and told him to take a walk with me.

We left the ICU floor and headed to the lobby. Once in the lobby, I grabbed a diet soda form the vending machine and we went outside to talk. Bramwell started by filling me in on Sal's condition (No significant change from the last time I talked to him), how many guys he had in the hospital (18), how he would use them (He decided on having six guys awake and in the ICU unit at all times in four hour shifts).

It sounded like he had the hospital covered. He told me about the local cops and the FBI coming in, what they asked, who they asked. Bramwell is an intelligent guy. I respect his opinion and insight. I asked him what his opinion was. He told me he didn't think the cops or the feds would spend a lot of time trying to find out who did this to Sal. He said if we wanted to find out, we were pretty much on our own. I agreed with his assessment.

"What do you think we should do about the meeting in

NY? Cancel it? Wait and see if Sal comes out of the coma?"

"No, I think if we cancel the meeting or don't show up, it will be taken as a sign of disrespect and weakness. Nothing good can come from us not being there."

"Ok, I kind of felt the same way, but I didn't want to do anything if there was a chance Mr. DiFlippo could go. I know I'm his underboss, but the families in NY aren't going to view me as that."

"You're right. They won't. Which is a good thing for us. Don't worry Bramwell, I have a plan." After telling him my plan, he smiled and shook his head. He asked a few questions, offered a few ideas and we had a rough outline.

"You really are crazy, aren't you?" He asked me.

"Some days I wonder that myself." I answered him truthfully.

"So if this plan fails, what next?"

"If our plan fails Bramwell, you'll be dead and won't have to worry about what to do next."

CHAPTER #12

By the time Primo made it to Erie, Pennsylvania, he was exhausted and picked the first budget motel he could find. He had hit a drive thru on the way and ate dinner driving. He had a restless night of sleep but he still felt pretty good.

He called his brother in Arkansas to let him know where he was. He told him he would be there in a day or two and to sit tight. He didn't want to get all the way to Arkansas until he was paid what he was owed to him from Moretti. He didn't know Moretti personally, only by reputation, and his reputation said he was an asshole.

Even though Primo had eight million dollars waiting for him, he was still owed another million from Moretti and he wasn't going to walk away from that. Using a different, pre-paid cell phone he called Moretti. His call was answered by a secretary and he was put on hold for almost 12 minutes.

Finally, the call was picked up but it wasn't by Moretti, it was his underboss, Bruno Conti.
"This is Bruno, who's this?"

Conti was the last person Primo wanted to talk to and he was starting to feel like he was going to get the run around. He took a deep breath "Mr. Conti, good morning. This is Primo."

Primo paused, giving Conti a chance to say something, or congratulate him for what he had accomplished, or to put him on hold to get Moretti.

"Yeah? So?"

"So? I thought there would be a little appreciation, some respect maybe? No?"

"Appreciation for what? For not following instructions? You were told to call us only when the job is done." They must not have heard the news. Maybe the old man's body was completely burned up in the fire. Maybe he hadn't been identified yet.

"That is exactly why I am calling. The job is complete…"

"No it's not." Enough was enough. Primo was tired of being disrespected, tired of being talked down.

"HEY Conti, don't EVER interrupt me again or I'll…"

"You'll what? Not kill me like you didn't kill DiFlippo?"

"What are you talking about? I stabbed him and burned him! He's dead!"

"You're pathetic. He's in the hospital, recovering. You failed." Primo couldn't believe what he was hearing.

"No, he was dead. There must be some mistake…"

"Yeah, the mistake was hiring a-has-been-that-never-will-be to handle an important job such as this. I hope you got some money from DiFlippo because we ain't paying you shit. Now, you can either go and finish the job, or you can disappear. Matter of fact, if you or your brother ever shows your face in New York again, we'll kill you. I mean, really kill you, not half-ass it like YOU seem to do. Capice?" Before Rock could answer, the line went dead.

Rock used the other phone he had and called his brother. "We have a problem…"

After leaving the hospital, I put together everything I promised Kate about the Brockport Federal Credit Union job. The job was done by two people in Augostino's organization. I knew the two people who pulled the bank job. I had them on video, with sound, talking about the job, in detail. This was about a month before the job took place.

The job was originally supposed to be pulled off by Sal's organization, but due to its proximity, namely being on Augostino's turf, Sal did the right thing and asked his permission, offering to give him a percentage of the take.

Augostino agreed, but he wanted to have two of his own people go in with two of Sal's'. Fine. The meeting was to go over the plan and for Sal's guys to meet Augostino's guys. Sal asked me to go along. He wanted my opinion on Augostino's guys. The meeting took place in a hotel room in downtown Buffalo. The room was wired for sound and video and I was in the adjoining room with someone's nephew who was running the sound and video through his computer.

I immediately didn't like Augostino's guys. They were loud, obnoxious, cocky and had more balls than brains. I called Sal and told him what I thought. He told me to give it more time. He said first impressions may not always be correct. So I followed his advice and stayed patient.

Our guys were instructed to not give away any details of the plan. Augostino's guys kept pushing for how they wanted to 'play this job'. The meeting was almost over and one of their guys asked one of our guys what was so important about the Federal Credit Union on that day?

All our guy knew was what he was told. That specific bank on that specific day was going to have over five million dollars passing through it. As soon as our guy told Augostino's guys that information, I could see the look that passed between them. I knew this would not end well at all.

After the meeting was over, I talked to Sal. I told him what I thought, what I felt about the two guys Augostino sent to go on the job. I told him it was a bad idea and to stay away from the job. Sal took a few minutes, weighed what I said and then picked up his phone and called Augostino. He told Augostino he had decided not to do the job and thanked him for the opportunity.

I told Sal Augostino was still going to go through with the job. He said he knew. He said we had the video from the meeting and he knew where Augostino's money would end up. Sal had a guy that worked for the U.S. Federal Government that had tipped him to the amount of money moving through the bank that day. He warned Sal that all of the bills serial numbers were accounted for and if Sal happened to come into contact with a large quantity of them, he should move them somewhere, outside the U.S. This was a piece of information Sal had kept to himself.

Since we knew who did the bank job, it was easy for us to follow the guys after the job was completed. So we knew which banks they stored their share of the cash in. We even had the safety deposit box numbers and keys to get into the boxes. We knew what storage unit they had left the weapons and clothing they used for the bank job in. We also had a key to that place. Why anyone would keep something that incriminating is beyond me, but these two idiots did.

I put everything I had together and put it in a large envelope. I left out anything that would specifically point to Augostino. I held that information back because I knew I would be seeing him soon and I had a different plan for him.

I had one of Sal's couriers take the envelope, now addressed to Agent Kate Riley, and drop it off at the FBI Office. It would be waiting for her on her desk when she came into work the next morning, as promised.

Once that was done, I called Geoff and had him get me a private flight to Florida later this morning. I didn't want to fly commercial because the airlines would not allow me to board with the items I would be bringing with me.

Once I was in my seat and had a glass of ginger ale, I booted up the laptop I had and installed the Assassin File Geoff sent me. I am very particular about my safety and have just started using laptops instead of going into internet café's.

The assassin file was a program that would destroy the computer and make certain if it fell into law enforcements hands, they would not be able to get anything from it. Once that was completed, I inserted the disc that Kate gave me.

About the time I was strapping my seatbelt on and preparing for lift-off, Bramwell was in a Lincoln Town Car with three of his associates heading to the meeting with the heads of the other crime families.

He was dressed in a pair of Joseph Abboud Charcoal Flannel slacks, a matching short sleeve Joseph Abboud Golden Haze Herringbone dress shirt, and a pair of perfectly polished Allen Edmonds Black Presidio Penny Loafers. He wasn't wearing a suit jacket or a vest or a tie because he never did. This was about the most he ever got dressed up.

He had his head shaved to the scalp with a razor earlier that morning. His long, blond goatee was neatly trimmed but still hung off of his chin a good two inches. The matching black, fiery skull tattoos were easily visible on his large, powerful forearms. He did not wear any jewelry, not even a watch. He never liked jewelry and only wore a watch when it was necessary.

They were not allowed to bring weapons with them into the meeting but they all had weapons on them for the ride to the meeting. The guys with Bramwell were bodyguards. Both were ex-military. Both trained in hand to hand combat and both had killed people before. They were dressed in suits and were told to be on high alert. They knew going in that they might not walk out. If that was to be the outcome, both of them were fine with it. They knew they would take others with them before they died.

The car was being driven by the third bodyguard and he would remain in the underground garage with the car and the weapons. Bramwell was told the meeting started at 10:00 am. He knew the *real* meeting started at eight or eight-thirty. Any decisions that the families were going to make were going to be made before he got there and without his input.

Bramwell knew this and expected it. He was prepared. He had a card or two up his sleeve. The final outcome would all depend on how well he played those cards. If he played them well enough and was believable, they would walk out of the meeting and return to Buffalo. If he misplayed them, or wasn't believable, he knew he would die in the conference room, or more likely, in the parking garage where he now sat.

Bramwell wasn't one to waste words so he got right to the point with his team. "Listen, I'm going to do the best I can to make sure we walk out of this meeting alive. If that doesn't happen, take as many of these sons of bitches with you as you can, got it? Let's do this."

I was starting to get spoiled and really enjoyed flying chartered, private flights instead of flying commercial flights. I got off the plane and picked up my pre-paid rental car without having to stop at the counter and I was on my way.

I wanted to go by Spree's townhouse and check out where she was taken. I didn't know if it would be helpful or not but it was where I wanted to start. It made sense in my mind. I knew I was going to need Geoff's help, but I didn't know exactly on what or where.

I didn't have any trouble finding the townhouse. I drove by it without slowing down. I watched the streets and surrounding areas. I wanted to make sure they didn't have a cop sitting on the house. I didn't see anyone or anything suspicious. I parked on the next street over and walked back to the house.

As I was walking towards the house, I called the home phone number. It rang four times then a machine picked up. I repeated the process and got the same result. I was going to lean on the doorbell but stopped myself and instead knocked on the door a few times, hard. I knew the house did not have an alarm system.

The street was quiet and the front door was partially concealed from view by the foliage and large palm tree. The lock was your standard Schlage. It wasn't the top of the line, but it wasn't cheap or flimsy either. Out came my lock picks and I went to work. It took me almost 90 seconds to have the door unlocked and I was in the house. I was definitely getting rusty using the picks. I think I said the same thing the last time I had used them. I chastised myself for not practicing and promised I would practice once this job was done.

"Hello? Your front door was open? Is anyone home? Hello?" I yelled into the empty house. I closed the door and relocked it. I took a quick walk-through of the house, clearing it. I now knew for a fact that the house was empty and I knew at least two other ways I could get out of the house unseen in case someone came home.

Sal had a guy in Florida (It seemed like Sal had a guy everywhere) and he scouted the place for Bramwell who gave me the information. Spree's roommate was staying at her boyfriend's parents' house until the shock and trauma from Spree's abduction wore off. I doubted she would ever live here again, even if I found Spree and got her home safe.

I knew the police had already been through here and I knew if the FBI hadn't been, they would be soon. Thinking about the FBI made me smile because I thought of Kate. I knew from the reports that everyone was in the dark on how Spree went missing. No one was even sure she was abducted from the house. The last person to see her was her roommate and that was earlier in the day. The roommate was going on her boyfriend's parent's boat for the day and Spree was planning on staying home and relaxing. The last time anyone other than her kidnapper saw Spree was around 7:45 in the morning.

A long time ago, the United States Army taught me how to hunt and track people. Then, for the next several years, they kept bringing me and my team to different places around the world where we got to put those skills to use. To a lesser degree, I was still using those skills in my current occupation.

This would be a little bit different but the idea and the general concept was the same. A successful tracker is someone that is patient. I could be very patient. I started my search in Spree's bedroom. I didn't feel the need to toss her room looking for clues. This wasn't a random kidnapping or done by a jealous ex-lover. This was a professional job.

Her room was neat and organized. Her books and DVD's were all in alphabetical order. Her bed was made and all of her clothes were either folded on shelves or hanging in her closet. I knew she was an honor roll student and seeing the meticulous way she kept her personal belongings told me a lot about her.

There were no signs of forced entry; there were no signs of a struggle. The police were leaning towards her knowing her attacker or leaving with him in his vehicle. Her car was still in the garage. The second theory was she walked somewhere to get the mail, or up the street to the juice place, and someone took her then.

I didn't have a theory yet. I wanted to read the scene without any preconceived ideas about what might have occurred here. I checked every door and window looking for signs of a break in. Chipped paint, a slightly bent lock, pry marks near a lock but I didn't find anything.

Assuming she was taken from this house, how would someone do that without standing out? How would they get her without her fighting or screaming or leaving some sign that she was under duress?

First, someone would have to have a vehicle that blended in with the area. A landscaping truck? Maybe. Most of the landscaping trucks I have seen are pick-up trucks towing an open trailer. It would fit in, but it wasn't the ideal vehicle to hide a person. The same could be said for a pool cleaning service. I eliminated them from my list.

Remembering the video from Sal's abduction, the kidnappers used a laundry delivery van. A laundry delivery van wouldn't fit in this neighborhood, but a food deliver truck or van would. A van with a pizza delivery decal on the outside would be unnoticeable here. I was close to the university so I knew there would be literally hundreds of food places, most of which delivered to college students in this area.

I'd have to figure out how to cut it down some. I went outside to the front of the house. The street was quiet. I waited exactly five minutes and did not see one car drive by. No one was out jogging or walking. Interesting...

I knew none of the police vehicles parked in the driveway when they responded to the scene. The entire house was wrapped in yellow crime scene tape. I bent down and got into the push-up position. I looked at the ground and the driveway. I wasn't looking for anything specific. I was just looking.

At first I didn't see anything. Then, I started to notice things. There were a few drops of oil on the driveway. It appeared to be somewhat fresh. When I touched it, it was still tacky and slick. I don't know if it meant anything. Spree's car could have an oil leak or her roommate or a visitor or boyfriend. It was just something I filed away.

There was nothing else to see. Sometimes you get lucky. Sometimes you find something that shouldn't be there, a receipt, a cigarette butt, something. Not this time. I stood up and walked to the front door. I examined the lock again, but came up dry.

I looked at the door bell button. I avoided using it when I first got to the house because it did not appear to have been dusted by the police. I wondered...

Bramwell was shown into the over-sized conference room. The first thing he noticed was the floor to ceiling window view of Central Park that ran across the entire back of the room. The next thing he noticed was there was only one seat left, and that was for him.

The other heads of the family were already seated and each underboss was seated next to them. The underboss and head of the family each had a bodyguard sitting next to them. Bramwell smiled to himself. This was how it was going to be?

He casually took the only remaining seat and his bodyguards stood next to him on either side. They firmly forced themselves in and the people on either side of Bramwell had to slide down to allow them room. They were the only two people standing in the room.

After the pleasantries were exchanged, it was time to get down to business. Bramwell was the youngest boss at the table. He was also the largest and least dressed. All the other bosses had on suits and ties and even the underbosses were wearing suits and ties. The way that everyone was looking at him, Bramwell felt like the turd that was floating in the punch bowl.

"Mr. Bramwell..." Ricci started to say. Bramwell held up his hand like it was a stop sign.

"Mr. Ricci, I appreciate the respect you've shown me but please, just call me Bramwell. Mr. Bramwell is my dad." Bramwell could tell Ricci was annoyed that he interrupted him. Good.

"Ok, Bramwell. Thank you for being here. It's a tragedy what happened to Salvatore. He was a good friend to all of us in this room…" Bramwell interrupted him again.

"Was? You mean he's not anymore?" Ricci actually made a face this time before answering. Bramwell noticed Moretti lean over and whisper something to his underboss. His underboss shook his head sadly.

"Bramwell, please let me finish, without interrupting. The reports that we have gotten have told us Salvatore is on his way out. That is why we are having this meeting. So…" Bramwell interrupted him again.

"Wait, reports? What reports? Where are you getting these reports?" This time, Moretti spoke up.

"Bramwell, you're new to this. We understand that. But show some respect. Don Ricci has asked that you not interrupt him and you keep interrupting him. For Christ sakes, I can tell my 6 year old nephews not to interrupt and they won't interrupt." Bramwell held up his hand in the stop sign motion again and apologized.

Ricci continued "You've been Salvatore's number two guy since that Mazzio incident? I don't know what you did prior to being the underboss, but running this business, this takes a lot of tact, and finesse and…" This time, Moretti interrupted Ricci.

"…It takes a high level of intelligence and ruthlessness."

"Yes, thank you Marcello. It's like he said, it takes a lot to be the head of a family. Even one as small as Salvatore's." Bramwell ignored the slight towards his organization and smiled like an idiot and shook his head up and down signifying he was following Ricci's every word.

"The people that respected Salvatore, worked with him, had arrangements with him, they don't know you. You've only been around for six months. This is a dangerous time for you and your family. Other gangs will look to move in on your turf. Your weekly envelopes will get lighter. Some people in your family might turn on you. Now is not the time to show weakness. Now is not the time to be indecisive."

This time Augostino picked up where Ricci left off. "I've known Salvatore a long time. We're close, like brothers. I met with him a few months back and talked to him more recently on the phone. He was thinking about retiring. Did you know this?"

Bramwell shook his head no and put on his best surprised face. He knew Augostino was lying and DiFlippo would never retire. So far, this conversation was going exactly the way Rick told him it would. Like clockwork, it was Moretti's turn to pick up the sales pitch.

"Listen, Bramwell, you're a straight shooter. I can see that so I'm not going to try to bullshit a bullshitter. I'll be honest, we're not only concerned for you and your family, we're also concerned for us as well. Since 9/11, the FBI has shifted their entire focus to terrorists. That leaves us with some breathing room, and more opportunities to make money. The last thing we want to do is have a war go on between families, you know?"

Bramwell shook his head up and down and smiled again. He saw through Moretti's bullshit. The thinly veiled threat of going to war if he didn't agree with whatever their proposal was. Moretti was rattling on about business and how hard it was to make decisions. Bramwell paid attention and shook his head when he should have and smiled when he should have.

He was waiting to hear the actual proposal before he went on the offensive. These old timers really liked to hear themselves talk. That was the issue with the mafia today. Nobody ever got right down to business. It was like going to a church service. You've got 45 minutes of filler to cover for a 15 minute sermon. It appeared they were running out of steam.

Ricci said "So here is what we are thinking would be best for you and your family…"

It was a longshot, I know, but it was better than nothing. It would only take me a few minutes to try and every gambler loves the longshot. I went into the house to gather the few things I would need.

I found the first two items in Spree's bathroom and the last three items were in a drawer in the kitchen near the telephone. I brought the stuff outside and followed through on my theory. My theory was whoever abducted Spree, used a commercial vehicle, parked in the driveway, and rang the doorbell.

I was hoping that when this occurred, they were not wearing gloves and left a fingerprint on the doorbell button. I didn't have a fingerprint kit with me, but I knew I could make one from a few common household items.

The first item I needed was a pencil. I was fortunate because Spree and her roommate used mechanical pencils instead of wood pencils. This would make my job easier. I removed the graphite from the pencil and used the second item, a nail file, and ground the graphite into a powder.

I used the third item, one of Spree's make up brushes to brush the powder onto the doorbell's button. I carefully blew the excess dust from the button. I tried not to get too excited, but there was a finger print on the button and few smudge marks around it. I didn't want to get excited because the fingerprint could have belonged to anyone.

I used the fourth item, a piece of clear packing tape and lifted the print off of the button. I carefully stuck the packing tape to the fifth item, a white index note card. I pocketed the card, cleaned the doorbell button and returned the items to the house where I got them.

I spent a few minutes walking through the house to make sure there wasn't anything I missed. When I was comfortable I wasn't forgetting to check something, I left the house. I walked casually up the street to the corner. I stood on the corner and took note of the traffic and the businesses around the area. I crossed the street and walked down the other side of the street. I passed directly in front of Spree's townhouse.

I walked down the street and stopped on the corner. Once again I just observed. My work on this street was done for now. I needed to call Geoff and then meet up with Sal's Miami contact.

"We have gone over the numbers, and have come up with what we believe to be a very generous offer." Ricci was still rattling on. He'd been talking about the generous offer for almost five minutes now. Bramwell couldn't take anymore.

He reached into his pants pocket and took out a package of cigarettes and a book of matches. He shook one form his pack and lit it with a match. The look of complete horror on everyone's face was priceless. Well worth the price of admission Bramwell thought to himself. Ricci had stopped talking mid-sentence and his mouth hung wide open.

Finally Moretti broke the silence "Hey Bramwell, put that out. You can't smoke in here."

"Really? I can't? Because, and correct me if I'm wrong, but I am smoking, right? So what, is me smoking a fucking miracle? That's what it must be since I *can't* smoke in here. You know, you invite me here and then do nothing but talk down to me and insult my intelligence the entire time I am here. You looked down on me because of the way I look and the way I dress. You automatically assumed I was an idiot and treated me as such." He paused to draw on his cigarette.

"But whose the real idiot here, huh Moretti? If we look at the word can't, which is really a contraction of the words can and not, and if we look at the word's definition and meaning, we see that can't is a model verb used to indicate that it is impossible for something to be done. So as I sit here and smoke, and you tell me I can't smoke, you sir, are incorrect." Bramwell continued to smoke.

"Now, Moretti, if you want to use the term, can't, correctly, this would be a more accurate sentence to use. If I put you through that fucking window over there, I'm betting dollars to donuts that you *can't* fly and you *will* fall to your death. You see the difference now asshole?" The entire room stiffened. Bramwell's body guards took two steps back and prepared to attack anyone that stood up.

Everyone was shocked into silence. Mario Costa, head of the Marino Family, actually had a smile on his face. Before anyone could speak, Bramwell said "Now let's stop the dog and pony show here and get right to business. No one in this room gives a shit about Mr. DiFlippo and I know this because no one asked about him. We all know this meeting is bullshit. You invited me here to buy me off so I would turn over Mr. DiFlippo's business interests and, if I don't do that, then I'm sure you're all planning on having me killed when I return to the secure, underground parking garage, right?"

"But you guys made a mistake. Two mistakes actually. The first mistake, was assuming Mr. DiFlippo was on his way out. Sadly, for you, this is wrong. He's actually doing very well. On the drive up here from Buffalo, I got word from the hospital that he had come out of the coma. He did not suffer any brain damage. He is in pain, and he is weak, but he can talk, and that's exactly what he's doing."

Bramwell had them all. He knew he had them. You could hear a pin drop. It was a lie. DiFlippo was still in a coma and wasn't talking to anyone. The prognosis wasn't very good he would ever talk again but Bramwell had sold it. Now, it was time to close this show. If his father was still alive, he would say it was time to shit or get off the pot. Well pop, Bramwell thought, this one's for you: I'm going to shit.

"Who is he talking to? Right? That's what you're wondering now, isn't it? I would be if I was in your shoes. Sadly, the answer again is not good for any of you. He's talking to Rick Stevens. You might know him better as The Reaper."

I needed to reach out and find someone that could run this print through the law enforcement database. I thought about asking Geoff, but I had him working on a bunch of other stuff. I knew I was wearing him thin with everything I expected him to do, but he never complained.

Maybe Sal's Miami guy, Manny Rios, would have a cop or a detective in his back pocket. I called the number Bramwell gave me but got voicemail. I left a message. I wanted to go to the other crime scenes and walk through them as I had done at Spree's house.

It would give me something to do while I waited for Rios to call me back. I was closer to the garage where Angiola was murdered so I would hit that place first. I wondered if the FBI had taken control of the scene yet and released it or if it was still under local jurisdiction. All of a sudden, a light clicked on.

I pulled out my cell phone and dialed a number. After three rings, the call was answered.

"This is Agent Riley" Clear, concise, direct and to the point. Just hearing her voice made me smile again.

"Hello Kate, this is Rick, you have a minute?" For a few seconds there was only silence. Then she said

"Yes, Mr. Stevens. How can I say no after the wonderful gift you left for me today." At first I didn't know what she was talking about but then I remembered the Brockport bank job.

"Good, I'm glad you got it. I hope everything is there that I promised would be. If it's not enough, let me know and I'll see what else I can dig up."

"No it looks great, thank you. Unfortunately, my boss told me I had to sit on it until we wrap up the DiFlippo case so it has been moved to the back burner. For now. Are you just calling to see if I got your envelope or is there some other reason?" Her voice was light, and I could sense an unfamiliar undercurrent to her words.

"Actually, I was calling to see if you could do me a favor." When she answered me, her voice was flat, emotionless, and professional again.

"Of course Mr. Stevens. I am here to serve. How many laws will I be required to break for you this time?"

"Agent Riley, sarcasm does not become you. This is regarding a possible lead on the DiFlippo case." I realized I was still smiling when I was talking to her.

"What Rick? What do you need? My schedule is packed full today and I am getting ready to go stand next to my boss at a press conference. As much as I enjoy our conversation together, and yes, that is sarcasm, you need to stop being cute and wrap it up." I didn't even realize I was being cute. Was that intentional?

"I have a fingerprint and I need to know who it belongs to." Once again she was quiet. She covered the mouth piece of the phone but I heard her say she'll be there in a minute.

"Ok, I don't have the time to get into this right now. The press conference is literally starting in 90 seconds. After that, I am on a plane headed to Miami. I don't know how long I'll be down there. I will call you back after we land."

"Miami? Kate I'm in Miami right now…"

"Of course you are. Why would you not be? Still trampling all over my case."

"Call me when you land and we'll meet up and compare notes on where each of us is on the case. Deal?"

"Ok, I'll call you when I get to Miami. Bye Rick." And she was gone. She was coming to Miami and I was in Miami. It appeared that Kate and my paths were destined to cross again.

Bramwell was trying to see who reacted first and most dramatically. He immediately noticed all the color from Moretti's face drained. The next thing he noticed was Augostino's reaction. He immediately started staring laser beams at Moretti and would not stop looking at him. Moretti didn't even notice. Costa still had that smile on his face like he was waiting for the punch line. Ricci looked pissed off and bored all at the same time.

Finally, Moretti spoke "Bullshit. Stevens is dead. Mazzio killed him last winter." Guilty, Bramwell thought to himself.

"No, he's alive and well. Someone started the rumor that he was killed and everyone bought into it."

Now it was Augostino's turn to talk. "How come we haven't heard about him or any of his jobs? Six months Bramwell, and nothing. He never goes six months without doing work."

"He just did a job in Texas. Who do you think took out

Collucci? It wasn't anyone from any of *your* families, that's for damn sure! The Reaper was on a vacation in Brazil or wherever the hell he goes in-between jobs. It took Mr. DiFlippo all of about 10 minutes to locate Collucci and hours later, the Reaper took him out. How long were you guys trying to find him? How did that work out for you?"

"I still say bullshit!" Moretti said again, but this time, he said it like he was trying to convince himself.

"You can say whatever you want. Here is what will happen next. The Reaper is going to come and do what he does. He's going to find Mr. DiFlippo's granddaughter and get her back. He's going to find out who was responsible. He's going to fucking work baby! It's time to harvest! Anyone involved will be killed. Your loved ones, your family, your friends, he'll fucking kill every single one of them." Bramwell paused to light a new cigarette. Amazing, no one said anything about him smoking now.

"If you had anything to do with this, you're a dead man as you sit here right now. Go home, kiss your wife, kiss your mistress, kiss your kids, whatever. Your time is done. If you even knew anything about this plot against Mr. DiFlippo's family, you're fucking done too. He's wiping the boards clean."

"What the hell? Are you threatening us with a war?" Ricci was really pissed off now. Bramwell didn't care. He was having too much fun. He estimated his odds of walking out of here alive at less than 50%. The hell with it he thought, in for a penny, in for a pound.

"A war? No. Not a war. I'm talking about Hiroshima and Nagasaki all over again. I'm talking about a fucking atom bomb blowing up in YOUR world and killing YOU and everyone you've ever cared about. There's not going to be a war." Bramwell put his cigarette out right on the top of the conference room table and stood up.

"Gentleman, get your shit together because the end is upon us. One last thing before I leave. If anyone has any information, any at all, even a suspicion; I strongly suggest you get in contact with me ASAP." Bramwell turned his back on the room and walked out with his bodyguards. He would know in about two minutes if he had pulled it off. Once the elevator doors opened in the garage, there would either be people there with guns or not. They stepped into the elevator and hit the G2 button, signifying the lowest level of the garage. As the doors slid closed, Bramwell thought it was out of his hands at this point.

CHAPTER #13

Kate hung up her call with Rick and walked out onto the stage with Phillips where the press conference was about to start. She stood next to Phillips as he made the task force sound courageous and brilliant and even a little humble all at the same time.

He played up the bit about rescuing DiFlippo, making his agents sound like superheroes. Instead of saying an unnamed witness carried DiFlippo out of the fire, Phillips gave the recognition to an unnamed Buffalo Police Officer. This led him to the end of his speech where he finished up by thanking the Buffalo Police Department and all their officers for everything that they had done to help close this part of the investigation. Then he took questions.

Like most politicians, Phillips had that knack for listening to a question, then talking about the question for two to three minutes without actually answering the question. Then he would go on to ignore the next question.

Once the press conference had ended, Phillips and Kate got in Phillips' car and his driver drove them to the airport where the FBI had a jet waiting to fly them down to Miami. Kate smiled when she thought about seeing Stevens again. She didn't understand it, but for some reason, she kind of liked him. Kind of, she thought to herself again. She was still curious about what he really did for DiFlippo and was almost afraid to learn the truth.

Primo was angry and felt like a fool for failing to kill DiFlippo. He had to decide if he should go to Arkansas or head back to Buffalo to see if he could finish the job. The issue wasn't letting Moretti down or the empty threat about them killing him and his brother. Now, it was a matter of pride.

He had fantasized about killing DiFlippo for so long and he thought he had finally done it. He was confused because he didn't understand his own motives. His first thought was maybe DiFlippo would die in the hospital. Even if he went back to Buffalo, would he get another opportunity to kill him? DiFlippo would be heavily guarded.

Maybe it would be better if DiFlippo lived. Knowing he was responsible for his daughter being killed and his granddaughter being kidnapped and abused. If he kept his granddaughter, he could send him pictures of all the horrible things he was doing to her, If he did this, he could kill DiFlippo a million times. Every day, when the mail arrived he would wonder, is today the day I get another picture?

He wasn't supposed to keep her butPrimo liked the idea of it. The old man would be tormented for the rest of his days. His life would be a living hell. Primo smiled. He could only hope that DiFlippo survived and got better. He would enjoy killing him again and again and again.

Geoff had worked most of the night trying to track the vehicle. After several hours, he was able to get the plate number. He hacked his way into the New York State Department of Motor Vehicles and checked who owned the vehicle.

It ended up being a dead end. The car was registered to a 78 year old person who was deceased. Geoff figured there was some social security scam in play here, but that wasn't what he was looking for. He took it a step further and tried to link the deceased owner to one of the four mafia families but couldn't find the connection.

He was still running different programs trying to find missing or moving money to see if he could figure out who was responsible for the abductions. Rick also wanted him to keep track of the money that originally flagged him as to where DiFlippo was being held. That money was on the move and he was trying to keep a trace on it to see where it eventually ended up.

Rick also had three or four other projects that Geoff was trying to do. Rick didn't want excuses, he wanted results. Geoff was going to give him exactly what he wanted.

The underground parking structure was promoted as a secure structure, but I could immediately find several easy ways to get in or out of the garage without being seen or being suspicious. There were two unmanned credit card exits anyone could walk through to gain access, there were the elevators from the building leading to the garage or they could have just drove in the regular entrance and got a ticket to park

He walked the parking garage and saw that there were several cameras. He spoke with the lot attendant and discovered there were eight cameras that recorded on one VCR tape that was held for one week until it was recorded over.

The VCR was hooked up to a multiplexer and the multiplexer would tape one camera for two seconds, and then switch to the next camera for two seconds, etc. So if you were watching camera #1, there would be 14 seconds from the first shot to the next. I figured whatever video there was from here was useless. The tapes were old and would be recorded over hundreds of times. The lot attendant didn't have any other useful information for me.

I made a mental note to ask Kate about it later tonight. She would definitely have access to the videos so I figured I should get a copy of it and at least watch it. This had been a waste of time I thought as I left the garage and walked back to my car.

I checked the time and thought I should be hearing

something from Bramwell soon, assuming he survived the meeting. I was also wondering when I would hear back from Rios. I typed the address of the restaurant where Spree's father was shot and killed into my car's navigation system. I cut across the city and by the time I had arrived, I was starving.

I planned on eating at the restaurant, but it wasn't open. I left my car in the parking lot and walked around the building. I was just getting a feel for the area and the surroundings. This was the hit that didn't make sense to me. Not the way it went down anyway. How did the shooter know who would open the door? The restaurant wasn't open for lunch on Sundays, but most of the kitchen staff was here prepping for the dinner service.

What would the shooter have done if someone other than Gallo opened the back door? Shoot his way into the place until he found Gallo and execute him? This was an attack against Sal. Taking out Sal, his daughter and his granddaughter made sense if this was some sort of vendetta, but the risk versus the reward to take out his son-in-law just didn't seem worth it.

I noticed the camera above the back door and knew the police would already have taken the video. I made another mental note to follow up with Kate about it. I walked around the restaurant and the block but I didn't see anything else that needed my attention. There was a camera at the intersection, and we knew the time the shooting occurred but the shooter could be driving anything. He wouldn't be restricted to just a van or something because his job wasn't a kidnapping. Wait....

I ran back to my rental car and pulled the file on everything we knew about this case. Sal, his daughter and son-in-law were all killed within minutes of each other. That meant there were two shooters in Florida and two in Buffalo. This gave me a better timeline of when Spree was taken.

Kidnapping Spree and Sal were the main objectives so the shooters here in Florida would have taken her *before* taking out her parents. That didn't feel right though. If something went wrong during the kidnapping, they might not have been able to get to Gallo and Angiola. Plus, one of them would have to have Spree gagged in a vehicle or stashed somewhere when they went to finish the next target.

That didn't seem like the plausible thing to do. The plausible thing to do was have the shooters hit the parents first. Hit Anthony at his restaurant and Angiola at her office, then grab Spree and disappear. That made more sense. What didn't make sense was why the hell Angiola was at her office on a Sunday? Accounting firms weren't open on Sundays, were they? My thoughts were distracted when my phone started ringing.

Bull had just gotten off the phone with his brother. The plan had changed a little bit. That was fine. They had eight million dollars to split three ways. He was a happy guy.

"Roman, you want to go out and grab a beer or something? I feel like getting a burger and a beer."

"I could eat. I can always eat." Russo replied with a smile, patting his hefty stomach. Russo was a large man. He stood over six feet tall, had thick, broad shoulders and arms as heavy as tree trunks. Bull and his brother had met Russo when they were all serving time together. Russo wasn't connected with any of the families and he and Vito Tommaso were cellmates. Tommaso was connected and ran with the Cosimo Family. This was good because Bull and his brother were with the Camarillo Family, and the Camarillo and Cosimo families had always been close.

The four of them all ran together in prison and formed their own gang or family. Russo and Tommaso were released before Bull and Primo, but they all stayed in contact with each other. Eighteen months later when they were released, they all got together to celebrate. That's when they started talking and planning. Word got around that they were looking to make a big score and Moretti called them in for a meeting. Augostino was also present.

They had come a long way since that meeting a few short months ago. They were no longer connected with either Moretti or Augostino. Tommaso had been killed in DiFlippo's abduction, but they had eight million dollars, the granddaughter tied up in the basement, and they would be leaving the country in a little less than a week. The way Bull had it figured out, they were ahead of the game.

"I know you can, you ox. Before we go, we got to get the girl cleaned up and feed her something."

"I'll take her with me in the shower, no problem!" Bull had to laugh at Russo. The guy was a giant hard-on all the time. They had to find some girls and soon, or maybe Primo wouldn't be the first one to have a go with the girl in the basement.

"Come on Roman, you know what my brother said. Just empty her bucket and I'll bring her down some food in a few minutes." They had been busy the first day they arrived at the house. The basement had a separate, smaller room that was used as the laundry room. The room was against the back corner of the and did not have a window.

They removed the washer and dryer and the shelving unit from that room. They drilled into the concrete wall and set in a new stainless steel bolt. They mixed up more concrete and made sure the bolt was set securely into the wall. After the mix had dried, not even Russo could yank the bolt from the wall.

They cut Spree's clothes off of her and left her naked.

They gave her two small blankets they found in a closet. They shackled her legs together and attached a five foot chain to the ring in the wall. They left her hands handcuffed in front of her naked body.

All the room had in it was a five gallon bucket that had sand in it and a roll of toilet paper. She wasn't allowed to wash or shower and they fed her at sporadic times throughout the day and night. They left the light, which was out of her reach, on all the time. They took turns tormenting her. Sometimes one of them would go into her room and just watch her. Sometimes they would go together and tell her the things they had planned to do to her.

All Spree knew was she needed to figure out a way to escape before they did the horrible things to her. She heard someone walking through the house. She recognized the sounds as the big one. That's how she referred to them, her capturers. One was bigger than the other one so she called him the big one and the other guy, the small one.

She was very afraid because they didn't bother to hide their faces from her. She knew the horrible things they said they were going to do to her were true. She knew when they were finished with her, when she was used up, they would kill her.

She didn't like either of them but she really didn't like the big one. The way he looked at her and licked his lips. The things he said he was going to do to her were more horrible than she had ever imagined. She could tell he was excited when he talked to her.

The last time he came into her room, she thought he was going to rape and kill her. He came in and brought a chair into the room. He closed the door and placed the chair in front of it. Then he took off his pants and started telling her what he couldn't wait to do. He masturbated in front of her and told her if she didn't watch, he would put out one of her eyes. When he was finished, he put his pants back on and left the room. He didn't bother cleaning up his semen from the floor.

The door opened and he was standing there with that awful smile on his face. Spree wished she was any place else in the world right now. She even wished she was dead.

The doors were closed and the wheels were up and they were airborne. Kate was sitting in a window seat of the private FBI jet heading to Miami. She was alone in the row and had the case file spread out around her. She was half thinking about the case and half thinking about Rick.

Where the hell had he gotten the finger print from? Was it something that one of the locals already took or was it something he found on his own? She was guessing it was something he found on his own. He was the resourceful type.

Her eyes were tired and she thought about removing her contacts and putting her glasses on. She rarely wore them at work. She was too self-conscious when she wore her glasses. They had gotten the ID on the body that was left behind when DiFlippo was taken. Vito Tommaso. The OC guys were running him every which way. With a name like that, everyone knew he was connected to one of the families. Once they figured out who he was with she thought it would be easy to figure out who his accomplices were.

Her thoughts drifted back to Rick. She thought about how intense he could be. How fearless and stupid he was when he raced into the burning house to rescue DiFlippo. There were times she could feel, well, what could she feel radiating off of him? She felt something, danger? She couldn't put it into words.

She was happy he was in Miami and she was going to see

him. She knew she was happy, but she didn't really know what that meant or why she was happy. She shook her head. Nice Kate. Real nice. Like you don't have enough issues, she thought to herself. You go and start liking a criminal. Start liking? Umm, no, she thought. Maybe I'm interested, but it's not like or anywhere close to that. She shook her head again. Ok, no more Rick. It would be Mr. Stevens and any interest beyond professional would end right now. She went back to work on the case file.

I didn't recognize the number that was calling me. I answered cautiously "Hello? Vegas Pizza?"

"¡Hola, Umm, yeah, I'm returning a call…."

"Manny Rios?"

"Yeah, ¿quién es este??"

"I'm the guy that's been calling you. I'm Sal's friend from Buffalo."

"Bueno, chico, Yeah. Sorry I missed your call. I was working on something. Who is this again? How do I know you're the guy?"

"Rios, you called me. I'm from Buffalo. Sal and Bramwell are friends. I know all about you and what you're doing or supposed to be doing. Bramwell told me you were running down every lead you had, calling in every favor that was owed to you. I don't have time to bullshit around here Manny."

"Ok, ok, I'm just making sure, you know, confirmando que usted es quien dice ser, how you say, establish bona fides, yeah?"

"I get it. I appreciate that. Listen, I'm pressed for time and we need to meet…" I hated what I was about to say next, it went against everything I abided by, but with Rios being shy and me not being able to reach out to Bramwell or Sal, I had to do something.

"So pick a nice, public place you and I can sit down and get a cup of coffee. Ok?"

"Bueno, chico, I can do that. There's a great place called Gaby's Café on SW 1st, in Little Havana. You know the place?" No, I didn't know the place. I don't think I had ever been to Little Havana but I had a GPS and wasn't afraid to ask for directions if I needed to.

"I know the place. I'll be there in 30 minutes…" I didn't like what I was about to say next either, but it needed to be said. "…And Manny, if you don't show up, if you show up and you're not alone, or if you try to do anything else I find unsavory during our meeting, I can promise you, I will kill you and leave your body there. We understand each other?"

"Holy Shit! ¡Sí! No se preocupe! I'll be there alone! I won't even be with a weapon!" Manny then described what he would be wearing. I told him I would see him soon.

I hated to be like that but it was how I stayed alive. I always had to be the asshole, the aggressor, the one threatening violence. I could tell by Manny's voice he would come alone and not be armed. I still took precautions. I was still armed.

I typed the name of the coffee place in my GPS and found it. It wasn't far from where I was and I would easily make it there in 30 minutes. I parked a few streets over and walked towards the place. I forgot how hot and humid Florida was this time of the year. I wished I was in Southern California on a job instead of Miami.

It's like Sal always said: You could wish in one hand and shit in the other, then see which one gets filled up faster. I didn't want to walk in the front door of the coffee place. I strolled around the rear and found a back door and a small parking lot. I didn't see anything suspicious and nothing spiked my radar.

I entered through the back door. I was wearing the same UnderTech UnderCover white t-shirt and carrying the same H&K pistol. I had on a pair of tan dockers, matching boat shoes and an unbuttoned blue short sleeve Tommy Bahama shirt. I had my hand on the inside of my shirt, touching my pistol.

Manny was seated at a corner table, alone, wearing exactly what he said he would be wearing. He had both of his hands flat on the table in front of him. I watched him for a few minutes and didn't see anything suspicious. Every once in a while he would use his left hand to pick up his coffee and take a sip. He also checked his watch each time he did it.

I walked to the counter and was happy to see they had normal sized coffee: small, medium or large. Those other places that have the fancy names for their coffee size irritate the hell out of me. It's bad enough to pay $5.00 for a cup of coffee but even worse when you have to order it by such a pretentious name. The coffee was a quarter of the price of the big national chain stores and I was willing to bet a lot better tasting. A few minutes later, after I had my large house blend, I took a sip and was correct. It was delicious. It made those chain places taste like they were serving burnt, muddy water.

I walked over to the table and sat down. Manny Rios had a full head of thick, black hair that was naturally slightly curly. He had a dark tan and his face was lined and weathered and had the look of someone that spent a lot of time on the ocean. He smiled at me and extended his hand. I shook his hand and felt the hard calloused skin and smiled back. I immediately liked Rios.

I told him why I was in Miami and what I had accomplished so far, which wasn't much. I was hoping he had more information for me. Rios had a habit of of blending the Spanish and English language together when he talked. I didn't speak a lot of Spanish, but I understood everything he was telling me.

Rios was very connected to just about everything in Miami. I could see why. With his good looks, charming personality and being associated with Sal, it was easy to see how much weight he had down here.

One of the buy-here-pay-here car places he was connected with told him about a big guy that had come around asking some odd questions about buying a vehicle. At first, the workers pretended not to understand what he was talking about because they were worried he was an undercover cop.

Rios explained that this was a legitimate used car dealership and body shop, but they also dealt with stolen vehicles and car parts. Basically, the dealership and garage were a front for a chop shop. This place employed enough felons that they recognized the big guy for what he was: a fellow graduate from the Gray Bar State University.

He was looking for a windowless panel van, neutral in color, preferably white that he could pay cash for. He was willing to pay extra if there was a way they didn't have to do any paperwork and if he could get a current license plate and registration with the deal. Some questions were asked; specifically, how long would he need the van for and would he stay in the immediate area.

Once the person in charge at the dealership realized the big guy was willing to pay a lot of money and would only need the van for 12-14 days and would be out of Miami in two weeks, a deal was struck. The van was prepped and washed, cash exchanged hands and the big guy left. After 14 days, the dealership would notify the police department the van had been stolen. Once they had a police report, they would report the theft to their insurance company and make even more money.

As interesting a story as this was, it didn't help much other than the fact that I now knew what kind of vehicle to look for. "So, that's it Manny? That's all you got?" I said, trying to keep the disappointment from sounding in my voice.

"Sí, eso es bueno ¿no?"

"It's good, it's helpful, sure, I just wish we had more. I don't know if that will be enough for me to get a lead on these guys with."

Manny said "Bueno, chico, I been saving the best for last." And then he flashed that big smile of his. I couldn't help but smile back at him. He continued "When the workers thought this guy was uno en la oficina de la cubierta de la policía federal..." He paused when he saw the confused look on my face, then said "umm, secret policeman?"

"I get it now, undercover police officer, yes I get it."

"Si, si, they were worried. They wanted to be safe, you know? One of the workers, he took los chicos de la foto, you know, with his phone? Then he sent me the picture on my phone. Here, look" Then Rios slowly pulled out his phone and pulled up the picture of the big guy that purchased the van.

CHAPTER #14

Kate called me a few hours later. After my meeting with Rios, but prior to receiving Kate's call, I called and touched base with Geoff. He was making great progress on the projects I had given him. He didn't have any tangible results, not on anything that I could immediately use. Neither one of us had heard back from Bramwell. I was starting to get worried.

I texted Geoff the picture from Rios and asked him if he could find out who the guy was. He didn't sound confident. He said he would have the picture scanned in and then run it through a facial recognition software system and then use that to start searching every database he could find that had pictures, starting with the New York State and Florida State Department of Motor Vehicles.

He said since the pic was of low quality from a cell phone, he would get a lot of false positive hits and have to go through each one to determine if it was the correct guy or not. I told him it sounded like a lot of work and I didn't want to keep him from doing it and to call me later.

Kate said she was meeting with the task force and going over the case. I had a lot of questions for her but she said she didn't have time to answer them but would later on at dinner. She told me to text her where she should meet me for dinner and said to make it after 8:00 pm. Dinner? Kate was as subtle as a 15 pound sledge hammer.

I was in Miami and really wanted to get sushi but I wasn't sure if Kate liked sushi or even sea food. I took a chance and made a late reservation at Doraku. I texted the name, address and time and said sushi/seafood with a question mark. She responded by saying it was an excellent choice and she would see me later.

When I came down to Miami, I didn't know how long I would be here so I didn't make a hotel reservation. All I had to do was give the private jet 60 minutes' notice and I could leave. I decided to get a room since I was having a late dinner.

I had a few hours to kill and decided to relax. I booked a room and a massage at the Standard Spa, Miami Beach on Island Avenue. The hotel was located on Belle Isle Park and was a short distance to Doraku. I had an excellent room and an even better massage.

I took a nap after my massage, showered, put on clean clothes and left for the restaurant. I got there thirty minutes before our reservation and was surprised to see that Kate was not there waiting for me.

I scanned the room and my surroundings looking for anything out of place. Nothing triggered my internal radar and I felt as safe as I could, under the circumstances. I mean, how safe can one feel when they're meeting an FBI Agent at a predetermined location at a predetermined time?

I waited at the bar for Kate to arrive. I was tempted to order a drink, but I never drink alcohol when I am working a job, and I considered myself working, so I got a bottle of Perrier with a sliced lime.

I have a bad habit of never sitting at a bar. I stand, usually with my foot on the rail. I try to get into a corner so I can put my back against the wall and see everything out in front of me. I was able to get a corner spot and I was standing with my back against the wall, leaning on the bar with one arm and holding my sparkling water with the other hand, when she walked in.

I almost dropped my glass when I laid eyes on her. She was wearing a light blue dress, some sort of silky material that was hugging her body. The dress had one shoulder side strap that had intricate detailing on it. Her hair was up and I could see she had on a pair of sapphire earrings and her neckline was bare. She looked absolutely stunning. The dress revealed her beautiful figure.

When she came in, she was removing her sunglasses and tucking them and her valet receipt into a Tano handbag. Her eyes calmly scanned the crowd until she saw me. I couldn't help it, I was smiling. When she saw me smiling at her, she smiled back at me. Her smile lit up the entire room, her face, and my heart.

I felt underdressed. I was wearing a Hart Shaffner & Marx Navy Tonal suit with a white and blue striped shirt without a tie. I had on a Tag Heuer Grand Carrera watch on my left wrist and a two-toned white and yellow gold bracelet on my right.

I walked across the dining room and met her. There was that awkward moment when we weren't sure how we were going to great each other. Even though I wasn't Italian, I had spent enough time around Italians to know what to do. I pulled her into a hug and kissed her on the cheek. For a second I thought she was going to resist or pull away from me, but she didn't and hugged me back.

"Mr. Stevens…"

"Good evening, Kate, You look amazing."

"Thank you. I haven't eaten all day! I am starving!" I told the maître d we were ready and he escorted us to our table. Doraku has an amazing menu and we decided to get several different rolls and share everything. I ordered another sparkling water and Kate got a tropical fruity drink with an umbrella.

I asked her how her day was and how the investigation was going and she glared at me over the tip of the umbrella and said, "Rick, don't go ruining dinner with work talk. Let me drink some of this cocktail, eat a great meal, and then we can talk about work. Deal?"

"Deal"

So we talked about everything except work. I had already pulled a complete background on her using Geoff's resources, but all that did was tell me about her. Sitting across from her, listening to her talk, I learned who she was. I learned about her family and her upbringing and her time working in the jails while she was going to college.

Every once in a while I talked about myself but it was always my past. Everything was from my pre-Army days or very brief memories of when I was a pastor. I enjoyed listening to her talk. When the meal was over, we ordered dessert. I ordered the banana flambé and she ordered a dish of the green tea ice cream.

When the meal was complete, I paid the check and we decided to go for a walk to discuss the case. She started by sharing with me everything she had up to that point, which wasn't much. Other than identifying the kidnapper that was killed during Sal's abduction, there wasn't much else to go on. She was still reviewing the files from Miami.

When she talked, I interjected my thoughts and opinions. We discovered we both had similar days: both going to the various crime scenes, both seeing the same things and drawing the same conclusions.

She informed me they lifted over 45 different finger prints from Spree's town house. They were running the prints down and eliminating the ones that belonged to family and friends. Well, not exactly eliminating them, just putting them on the back burner. It was a slow tedious process and she didn't expect to receive promising news from the search.

I asked her if she remembered if they removed any prints

from the doorbell. Kate had an amazing memory, almost photographic I found out. She stopped walking, closed her eyes for a few seconds and then shook her head no. She would go back and check the file to see if the doorbell button was ever dusted and there wasn't anything usable, or if it was overlooked.

I pulled the fingerprint card I made up out of the inside pocket of my jacket and gave it to her. At first she looked confused, then she saw what was on the card, then she understood the significance and then those beautiful soft green eyes lit up and she said, "You tampered with a crime scene? Are you kidding me?"

"I wouldn't say tampered, not exactly, no. I pulled a print off the doorbell button and I am hoping you can tell me who it belongs to."

"Damn it, Rick! It doesn't matter who it belongs to! I can't use it! It's useless! Thanks, thanks a lot for destroying what might have been our abductor's fingerprint and the only piece of evidence tying him to the crime scene!"

"It's not destroyed. I think I lifted a decent print, considering I was using a makeup brush and pencil graphite." I tried a wink and a smile. They both failed.

"This is NOT funny! I am really pissed off here!"

"I know you are but I don't understand why. You can still run the print and find out who it belongs to, right?"

"Yes, I can, but if it belongs to our abductor what then Rick? Huh? It's useless! I can't mention it, I can't use it to get a warrant and I sure as hell can't use it as evidence or proof in a trial!" Now I understood her frustration and anger. I was such an idiot! For a moment, I forgot that Kate and I were on opposite sides of the law. I forgot we had differing goals and ideas. For a moment, I felt like I was a part of the real world again. A sad mistake on my part.

"Kate, I'm sorry, but there isn't going to be a trial. Not for the people that took Sal or Spree and killed his family."

"Well, no shit Sherlock! Not now with you trampling all over my case and contaminating it!"

"No, you don't understand. Regardless if there was evidence or not, the people that did this, they would never make it to trial."

"Why not? Why the hell not?" It was decision time. I could continue to pretend that I was something I wasn't to Kate and lie to myself or I could lay the cards down on the table. We had both stopped walking and she was looking at me with those striking eyes of hers. I almost faltered, I almost backed away from what I had been wanting to tell her. But I didn't. I told her the truth.

"Because I'm going to kill them Kate…I'm going to kill them all."

PART TWO

CHAPTER #15

20 years ago…

Salvatore DiFlippo was sitting in his top floor, corner office located in the Rand Building in downtown Buffalo, New York. He was smoking a Cuban Partagas Series P #2 cigar and drinking a glass of 20 year old Pappy Van Winkles Whiskey. It was great to be the boss!

Business was great and he was making more money than he could count. His number two guy, Dominick Mazzio, had a tight leash on the crews that worked for them and everyone was happy. Sal didn't have any meetings scheduled that day and was considering calling Mazzio to see if he wanted to hit the country club for a round of golf and a late lunch. He was about to pick up his phone to buzz Mazzio in his office when his secretary buzzed him.

"Mr. DiFlippo, there's a Mr. Dennis Saville here to see you."

"Maria, I didn't think we had any appointments scheduled for today."

"No sir, we don't. He says it's important that he talks to you today…" Sal could hear Maria cover the mouth piece of the phone as someone in the background spoke to her. He couldn't hear what was being said, only murmurs.

"Sir? He says it's about the loan you gave him."

"Ok, Maria, tell him I'm tied up right now. Call Dom and have him talk to him. If it's important, then have Dom call me, ok?" He disconnected before she could respond. I bet it's about the loan he owes. Probably more about why his weekly payment will be light or non-existent, Sal thought to himself. Dennis Saville was nice enough guy, but Sal knew he would struggle to make the payments on the loan. Saville was a contractor and work was hit or miss in his business. Sal had thrown him a few jobs, more as a way to protect his investment but Saville went over time and budget on each job so Sal stopped throwing him work.

Sal puffed on his cigar, took a sip of his whiskey and went back to reading the race report from Fort Erie, Canada. A few minutes later, there was a knock at his door. Frustrated, Sal said "Yeah?"

Mazzio walked in, "Sorry to bother you boss, but this Saville has a pretty good idea. We could make some quick scratch, but it's something we need to move on quickly." Mazzio held his breath. Sal wasn't prone to making snap decisions. He liked to evaluate a situation, then reevaluate it, think it through, and try to figure out all the odds and angles involved. Mazzio could tell he was losing Sal's interest by the frown on his face.

"Listen Boss, I think this is at least worth hearing." Sal put his racing form down, drank some more whiskey, puffed his cigar and just stared at Mazzio. He continued, "Saville is a week behind making his payments. The last six payments he's made, have all been just the vig, and three of those were late."

The vigorish, or vig as it was called, is a fee charged by a bookmaker on a bet. The way Sal ran his loan operation was simple. He would loan out any amount of money, pending a review of your financial situation. Sal didn't like to loan large amounts of money to people who couldn't pay it back. His captains were responsible for reviewing and approving the loans.

Sal would charge a minim of 10% per week (eith the max being well over 50%), plus a standard, one-time, operating fee. He charged $25 per every hundred dollars borrowed. For example, if you were to borrow $100 from Sal, you would owe him the original $100, plus the one-time fee of $25, plus the interest, or the vig. So after one week, with a 10% vig, you would have to pay back $137.50.

Dennis Saville borrowed $6,000. After the first week, he went from owing $6,000 to $8,250. He had managed to pay back the $1,500 service fee and keep current or almost current on the vig payments which were in the $750-$800 a week neighborhood. Mazzio and Sal knew Saville was a drowning man and it would only be a matter of time before they took everything he owned and probably killed him.

Sal wanted to avoid that because of Saville's father, Jack. Jack Saville worked for Sal when he was younger and even went to jail for 8 months covering for Sal. Jack later was killed in a gun fight with the police. Sal hated doing the loan for Jack's kid because he knew he and Mazzio would be sitting in a room, like this, having this same conversation, like they now were.

"Ok, Dom, I'm listening. What's his deal?"

"Alright Skip, he's got a kid that works for this armored car company, Atlas Armored Cars. They're based out of Rochester and his kid is on this convenient/corner store and bar run that he does. He says that on Thursday, the car is going to be packed to the gills with cash…."

"Thursday, Dom? As in, two days from now, Thursday?"

"Yeah, I said we needed to move fast…"

"I don't get it. What's the significance of Thursday? Why is the car going to be packed on Thursday?," Sal asked.

"Well Boss, Thursday is the 14th. That means Friday is the 15th, welfare day. All the 'coloreds' get their government handout on Friday. He says all these businesses load up on their cash Thursday so they have it on hand to cash all the checks they get on Friday." Mazzio could tell Sal was interested now. He could see the man thinking through how to take the car.

"How much we talking, Dom? Roughly."

"Saville said according to his kid, the lowest he's ever seen was $500,000 and a few times there was over a million dollars."

"Why do we have to do it this week? Why not wait two more weeks, or a month. Welfare is paid out twice a month."

"Saville said this week is best. I think because he knows when Saturday rolls around he won't have the cash and we'll have to take something from him, you know, like his life."

"Ok, I can understand that. How many guys in the truck?"

"That's the best part. Just Saville's kid and one other guy. Saville's kid will be driving the truck this Thursday. He said he would delay hitting the panic button and calling the heist in."

"What do they want?"

"Saville said he wants a percentage of the overall take, and as a finder's fee, for us to forgive the debt he already owes us."

"What percentage we talking Dom?"

"He said 25%." Dom could tell Sal was not happy as the frown returned to his face.

"Is he still here? Call him in here." Mazzio left to retrieve Saville. Sal opened one of his desk drawers and removed an item and put it in his jacket pocket. Mazzio showed Saville into Sal's office. They greeted each other and shook hands. Sal took a seat on the couch in his office right next to Saville. Mazzio calmly closed the office door and stood in front of it.

"Dennis, Mr. Mazzio tells me you're having trouble repaying the loan. I told you this would happen, didn't I? This is why I didn't want to loan you that amount."

"Yes sir, you did, I know, but did he tell you the other thing?" Sal gave Mazzio a look. Mazzio told Sal that Saville was clean, meaning he wasn't wearing a wire or recording device.

Sal put a little steel into his voice and said, "He told me the other thing, yeah. What I don't get is why you brought it to me? Go do the thing yourself and pay me off."

"Mr. DiFlippo? I, I can't do that. I don't have the experience, or the know-how, you know?"

Sal dropped his voice and said "Exactly. You don't know how to do it nor do you have the intelligence or the stones to pull it off. That's why you came to me. For this idea of yours, you want me to, what did you say it was Dom, oh yeah, you want me to forgive the 8 G's you owe me AND pay you 25% of whatever the take is. So basically, I take all the risk, do all the work, and you sit back and take 25% of my profits and another $8,000 on top of that. That about right, Dennis?"

"Mr. DiFlippo, I didn't mean no disrespect…." He stammered. Sal removed the item he had in his pocket and held it up to Saville's face. His eyes flashed wide and showed how afraid he was.

"You know what this is Dennis? This is an Ice Pick. Very useful tool. You don't see them used a lot now a days. Back in the day, they were used to break up, pick at, or chip at ice. It resembles a scratch awl, but is designed for picking at ice rather than wood. Before the invention of modern refrigerators, ice picks were a ubiquitous household tool used for separating and shaping the blocks of ice used in ice boxes. Now Dennis, I still use my ice pick, just not on ice." Then Sal gave him his hardest look. Dennis looked like he was going to cry.

"If your information is correct, and there is $500,000 in the car, you want $125,000 plus another $8,000 on top of that, bringing you to $132,000. It seems a bit high to me, don't you think Dom?"

"Absolutely. Seems very high to me. I mean, after we pay

him, and the crew we'll need to do the job, that leaves hardly anything left for us." Saville was looking back and forth between the two men with wide, panicked eyes.

"I'm thinking more in the 8% neighborhood. Wait, you know what? I like you Dennis. I loved your father. He was a good man. Loyal. Let's call it 10%. I'll give you 10% of the take on two conditions: Condition #1 – There has to be at least $500,000 in the car. If not, the deals off, and I'll kill you and everyone you know. Condition #2 – After paying you $50,000, you will immediately hand over, back to me, the remainder of what you owe me. Do we have a deal?"

After agreeing to Sal's terms and providing more information, Saville was escorted from the office.

"Call Augostino. Tell him to talk to DeMayo, tell him we have some work in his area and we want a work permit to do it. Tell him we'll pay him $50,000 up front, no questions asked."

Mazzio left Sal's office and Sal went back to his racing form. He was reading the racing form and thinking about how he wanted to pull off the heist and who he wanted to use to do it. A few minutes later, Mazzio buzzed him, "Hey Boss, I got DeMayo on line 2 holding for you. He's being a prick."

"Thanks Dom, I'll talk to him." He hung up with his underboss and picked up with the head of the Camarillo Crime Family, Anthony "Tony the Butcher" DeMayo. "My friend, how are you?" Sal said as a greeting. After the two bosses exchanged pleasantries for a few minutes, they got down to business. Sal told him a rough outline of what he wanted to do, without giving away specific details. DeMayo was told Sal wanted to perform a heist in his neighborhood and pay him for the opportunity to do so.

"Listen, I don't have an issue giving you the work permit.

I have a favor to ask though. I have two guys, brothers actually, that are still wet behind the ears, but they're hungry, you know? These are good guys; they're ready for something like this, to prove themselves. They're related to me through my wife, cousins of cousins or some shit, whatever. Can you let these guys go along with your guys, you know, expose them how to run an operation, as a favor to me? Listen it's none of my business Sally, what you're doing, you know that, but $50K sounds a bit light…"

The nerve of DeMayo Sal thought. "How much are we talking here? You know, I have to pay an inside guy on this and his partner, then I got to pay my crew, then I got to pay you, all of a sudden, by the time I get a piece of the pie, it's smaller than everyone else's pieces."

"I understand Sal, I do! Business costs are going up and eating away at everyone's profits! What were you going to pay the guys in your crew to do this?" Sal was planning on using two of his best guys and paying them $50,000 each. He figured that would be $100,000, plus another $50,000 to DeMayo and another $50,000 to Saville and he would be left with at least $300,000 for himself.

"I was planning on paying two guys $10,000 each to do the job and you $50,000 for the permit." DeMayo cut Sal off.

"Ok, here's what we'll do. I'll take $80,000 for the permit, you send along one guy, I'll send my two guys, they'll get $10,000 each and you'll still be able to enjoy a nice slice of pie at the end of this. That sound good to you?" It was the best offer Sal was going to get from DeMayo. If Sal had more time he might be able to chop DeMayo down but he was on a time crunch so he agreed. He told DeMayo he would have one of his couriers leave immediately with the $100,000 and deliver it to DeMayo's office. He also told DeMayo that no one was to be hurt or killed on this job. DeMayo agreed.

Sal didn't like only having one of his guys on the job where DeMayo would have two but it was business. Since DeMayo would already have been paid before the heist, there would be no reason for either of his guys to look into the sealed cash bags to see how much had been stolen.

Sal thought that the day after the heist, he would send his courier back out to DeMayo's office with an additional $20,000 and a note saying he did better than expected on the grab and wanted to share. It would be a good relationship builder between the two organizations. That's how Sal was: always thinking about and planning for the future.

Wednesday, the day before the heist.

Sal wanted to meet the two guys DeMayo was sending on the heist. He personally wanted to meet them. It was the only stipulation Sal made and DeMayo finally agreed. They would be meeting at Salvatore's Italian Gardens. Although they share the same first name, there was no connection between the famous Italian restaurant and the infamous mafia don.

Sal was well known there and reserved a private room in the back of the restaurant. Out of respect, Sal invited DeMayo to the dinner, but he declined. So it would be Sal and his underboss having dinner with the Patrizio brothers.

The brothers arrived on time and were dressed for the occasion. Sal wanted to see how they would react to being put off a bit. So he made them wait. He watched from the private room. At first the brothers were calm and polite. Then, as more time elapsed, he could sense their impatience growing. Something about them triggered a memory in Sal. He couldn't put his finger on it though.

He was about to have Dom go retrieve them when the bigger brother went back to the hosts stand and started complaining, very loudly. He was punctuating his words by tapping his finger first on the host stand and then, finally, on the host's chest. DiFlippo was not happy. He spoke briefly to the restaurant's manager and sent him in to diffuse the situation.

The manager pulled the brothers aside, apologized for DiFlippo's lateness and offered them free drinks at the bar. Both brothers accepted. DiFlippo continued to watch as the brothers drank several drinks. The bigger of the two brothers continued to get even more angry after every drink he took.

He sat at the main table in the private room and sent Dom out to get the brothers. When they entered the room, Sal could tell the older, bigger, brother was still furious. Sal found this unsettling. If there was more time, he would cancel the job. He was still considering it as an option.

After the introductions were made, the older brother seemed to settle down a little. During dinner, the brothers were very polite and respectful. They had been brought up the right way. Right before dessert was served, Sal made the connection. He had met the brothers before. Years before actually.

It was before Sal was a boss. He was a captain of a crew and working his way up. He was out in an unincorporated area between Buffalo and Rochester, NY. Two of his guys had just stolen an 18 wheeler full of electronics bound for a department store. They were running the load hot and had to get the truck off the street.

Sal was told to secure a garage and meet his guys there. The truck was stolen from a truck stop between Buffalo and Rochester. Sal's family, the Accardo Family, had control of Buffalo and the Camarillo Family had control of Rochester. Technically, the theft occurred in an area where neither family had control, a gray area or open area of sorts.

However, acting boss for the Camarillo family, Anthony DeMayo, was making a big deal to acting boss of the Accardo Family, Peter Massino. The two bosses argued a bit and decided on an agreement: The Butcher would send someone to pick up the truck and move the merchandise and give Massino a cut of the proceeds. Massino knew he was getting the short end of the stick and was being bullied but he decided a few thousand dollars' worth of stolen electronics just wasn't worth the headache.

He sent Sal out to secure a warehouse and help inventory the truck before DeMayo's guy got there. He wanted to get an idea of just how bad DeMayo was screwing him. They were just about done inventorying the truck's contents when they heard a car pull into the lot and start honking its horn. Sal looked at his two guys and sent one of them outside to see what all the noise was about.

He returned with the Patrizio brothers. Both were young and full of piss and vinegar. They swaggered in and asked Sal, "What the fuck is this? Why isn't the truck ready to go?"

"I'm taking an inventory. Getting an idea of what's here and what our end of the take will be?"

"Who told you to do that?" Before Sal could answer, the second brother spoke up. "Your end of the take? Your end is whatever we say it is. That's your end!" Sal thought about responding, but realized it would only lead to death: both of the brothers' death. He didn't want to cause a problem between the two families over stolen electronics so he just smiled in his self-depreciating way.

"Sorry fellas. No harm, no foul." Then he motioned to his guys to follow him out.

"Hey, where the fuck ya going?" Sal stopped. Took a deep breath and turned around.

"The truck's yours now. You two can load it back up and bring it wherever it is you're supposed to bring it." Sal said smiling. The bigger brother walked aggressively towards Sal.

"Listen here, I don't know who the fuck…." His words were cut off as Sal chopped him with the blade of his hand to his throat. Then he kicked his knee out and dropped the brother to the floor. Before anyone else could react, Sal was laying on his chest and had an ice pick poised above the bigger brother's eye as he sprawled on the floor.

"You're right. You don't know who I am. I'm a captain in the Accardo Family. Your actions here today have made it ok for me to kill you and your brother. I don't need a sit down, I don't need permission. I'm going to give you a pass. I can see you've got more balls than brains and everyone makes mistakes. You ever disrespect me again like you have today, and I'll tie you to a chair as I cut your brother to pieces. I'll feed the smaller pieces of him to you. You understand me?"

Sal and his crew then left the warehouse. The NY State Police received an anonymous tip regarding the stolen 18 wheeler and where it could be found. Both brothers were arrested for the first time in their adult lives. Since it was their first arrest as adults, DeMayo's connections and lawyers got them a reduced sentence and they only served a few months each. Neither one ever suspected Sal phoned in the tip himself.

Sal asked the brothers if they remembered meeting him years before. Neither one did. Sal chuckled out loud and told the story to Dom about their first meeting and about how he embarrassed Primo and how scared he was. He could see how angry the brothers were getting with the retelling of the story. He could feel their embarrassment.

Sal knew neither brother would say anything because if they did, they would be signing their own death warrant. Sal enjoyed rubbing the arrogant brothers' faces in their past failures. He left out the part about him phoning in the tip to the police. Sal thanked the brothers for the trip down memory lane, folded his napkin, got up and left the room without looking back.

Sal rudely and disrespectfully, dismissed the brothers, on purpose.

Thursday, the day of the heist.

The armored car from Atlas left the garage right on time. The car was packed with $685,000 to be delivered to various banks and businesses along their route. Whoever had seniority got to choose between driving the truck and running the money. John Saville was supposed to be driving, as he had seniority over his partner but his partner called in sick. That left Saville working with an old-timer with a bad knee, who had more seniority. Saville was bumped to being the runner.

This was in the days before cell phones so there was no way to notify his dad of the switch. John was a little nervous because when he proposed this idea to help his father out, he thought he would be behind the safety of the bullet proof glass.

The truck arrived at the first drop off point. The truck pulled up behind a city owned garbage truck. The second the side door was opened and as John was stepping out, two things happened almost simultaneously: The first thing that occurred was the city garbage truck backed into the front of the armored car. The second was a masked gunmen shooting John in the face at point blank range with a .357 magnum.

The driver jumped from the garbage truck as the first gunmen entered the armored car and opened the back doors. The door leading to the cab of the truck was secured from the inside and the gunmen couldn't kill the driver.

A second masked gunman backed a SUV up to the back of the truck and joined the first gunmen in emptying the armored car out. The driver of the garbage truck ran towards the back of the armored car, "What the hell are you doing? No one was supposed to get hurt!" Before he could reach the back of the armored car, the first gunmen stepped out the side door and shot him four times with a 9 mm pistol. The garbage truck driver fell to the ground, dead.

The masked gunmen dropped his .357 into the garbage truck driver's hand and put the 9 mm back into the dead armored car officer's hand. Perfect, he thought. He went to the back of the vehicle and helped the other masked gunmen finish loading the back of the SUV. When all of the money was removed, both gunmen got in the SUV and drove off. Total time from when the garbage truck backed into the armored car until the SUV drove off with the money? 2 minutes, 13 seconds.

Friday, the day after the heist.

"You son-of-a-bitch!"

"I would advise you to watch your tone when you're speaking to me."

Sal and DeMayo were in the backroom of the East Side Social Club in Rochester, NY. They were the only two in the meeting. They were both staring daggers at each other.

"Fuck you, DeMayo. Your craziness doesn't frighten me. You don't frighten me…"

"That's a mistake. You should be very afraid of me." Sal had known DeMayo's type his entire life. Sure, they were crazy and violent, but only when they had a crew of guys with them. Only when the odds and numbers were on their side and they were all but assured victory. Sal was 14 years younger than DeMayo and in much better shape. DeMayo outweighed Sal by over 50 pounds, but it was wasted weight, as the advantage was all in fat.

Sal pushed his chair back and stood up. He removed his suit jacket and started rolling his sleeves up. "I'm going to show you just how unafraid I am of you. You see DeMayo, you're a coward. Without your crew, you're nothing. I'm going to beat you from one end of this room to the other. When I'm finished, they'll have to carry you out of here in a fucking bucket."

DeMayo could see Sal was serious and he was afraid. He was very afraid. He knew Sal's background and pedigree. As Sal expected, DeMayo backed down. "Sally, come on, we're old friends here. I should be pissed at you. From what my guys are telling me, it was YOUR guy that did the shooting. The gun was found in his hand and Sal, let's not forgot, the guard killed your guy. So before we go to the mattresses on this, just know it was your guy that fucked up. My guys completed the job and got the cash, which by the way was a hell of a load!"

Sal was trying to blink away the stress and anger he was feeling. There were conflicting reports on what occurred during the heist. The evidence pointed to his guy killing Saville but Sal knew his guy would follow instructions. Sal took a deep breath. There was a time and place for revenge. This was neither.

"How much was in the armored car?" He asked DeMayo. As expected, DeMayo lied when he answered.

"You'll be happy to hear there was $410,000 in there! Once you minus the $100,000 you owe me that will leave you with $310,000!"

"I already paid you." DeMayo sat back in his chair and stared icily back at Sal.

"It's going to be another $100,000. Since your guy

committed murder, I have to pay my guys more. A lot more. They have a lot more to lose. Plus, you won't have to pay your guy or one of your inside guys anymore. So I think an additional $100,000, between friends, is fair. Don't you?"

Sal knew he was getting taken advantage of. He knew it. He knew how much was in the armored car because it was all over the news. He asked DeMayo about the discrepancy and he said the armored car company stole the difference and would hit their insurance company up for it.

Sal knew he would kill DeMayo. There was no doubt about it. He was a dead man walking. He just had to bide his time and do it in a way that wouldn't lead back to him. The quicker he got out of this meeting, the quicker he could get to work on planning DeMayo's death. So he agreed to take $310,000, all of which he planned to give to Dennis Saville. Unfortunately, he never got the chance because upon hearing the news of his son's death, Dennis hung himself.

Three days later, an outline of the armored car heist plan, who the contact was from the city that supplied the garbage truck, how much he was paid, where the money was, who the other two masked gunmen were, where they had their money stored, and where the SUV that was stolen and used during the heist could be found was hand delivered to a young prosecutor who was a NY Yankees fan and who would later become the governor of NY.

The Patrizio brothers were quickly arrested for the heist but not the murder. Any murder committed during a felony can automatically be and is, in most circumstances, murder in the first degree. However, DeMayo was a powerful boss; he had a long reach and friends in high places. Backroom deals were struck, money exchanged hands and the brothers went down for murder in the second degree, 15 years to life.

On the one year anniversary of the failed heist, the young prosecutor received another gift: enough evidence to put away Camarillo Crime Boss Anthony "Tony the Butcher" DeMayo for life. DeMayo was arrested and placed in the secure housing unit of Rikers Island. While DeMayo's lawyers were attempting to get him released, a young correctional officer that was on Sal's payroll walked up to DeMayo's cell.

He was carrying a glass Dr. Pepper bottle with a piece of torn fabric sticking out of the end. The prison guard said five words to DeMayo before lighting the fabric and throwing it at the old mafia don's feet: "Salvatore DiFlippo sends his regards."

CHAPTER #16

Bramwell and his bodyguards made it out of the basement alive. No one was more surprised than him. It was a hell of a gamble that had paid off! He had to get in contact with Stevens and get part two of the plan working.

The old dons were stunned into inactivity, but it wouldn't last. Like so many things in life, it was all down to timing. It would either work or it wouldn't. Bramwell would prepare his guys for war, because he knew it was coming.

On the drive back to Buffalo, Bramwell received a phone call from an unrecognizable phone number. "Yeah?" He gruffly said into his cell phone.

"Bramwell, please."

"You got him. Who's this?"

"Bramwell, it's Silk. I represent the Marino Family." Bramwell knew who Santo 'Silk' Silvino was and who he was with. This was interesting.

"Silk, I know who you're with. What's happening?" Bramwell said, as he lit a cigarette.

"I know we just met Bramwell, but damn son, you got some balls. I'll give you that. I'm surprised they're not wiping you up from the parking garage right now."

"You and me both Silk. No one is more surprised than me."

"Is it true? Is he still alive?"

"Why would I lie about that Silk? For what? It would only buy me a day or two at the most."

"It would give you a chance to get into the wind. A head start anyways…"

"Do I look like the running type Silk? No, I was being honest. Sal is making a recovery and the Reaper is alive and well. And really pissed off. You got anything for me?"

"In that case, allow me to share with you everything I know. This has all been approved by Mr. Costa himself, ok? All we ask is that whatever you have planned, you leave us out of, deal?"

"Let me hear what you have Silk, then we'll negotiate."

"That's fair. Ok, after you left, Moretti went ballistic! He was almost demanding that Ricci send someone to the basement to finish you off. Damn! Augostino agreed with everything Moretti was saying too. Which is interesting..."

"Ok Silk, you baited the hook. Now reel me in. Why is that interesting?"

"About a month, two months back, two of Augostino's guys came out of the pen. They had been away for a long time, almost 20 years. They went in back when DeMayo was running the family."

"Silk, skip the history lesson. I have a million phone calls I have to make here."

"These two guys are brothers. Patrizio is their name. They come out, get hooked back up with Augostino and start making a little dough. That's normal so far. This is where it goes off track. About three weeks ago, one of my lieutenants eyeballs the older brother and Conti having lunch together at a private club in NY, in the Cosimo Families' district."

"That's not really interesting Silk. Conti is the number 2 guy with the Cosimos'. You got anything else?"

"Let me finish man. We had a bit of work to do out in Augostino's area. Throw away shit, you know? Quick, easy cash, but not exactly worth the risk? It would be perfect for two guys that just got out of the joint though. So I call Augostino's underboss, Pasqual Gaccione. I tell him a little about the job, what's involved and tell him I want to use the

Patrizio brothers for it. All we want is a percentage of the take. Like a finder's fee."

"I get it Silk. Let me guess. Gaccione said they were unavailable, right?"

"Better. He said they were no longer associated with his organization. So I start bullshitting him a bit, we go back a ways. He finally tells me Augostino moved both of them to Moretti's family for a bunch of cash. He didn't know why, and didn't want to know why."

"It's interesting Silk, I agree. Not exactly a smoking gun, but I see where this is going."

"Bramwell, I'm not done man. I saved the best for last. The brothers are in the wind. No one has seen or heard from them in about five days or so. Guess the last place anyone ever put eyes on them? You got it baby, Buffalo, NY"

I was distracted. Which on a normal job is never good but on one as complicated as what I was working on, was downright deadly. I couldn't stop thinking about Kate and how good she looked the previous night at dinner. Needless to say, the evening took a turn for the worse when I told Kate that I was going to kill everyone involved in Sal's abduction.

I can't describe the look on her face. It was a cross between horror, disappointment and sadness. The sorrow I saw in her eyes hurt me in ways I am not even fully aware of yet. She asked if that's what I do: kill people for Sal. I told her it wasn't what I do, but who I am. I am an assassin, an executioner, a reaper. I am traveling hate, death personified.

I thought she was going to arrest me, or try to. I would have let her. For a moment, I thought she was going to shoot me. After seeing the depth of unhappiness I saw in her face, her eyes, I would have let her. I could see she had questions, but I stopped her.

I reminded her that when this was all over, she could ask me anything she wanted and I would tell her the truth. I gave her the finger print card and asked her to run it for me. When she found her voice, she told me she would run it, but she wasn't sure if she would share the results with me or not.

I shook my head trying to forget the look on her face as she turned and walked away from me.I had to clear my mind because I had work to do.

I was sitting outside a plain two story house on the outskirts of Rochester, NY. The house matched all the other houses in the neighborhood. It was the corner house at the end of a cul-de-sac. None of the other people living on the street had ever met the owners of the house. People would come and go at odd times of the day and night.

They were always quiet and their lawn was always mowed. The newspaper and mail were always removed on a daily basis and the trash cans were removed from the curb the same day after the garbage truck came. Whoever lived there was the perfect neighbor: quiet and unseen.

The house was actually owned by Augostino through one of his shell companies. The house was used as a refinery for designer prescription medication. Augostino would import the drugs in a powdered form, usually from China or Russia via a carrier through Canada. The powders were delivered to the house to be cut and refined, and pressed into pills or capsules.

This was one of three houses like this that Augostino had. Each house was generating a little over $75,000 in profit. Per week. Right now, I knew there were ten people in the house. I didn't know exactly what rooms they were in but that didn't matter because in 30 seconds, they would all be rushing outside. I knew at least five were armed.

That was fine by me because I was armed. I had two

H&K Military Issued Mark 23 pistols. Each pistol held 12 rounds in the magazine and one in the chamber. I had 26 rounds of .45 caliber ACP 230 grain jacketed hollow points and I planned on firing every single one of them.

I got out of the rental car I was using and started walking towards the house. I had on a pair of jeans, a black tee-shirt, a pair of black neoprene gloves and sun glasses. I looked and felt like death. When there was five seconds left on my timer, I drew my pistols and continued towards the house.

Right on schedule, I heard a small popping sound from the rear of the house. I stopped in the house's front lawn and shielded myself behind the large oak tree that resided there. A few seconds later, the front door opened and a large cloud of smoke poured out. Then, the residents of the house exited.

When the tenth person exited, I stepped from behind the tree. Everyone was disorientated and coughing from the smoke. I picked out the bodyguards from the crowd. That's where I started. I leveled the pistols and did what I was made to do: destroy life. Instinctively, without conscious thought, my guns bounced from target to target, flame, smoke and death were all dealt from my guns, my hands.

When the last person fell to the ground, I advanced towards the bodies, guns at the ready. I knew I had fired eight rounds from each weapon, or sixteen of my twenty six. I had ten rounds remaining, but they weren't needed. Everyone was dead. My aim had been true. My job, at this house, was complete.

I tucked the guns back into my pants and walked back to my car and then disappeared. 55 seconds after I left the neighborhood, a bomb leveled the house. At the same time, two other bombs leveled the other two houses Augostino had like this one.

Kate was still in Miami and working the case. The FBI was still processing Spree's townhouse but Kate wasn't hopeful they would find anything. She did submit the fingerprint that Stevens gave her. Rick Stevens. She was torn on how to feel about him.

The critical thinking part of her brain, the common sense part of her brain, told her to either stay away from him completely or arrest him and drop him in a hole somewhere for the rest of time. She was shocked that he admitted to her that his intentions all along were to kill the people that abducted DiFlippo and Spree.

Maybe not shocked. Maybe shocked wasn't the right word for it. She sensed something off about him. She knew he was dangerous and probably a little crazy too. The problem was, and she knew it was absurd, but she felt a deep connection with him. Her heart was telling her he was special, in some way. She shook her head. *Yeah, Kate, real nice* she thought to herself. She thought her last boyfriend was a mistake. That relationship didn't even register compared to how bad of an idea it was for her to feel *anything* for a mafia hit man. If that was what Stevens was. Well, of course, he was! Why else would he so casually talk about murdering people? Her thoughts were interrupted when her cell phone rang.

"This is Kate," she answered.

"Agent Riley? This is Dale from the lab. I have the results of the fingerprint you dropped off." Kate was surprised to be hearing back from the crime lab so quickly. She had scanned the print card into a digital record and e-mailed it to the lab back in Quantico. She had Phillips call the head lab tech and throw his weight around to get the print ran right away.

"Dale, that was very fast. I mean, fast like a television crime scene show fast."

"It wouldn't have been so fast without the filters you requested. How did you know where to look?" After Phillips got the green light to have the print immediately ran, Kate spoke to Dale and asked him to start the search looking at all convicted felons in New York State. She was following a hunch that the person whose print Stevens found would somehow be connected to the dead kidnapper in NY and the most plausible connection would be through the NY State Department of Corrections.

"I was following a hunch is all. What have you got?" Dale told Kate about the hit on the fingerprint and that he was 99% certain they had a positive hit. She asked him to e-mail her all the info. When she hung up with Dale, Kate had a minute of indecision. Should she tell her boss about the hit on the fingerprint or call Stevens first?

Vince Augostino was finally starting to feel comfortable after the failed meeting in New York City. Moretti was finally able to convince Augostino that Bramwell was lying about Stevens being alive. Ricci decided to put all decisions on hold regarding DiFlippo's organization until they had more information. Was DiFlippo in fact making a recovery or was Bramwell simply stalling for time?

Moretti and Augostino decided to wait a few days and then meet to put together a plan on how to eliminate Bramwell and then the rest of DiFlippo's organization. Ricci might have put things on hold, but it wasn't his ass on the line if, and it was a big if, Bramwell had been telling the truth.

He drank another swallow out of the horrible pink tasting medication that was supposed to settle his stomach. He felt like he spent the majority of the day sitting on the toilet. He was starting to get his appetite back; that was a good sign. He was trying to think if he wanted to chance eating something, maybe some toast, when his phone rang.

Two of Augostino's legitimate businesses were a butcher shop and a funeral home. Each place provided an excellent opportunity to make a body disappear with little to no suspicion. My business this afternoon was at the butcher shop.

Vic's Chop Shop, with the unoriginal slogan of "Where nobody beats our meat", was located in the corner of a commercial building in the business district in Rochester, NY. It was an old school butcher shop in that it sold deli sandwiches and had a handful of tables scattered around the front room where customers could eat their lunch. From the backroom of the shop, there was a staircase that led up to where the real money maker was, a 12,000 square foot gambling house.

Augostino made a lot of money from this one location and the place was always hopping, twenty-four hours a day, seven days a week. I knew there would be armed guards in and around the casino and it would be harder to hit this place than the three houses I had already blown up. That was ok though because I liked a challenge.

The first issue was getting through the butcher shop to the back room. I knew there would be one spotter in the shop. All of the butchers that worked there would be loyal guys to Augostino. They would all be armed with edged weapons and were very skilled in their use.

In the backroom, this was where I would encounter the first two armed guards. After that, it was anyone's guess. I figured there would be a doorman either on the staircase leading to the gambling house or working the door at the top of the stairs. Once inside the gambling house, the room was broken into three sections. The first section was the main room that contained a bar, tables and chairs, a few big screen

TVs, and several couches and love seats. Off the main area, there was a small hallway that lead to the third floor and a set of bathrooms.

The second section contained a few table games: Blackjack, roulette and craps. The third section contained several poker tables. I knew there was a strong room located somewhere in there, maybe behind the bar, or on the third floor where all the money was kept. This is where the majority of the security and armed guards would be located.

I wasn't interested in robbing the miniature casino. I didn't want or need the money. My objective was mayhem and massacre. I was dressed differently. I was wearing the same jeans and black tee-shirt, but now I had on a black pull over windbreaker and a black & gold Rochester Rattlers baseball cap.

I entered the butcher shop carrying a newspaper and ordered lunch. In a place like this, you had to try the Italian sandwich. They piled on layers of prosciutto, hot supressata, capocolla, dry salami, and mortadella. They also added sliced Romano cheese, sweet and hot roasted red peppers and sliced cloves of roasted garlic. They finished it with a drizzle of olive oil and red wine vinegar and wrapped the whole thing up in white butcher's paper. I grabbed two cans of root beer and sat down to eat.

This was the best sandwich I had ever eaten. While I ate, I casually read the paper and surveyed the room. It didn't take long for me to pick out the spotter. He was the bored looking guy sitting at the table with a view of the front door and the side entrance.

He had an empty coffee cup in front of him and his own newspaper. He also had a cell phone that he never put down. I didn't have a plan when I walked into the butcher shop and sat down beyond eating lunch. I figured I had two options: The direct approach where I pulled the pistols and started killing everyone, or I could attempt to be discreet and secretly get up into the gambling house.

The direct approach would not work here.. I figured I would go with option number two knowing I could always go back to option number one if I needed to. I finished my lunch and threw the garbage away. I stopped at the counter and asked if they had a restroom I could use.

The butcher didn't look up from the meat he was carving, he just pointed to a hand drawn sign that said "No Public Restroom". I thanked him for my lunch and told him he was right, no one could 'beat his meat' and walked as if to leave the shop. When I got equal to the table where the spotter was sitting, I noticed he had the sports page open. I stopped and pointed to an article about the Buffalo Bills.

"You think they're going to do anything this season?", I asked the spotter. There are two things people from NY will always talk to you about: The hometown sports team and the weather.

"I doubt it. Probably be lucky to go 8-8. Whattya think?"; he replied. I took his question as an invitation and sat down across from him.

"I don't know. I was thinking the same thing until the other day but I caught the tail end of a sports talk radio show on WGR, and the host said they beefed up their offensive line a bit and picked up that free agent on defense so they might be able to squeak out 10 wins and maybe get a wild card into the play-offs."

"I heard that. I listen to that show almost every day, it's The Thomas Loop show. He's a local guy from Western New York, knows sports for sure, but I know a guy that knows a guy and he says that Loop guy is a Cowboys fan."

"That's God awful! I'm sorry to hear that. I like his show, but now, this kind of puts things in perspective." The shop was empty, there was only one butcher at the counter and he was on the phone and writing something down, either taking an order or placing a bet. I started to stand up.

I was lightning fast when I struck. One solid, forceful chop that crushed the spotter's larynx. His eyes bulged for a second and then he gripped his throat and fell to the floor. I rushed back to the butcher's counter "Holy shit, I think that guy is choking on something! Do you know the Heimlich maneuver? Can you please help him?"

The butcher hung up the phone and came out from behind the counter. By now, the spotter was nearly unconscious. The butcher went over to help and I told the butcher I would call 911. I went behind the counter and pulled the phone off the hook and pretended to dial the number. I faked a conversation, pulled the phone cord out of the wall and hung it back up. Then I quietly slipped into the back room.

Two other butchers were sitting at a table eating and playing cards with two body guards. I was already holding a silenced 9mm Walther P99 pistol. The gun danced, bodies jerked and in a matter of seconds, all four of the people in the backroom were dead.

The door leading to the front opened and the other butcher charged into the kitchen wielding a knife. The rouse was up. If I wasn't holding my pistol out in front of me and ready to fire, the butcher would have destroyed me. In the battle between gun and knife, in close quarters and especially if the knife was in hand before the gun was, the knife usually wins.

The first shot hit him in the chin and the second shot shattered his nose and skull. He fell to the floor dead, like everyone else in the room. I went out to the front of the restaurant and thankfully, no one had come in. I dragged the body of the spotter into the back room with the other bodies. I flipped the open sign to closed and locked each of the doors.

I had only brought one silenced weapon with me and had fired it several times already. With each shot, the silencer broke down more and lost its ability to do what it was designed to do: silence my gunshots.

I unscrewed the silencer and filled the magazine up again and tucked the gun into the back of my pants and pulled my windbreaker over it. I drew my Cold Steel, Recon Tanto knife from underneath my wind breaker. The knife had a 4.75 inch Kraton handle and a seven inch black epoxy powder coated blade. The entire weapon was less than 12 inches long, entirely black, and was simply designed to slay anything it came in contact with.

The stairwell leading up to the gambling house was without windows and had recessed lighting. The entire staircase was enclosed in shadows. I walked up the stairs like I was supposed to be there, my combat knife tucked nicely to my side and hidden within the dimness and blending perfectly with my windbreaker.

The first bodyguard I encountered stood outside the door. He smiled at me, and I smiled back. I wasn't acting suspiciously, and the guys downstairs should have already frisked me to make sure I wasn't carrying any weapons into the apartment. He was big, younger than me and definitely stronger than me. In a fair fight, it would be a close call. Like I said, I don't like close calls.

The combat knife slid effortlessly through his ribcage and

into his heart. I flicked my wrist back and forth a few times and he was gone. I don't think he felt much pain as his face only revealed a confused look and then nothing.

I understood that none of the people I killed today or would still kill today had anything to do with Sal's abduction. Killing them was merely a means to an end. A way to hurt the person who was responsible for what happened to Sal. I didn't know how many people were in the gambling house. I didn't know how many were guards or on Augostino's payroll and how many were just normal people, at the wrong place at the wrong time.

It didn't matter to me. I would kill them all. I would burn this entire city to the ground and kill everyone within it to get back at the people who had tortured Sal and still had his granddaughter. I pulled my windbreaker up so I had easy access to my weapons. The combat knife was tucked away into its sheath and the H&K pistols came back out. I took a deep breath and opened the door.

CHAPTER #17

It was time to leave Pennsylvania. Primo's original plan was to fly to Arkansas to meet up with his brother and Russo. After he hung up the phone with Conti, he had been in a funk. He spent the rest of the day in an alcohol haze. When he woke up this morning, he felt awful.

He decided he didn't feel like dealing with the assholes at the airport today. He took a long, hot shower, shaved and cleaned himself up. He still felt horrible and hung over, but he had a plan for that. He would go and eat a very large breakfast, do a few lines of cocaine, and get an escort to spend the rest of the day with.

Tomorrow he would rent a big luxury car or SUV and drive to Arkansas. It was roughly 16 hours away by car and he figured it would be at least a minimum of eight hours travel time if he flew and he would rather spend twice as much time and be comfortable by driving.

He picked up his phone and called his brother.

"How are things in The Natural State?" he asked his brother when he answered.

"They're going well. We're laying low, not drawing attention to ourselves. When did you get in? Today?"

"That's why I am calling. I've changed my plans. I'm staying another day where I'm at and will leave tomorrow. I plan on driving down instead of flying. I leave tomorrow; I'll be there the day after tomorrow."

"I don't blame you for driving instead of flying. Fucking TSA groping everybody. Fuck them. Roman's got me a little worried."

"Worried why? How?"

"He's pretty wound up. The way he watches the girl. I

caught him jerking off in there in front of her yesterday. He didn't even stop, wasn't even bothered I walked in on him."

"Bull, listen, we both did time with Russo. We both know he's a little off, right? All he needs is his pipes cleaned out. Why don't you guys head into Missouri tonight, find somewhere to go and take care of your needs? Get it out of your system because if either of you jump that girl before I get there, there will be hell to pay."

"I get you brother, I do. You don't have to worry about me jumping her. Missouri it is. We'll hit up somewhere a few hours away and get a room. Sometimes Roman can be a little rough, so it's better if we don't do it anywhere near where we're at."

"Excellent. I have a business opportunity where I can trade the girl for some crystal meth."

"With them hillbillies?" Bull asked
"Yes, to them. They deal in that stuff. We can use her up a bit and then trade them to her for some product. It could be useful down the road."

"Whatever you want to do, you're the boss."

"I'm going to make some calls. Set up the transfer for a day or two after I get there. I'll let the buyer know the merchandise will be used and well broken in." They chatted for a few more minutes than disconnected the call. Russo was an asset for sure. In a fight, there was no one Primo wanted on his side more, including his brother, than Russo. The downside was Russo was hard to control and clinically crazy. Oh well, you take the bad with the good Primo thought as he grabbed the yellow pages and flipped to section E.

Kate had called Stevens first but, of course, he didn't answer. Probably out killing people she thought. She shook her head in frustration and left him a very short, abrupt message.

She was trying to get everything wrapped up in Florida so she could get back to NY to chase down this newest lead.

She had done some digging on the name that was connected to the fingerprint Stevens found. Patrick Patrizio. The name didn't mean anything to her. She made phone calls, threw her federal weight around and discovered the dead kidnapper in NY, Tommaso, and the kidnapper in Florida, Patrizio, both served time together at the same prison in NY. That had to be the connection.

She had called Davis and Wilson back in Buffalo and asked them to run down which family the two kidnappers were affiliated with. Neither one answered, so she left them both a detailed message indicating that her request should be their top priority.

She called the prison in NY where Tommaso and Patrizio served their time and spoke to the warden. She told him she needed everything they had on each person. She wanted everything: old visitation logs, phone records, incident reports, health reports, parole and probation reports, and who they ran with while they served their time.

The warden said it would take him some time to get all the information together and he would get back to her. She stressed the importance of getting back to her sooner rather than later. She said she would owe the warden a favor if he could start getting her information by the afternoon.

That was the frustrating thing about working investigations: there were often times when the case seemed to stall out because you were left waiting for other people to come through with information for you, or for the crime lab results to come back, or waiting on something else. Typical government bureaucracy: hurry up and wait.

She hit the redial key and called Stevens back. She felt like whipping the phone across the room when he didn't pick up. She decided she would give him until noon to call her back. If she didn't hear from him by then, she would release the lead to Phillips.

She was a little startled when her boss walked into her borrowed office.

"Have you seen it yet?" he asked

"Seen what Tom? What are you talking about?"

"So you haven't seen it. Great! Guess what! For real, take a guess."

"Tom, if you knew how just not in the mood I am for this right now…"

"Ok, ok, I'm sorry Kate. Fine, be a party-pooper then. Three houses were completely leveled outside of Rochester, NY this morning."

"Tom, it's still morning. Three houses? All in the same neighborhood?"

"No. All in different neighborhoods." He replied with a smug smile on his face. She was so frustrated, now she wanted to whip her phone across the room at her boss' smiling, arrogant face. She calmed herself as much as she could.

"What do you mean leveled? How? At the same time or different times?"

"Very good Kate, very good questions! When I say leveled, I mean, destroyed, blown up, with military grade C-4. All at the exact same time or within one or two minutes of each other as close as our techs can tell. What else Kate, what are you forgetting to ask?"

"I haven't forgotten to ask anything *Tom*. Obviously all three of the houses are connected. All by the same owner is what I am guessing."

"Right again!"

"Yeah, and the fact that you have this shit eating grin on your face, it obviously connects with our investigation. Rochester is outside of DiFlippo's area if I remember correctly. One of the other families is based out of Rochester…" Shit! Wilson or Davis had told her which families had which areas but she was only half paying attention and didn't remember what was said.

"Do you need a hint Kate? I can't believe this, the infallible Kate Riley actually forgot something?"

"Shut up Tom. I didn't forget…Not exactly…" Rochester was the 2nd smallest area, just one step above DiFlippo's. She remembered Ricci had the largest area so she had a one in three shot of guessing correctly. "Augostino. Vince Augostino owned the houses. Right?"

Her boss responded by slowly clapping his hands. "Very good. He owned the houses through a shell company. Wrap it up here. We're heading back to NY in two hours. Unless you see some value in staying here."

"No, we're done here. We've gotten everything we're going to get. We need to get to Rochester. Tom, I think this is just starting. I think if we're not there soon, we won't have a shot at getting Augostino. I think he'll be dead."

Augostino had a safe house on Rock Beach Road East. It was a sprawling mansion, with a high fenced gated property that had a private dock that was on Lake Ontario. There was a state of the art alarm system, motion detectors, video cameras and armed guards. After receiving the phone call earlier in the day about three of his businesses being blown up, he decided to go there.

He had made several phone calls to Moretti but never got through to him. He was in full panic mode. Especially when two hours after he received the first phone call, he received a second one telling him that his butcher shop/casino was also burnt to the ground.

He had over twenty armed guards at his safe house. His yacht was fully fueled and anchored in the middle of Lake Ontario, just south of the US and Canadian border. He had two other speed boats gassed up and ready to get him out to the yacht where he could easily flee to Canada.

He was scared, angry and restless. He left Conti in the city to run the business as usual while he took a few days off. They needed to set a bounty on Stevens' head. If he could get Moretti and the other families to pitch in on it, they could put out a large enough figure that Stevens would have to leave the country. He called Conti and told him to reach out to the other families and get the bounty on Stevens in play.

Augostino poured himself a glass of scotch and sat down to worry more. Maybe he should call that Bramwell guy and explain what happened. Augostino thought he could sell the fact that he didn't know what Moretti wanted his two guys for. He could put all of the blame on Moretti and maybe still walk away.

If DiFlippo was alive, then he knew putting the blame on Moretti wouldn't work. There was no way DiFlippo would believe that the last two attempts on his life had been from people in Augostino's organization without his knowledge. Augostino smiled. He would put a million dollar reward out on Stevens and try to confirm if DiFlippo was alive.

He could play both ends of this he thought. He could have people hunting Stevens and if DiFlippo was still in a coma, or even better, recently deceased, he could convince Bramwell it was all Moretti's fault and even offer to help Bramwell eliminate Moretti. He picked up his phone to call a friend in Buffalo to see if he could get any info on DiFlippo's status. As he was dialing, the first explosion took out one of his armored SUV's in the driveway.

Fourteen people. That's how many people I gunned down in the gambling house above the butcher shop. There were only seven or eight people in there gambling at the time and as soon as I started shooting, they all hit the floor.

My original plan was to kill everyone in there, but I spared the gamblers. I don't know why I didn't kill them. I didn't have time to think much about it. I still had work to do. I walked through the three rooms dealing out death and collecting souls. The cash room was located on the third floor. There were six armed guards up there when I started shooting. Three were on their way down to see what the commotion was but they died quickly and violently in an empty, dark, dank stairwell.

The other three died in a room that had over $250,000 in cash in it. Once everyone was eliminated and the innocents had fled the building, I set it on fire. It would serve as another warning, another sign of what was coming for those that dared hurt my friend.

So far, my plan had worked out exactly like I wanted it to. There was only one more thing to do: confront Augostino. I knew by now he would be in hiding and protected. Once he found out about the houses I bombed earlier in the day, he would panic. Augostino was a coward and would react the way cowards do: run, hide, and pay someone else to fight his battles.

I knew how he would react and he was playing right into my hands. If he was frightened, he wouldn't be thinking clearly, and he wouldn't make the mistake I knew he would make. I'm a logical person and think in straight lines. If someone destroyed several of my hidden properties, properties that I owned but were not connected to me, the next thought in that straight line thinking is whoever that person was, would also know about *all* the hidden properties I own.

I wasn't surprised in the least when four, armor plated SUV's roared into the driveway of the mansion on Rock Beach Road. I was expecting them. I held a remote detonator. I figured Augostino would have 15 guards with him. I counted twenty. He may have had a few more I missed.

I'm good at what I do. Hell, I'm one of the best. I don't care what happens to me and haven't for a very long time. I'm fearless and confident in my abilities, but I'm not stupid or careless. This wasn't a movie, this was real life. One guy going up against twenty armed guards that were expecting trouble was suicide.

Everything had been prepared well in advance of Augostino's arrival. It was now time to direct him where I needed him to go. I hit the first button on the remote detonator. This blew up the bomb I had planted on the bottom of one of the SUV's as soon as I got back to NY earlier in the day.

I counted to sixty, and then hit the second button. The 2nd bomb was one I had planted on the back side of the garage. As soon as I heard the second explosion, I hit the third button. This detonated the bomb I had planted on the other side of the house, opposite of the garage. This was the smallest bomb I planted.

My goal with the bombs was to cause confusion and funnel everyone out the back of the house. That's why I detonated the bombs in the order that I did. I couldn't be certain of where Augostino would be in the house so the third bomb was the smallest and I doubt it even broke through the outside wall of the house. The back door flew open and out rushed several of the armed guards.

Her noon deadline had come and gone. She had given Stevens every chance she could to get in touch with her, but he still hadn't returned her calls or answered when she called him back. She finally received a phone call back from Wilson confirming that Patrick Patrizio was part of the Camarillo Family. She was also informed that his older brother, Primo, was also part of the family.

A few hours ago they barely had anything, and now they had two solid leads they were following up on. She was having Wilson and Davis pull everything they could on the Patrizio brothers. She also wanted to know where they were.

While they were on the FBI's jet heading back to NY, they were notified that a fourth business that was tied to Augostino had been burned. Early reports were indicating multiple dead by gunshot wounds.

Her boss was convinced that whoever was filling in for DiFlippo had declared war on Augostino. Kate wasn't so sure. Stevens had been one step ahead of them throughout the entire investigation. Maybe he still was. Maybe he was burning and killing his way across NY State until he found the Patrizio brothers.

Reports were still coming in from the fourth building. Apparently, there was a deli with an illegal casino taking up the top two floors above it. There was at least one witness that they were questioning. He was in the casino when the shooting started. Kate wasn't sure if the witness would be able to provide a description of the shooter, but Kate bet if she showed him a picture pf Stevens, he would identify him.

She had a queasy stomach thinking Stevens might have been involved. She really didn't want him to be but figured he was the cause. She was surprised that she was also worried about his safety. She was afraid that once they landed, the next reports they got would be about his death in another place owned by Augostino.

They needed to have a conversation very soon she thought. She just didn't know what she wanted to say. There were moments when he could be sweet and charming, where she could see his sense of humor and personality, and she loved all of that. There were also times when she was afraid around him, where she could tell he was dangerous, violent. She just wanted to know, which one was the *real* Rick Stevens?

With a sniper rifle, I could probably pick off at least seven or eight of the armed guards from the distance I was at. I would be able to cycle through my shots and clip one per second, maybe a little faster than that. Three or four seconds until some realized what was happening, three or four more seconds of confusion and then they would seek cover. I believed I could take out three or four more before they found cover.

On the low end, I could kill at least half of the guards protecting Augostino and on the high end almost three quarters of them. That would leave four or five guards remaining, plus Augostino. I could manage that, but that wasn't my plan.

Four guards set up a loose perimeter around Augostino and rushed him to the waiting boats. Two got into one boat and raced off. The other two got into the other boat with Augostino and followed them. The first boat ran directly to where the yacht was anchored. The yacht signaled the first speed boat by flashing its spot light in a predesigned signal. The speed boat responded by repeating the same signal. The yacht repeated the signal again.

The first speed boat headed back towards the second one and repeated the same signaling process as it did with the yacht. Talk about overkill I thought. The second speed boat raced up to the back of the yacht.

The back of the yacht was a few feet above the water line. It appeared to be a small, outdoor sundeck. The speed boat put out its bumpers and tied off to the sundeck. One of the guards jumped on the deck and retrieved a plank of wood and put it between the two boats.

Augostino climbed from the speed boat to the deck of the yacht. There was a seven foot ladder and an electronic lift that would take a person from the sundeck to the main deck of the ship. Augostino walked over to the lift and started it up. The guard put the wood plank back from where he retrieved it from, jumped in the boat and they took off.

I imagined the two boats would make the run to Canada and make sure they didn't run into the Coast Guard or customs officers. They would act as a buffer for Augostino's yacht. Thirty-five seconds after Augostino got on the lift, he was getting off of it and onto the main deck. As soon as both his feet were planted on the main deck, I stepped out from the shadows and punched him as hard as I could in his fat stomach. He dropped to the deck like he had been shot.

Before he even had a chance to realize what was happening, I kicked him in the head. I kicked him hard, but not hard enough to kill him. I would kill him, no doubt, but I needed information first.

I felt myself slipping away, again, as the other side of me came out. I didn't think I would have to torture the truth out of Augostino. He was too much of a coward for it to come to that. My problem was that I wanted to torture him. This thought alone frightened me and sickened me all at the same time. What had I become?

I knew at the first sign of trouble Augostino would run to

his safe house and use his yacht as his fallback position. So I planted my bombs earlier in the day. I wanted him on this yacht, in the middle of this lake, without witnesses. He could be as loud as he wanted and no one would hear him.

After I burned the casino down, I had raced out here to the lake. As an Army Ranger, I went through aquatic training and tactics. Throughout the years, when I am in-between jobs, I spend a lot of time around the water and on the beach. I've scuba dived for years and am a competent diver.

Geoff was able to tap into the Yachts GPS system and he gave me the exact coordinates. I had a boat of my own and anchored it out just a little over a mile away from the yacht. I entered the coordinates into my underwater wrist GPS unit, donned my wetsuit and swam to the yacht. There were four guards and two crewmen on the yacht.

No one was paying attention to the sundeck. I climbed on the deck, shed my scuba equipment, climbed the ladder to the main deck, pulled out my pistol and killed everyone with the exception of one of the crewmen.

I kept him alive and told him he would remain alive as long as he did exactly what I said. I had over an hour to question him about the correct signal. He told me they had decided on using one signal and anything else would mean trouble. Throughout our hour together, I asked him at different times what the signal was and to do it. He said and did the same thing every time.

I told him if he didn't do it right when Augostino was heading out here, I would slip my Tanto combat knife into the center of his back and sever his spinal cord so his legs would be useless. I showed him the knife, and sliced a slit across his forearm. I wanted him to know how serious I was. After I did that, I told him I would toss him into the water to see how long he could tread water using only his arms.

Once Augostino climbed on board the boat, I knew the crewman had been honest with me. Instead of making him suffer, I stabbed him in the back of the head, in an upward thrusting motion that killed him instantly.

Augostino was gasping for breath on the deck. I grabbed him in a head-lock and dragged him to a sitting area that was off to one side. He wasn't trying to struggle, but I viciously punched him in the face twice, just because it felt so damn good.

I picked Augostino up and threw him onto a wooden deck chair. I grabbed the roll of duct tape I had brought along and taped his arms and legs to the chair. He was coughing, wheezing, bleeding, and out of breath. He still hadn't looked at me. For some reason, this pissed me off.

"Hey Vince, look at me." He still sat with his head hung low, refusing to look at me. I was really starting to get mad. "Vince? HEY! Look at me I said? What, you can't hear me?" I asked him.

Then I braced his head with one hand, and I grabbed his left ear with my other hand. I squeezed the ear tight. In one explosive moment, I pulled my arm back hard and fast and tore his ear off. I heard it takes anywhere from seven to twelve pounds of pressure to tear an ear from the human body. Well, not exactly pressure, but sheer force. I don't know if that is true or not, but I can say it's absolutely possible to generate enough force, whatever the number is, to do it.

Augostino yelled and howled louder than anyone else I have ever heard. He looked up at me now with pain and fury in his eyes. I held his ear I was holding to my lips and said "Can you hear me now?" and smiled. Then I tossed the ear overboard.

"Fuck you! Fuck your mother! You're a son of a…" I open hand slapped him on the side of his head where his ear used to be. Hard. He almost passed out from the shock of the blow and the pain it caused. Either way, it stopped him from talking.

"This is how this works. I'm going to ask you questions, you're going to answer them. If you say anything else other than an answer to a question I asked you, I will tear, break or cut a piece of you off. You will tell me what I want to know, Vince. There is no doubt about that. After I have everything that I want and need from you, I will leave. I'll leave you tied to the chair where you're at." I pulled out my Tanto knife and sliced him across the chest, tearing his shirt, and drawing blood.

"Eventually, one of your guys on the boat will come back and find you. They'll rescue you, that is, assuming there's any of you left to rescue. The choice is yours. I assume you know who I am and why I'm here. That's the first two questions, Vince. Who am I and why am I here?" I thought for a second he was going to curse at me more, or attempt to lie. Any bravery or bravado he had was gone. He lost it a long time ago.

"I know who you are. The Reaper. I knew you would come but I didn't do this. I didn't have anything to do with this." No, he wasn't brave, but he was a liar and a coward. Liars lie. He was doing it now.

I calmly reached over to his left hand, selected his pinky finger, put the edge of my Tanto blade to the middle knuckle of the finger and used my thumb to force the blade through the bone and gristle. Blood spurted, Augostino yelled and I smiled some more. I tucked Augostino's severed pinky into the top pocket of his shirt. "Save this. You might need it later." I said to him.

"Vince, you just lied to me. I know about the Patrizio brothers. I know that they work for you, or did. They're probably with Moretti now. I don't give a shit, Vince. Moretti is next on my hit list. He won't survive the night, I can promise you that. All I want to know is where they are."

I knew about the Patrizio brothers from Bramwell who got it from Silk. Silk was a straight up, old school gangster. He would take a bullet or a 20 year federal rap for his boss without changing his facial expression. I had met Silk on two occasions and liked him.

The look on Augostino's face told me everything I needed to know. He had no idea where the Patrizio brothers were. He was trying to decide if he should lie to me by giving a false location or to tell the truth. I think he was afraid to do either one.

I jabbed his severed pinky finger with the blade of my knife. "Vincent, stop. I can see the wheels turning. You're trying to decide if you should lie to me, or tell me the truth. You can tell me nineteen more lies and then you won't have any more fingers or toes. Twenty lies and your ears will be gone. Twenty-one lies and you won't have a nose either. If you are still alive at that point, and still telling lies, I'll have to think of something else to cut off." I casually let the blade of the knife point to his genital area. 'Or maybe, I just start in the middle and work out from there, yeah?"

Augostino's eyes flared wide as he got my point. A few tears streamed out of his eyes and he sniffled, once, and then he started talking.

CHAPTER #18

A little after twelve thirty in the afternoon Moretti had received a call from Augostino's underboss, Bruno Conti. He told Moretti he had just gotten off the phone with Augostino and they wanted to put a bounty out on Stevens. Augostino was offering to pitch in one million dollars and asked if Moretti would be willing to contribute.

That was the last contact anyone had with Augostino. He had gone into hiding. Moretti liked the idea of having Stevens hunted. If he was still alive, the contrct would take some of the pressure off of him and put it on Stevens. He called Mario Costa to get his take on the situation, but Costa said he didn't have any issues with Stevens or DiFlippo and didn't understand the need for a bounty.

Moretti said it was clear Bramwell had declared war on Augostino without getting it sanctioned first. There were consequences that had to be addressed. Costa countered by saying maybe Augostino shouldn't have tried to kill DiFlippo twice. Yeah, consequences were being addressed right now and he didn't want any part in it. He enjoyed making money, running his business and staying alive.

Crossing DiFlippo or Bramwell guaranteed one thing: The Reaper. He wanted no part of The Reaper. Moretti said he would remember this when he was holding Stevens head. Conti told him good luck and hung up the phone.

Moretti was angry with Conti's response. He was hoping to have a combined front when he spoke with Ricci to get his input and approval. Before he called Ricci, he decided to tip the scale to his favor. He picked up his phone and called his underboss.

When Kate and the rest of the task force got off the jet in

Rochester, they were told there had been more developments. *Shit*, Kate thought. Here it comes; this is where I learn that Stevens is dead.

To her surprise and relief, the news wasn't about Stevens' death. It was about another bombing that occurred at a different property that was also owned by Augostino. When the police got to the bombing site, they were met by several armed security guards on Augostino's payroll. So far, they had been less than cooperative.

All of the guards were being held in a secure federal holding facility fifteen minutes from where they landed. They were going to split into two teams: The first team would go to Augostino's safe house and the second team would go to the federal detention center to question the guards.

Kate wanted to be at both places, but she felt the most promising lead would come from the guards and not the house. She would be the lead once the interrogations started. She was on the phone making sure someone was running full background checks on each of the guards.

If everyone she questioned didn't say anything to her or they all told the same story, which would be an obvious lie, she wanted to find something on one of the guards she could use so he would give up whatever he knew.

She wanted to know where Augostino was and who was responsible for the bombings at the safe house. Secretly, she wanted to know if the bomber had succeeded and gotten away or if he was gunned down and left to die somewhere.

Amongst other legitimate and illegal businesses, Antonio Ricci owned over one hundred massage parlors in New York City. Some were licensed places in upscale shopping centers and others were storefronts used for prostitution.

At exactly 4:00 pm, three of the storefront locations in

less desirable neighborhoods all were blown up, killing everyone that was inside each location. Chaos ensued. There were not any witnesses, partially because the person responsible for the bombings was very good at what he did and very careful, and partially because people minded their own business in the neighborhoods where the massage parlors were located.

It was too early in the investigation to tell for certain, but the predominate thought was that the bombings in Rochester were connected to the bombings in NYC. As per procedure, the FBI was notified. Phillips was examining the safe house on Rock Beach Road when he got the call.

Phillips felt like they were close to catching the bomber. They were at least in the same state and would be on their way to NYC once he cleared the scene and Kate was done with her interrogations.

"Ok asshole, just sit there with that smug look on your face. Go ahead, keep smiling. We'll see how funny all this is when you're serving time in a federal prison." None of the guards were talking to the FBI, or anyone else. They all kept saying the same thing.

"Lawyer. I said I want my lawyer. Do I need to spell it out for you?"

"You flatter yourself. Lawyer has six letters in it. You think you can spell six letter words?" Kate was getting angry, which was never good during an interrogation. She was technically breaking the law by continuing to ask him questions after he requested a lawyer. She didn't care because she knew he had information she needed and she was determined to get it.

He didn't respond to her baiting. He just sat back and smiled. It was time to shake him up. "I wouldn't be as confident as you are. I mean, you were just arrested and you are already on parole. You can kiss your freedom good-bye…"

"L-A-W-Y-E-R. I can spell. You understand English? I'm going to own your badge after the way my rights have been violated here. I'd hate to be you! I've been arrested and you haven't told me why. I've requested a lawyer, repeatedly, and not only have you refused, but you continue to ask me questions. This is getting good. I'm gonna be rich, compliments of a shitty FBI agent and the US Government." He said with a big smile on his face.

Kate smiled right back at him. "Technically, you haven't been arrested. Not yet. You're being held under the Patriot Act and, as of this point, you are classified as a domestic terrorist. The Patriot Act supersedes the US Constitution so you no longer have any rights whatsoever. You can yell lawyer until your vocal chords are raw and I still won't have to provide one to you."

"Bullshit! You're good. You almost had me there for a second" he said, smiling, but less sure of himself than a minute ago.

"Take a look around you. Are you at the Sheriff's Dept., or in a city jail? Did we take you to a trooper barracks or other state run facility for questioning? No. You're sitting in a federal detention center. I can keep you here for as long as I want. I don't have to charge you with a crime, let you make a phone call or tell anyone where you are. I own you. I can drop you in a hole forever."

The smile was gone now. Fear had replaced it. He cleared his throat "What do you want to know?"

Ricci was furious. He could not believe someone, anyone, would have the audacity to cross him by destroying three of his businesses. He had been following the news reports and listening to his people on the street. He knew of Augostino's problems earlier in the day.

It was time to get Bramwell on the phone. It was time for answers. He had his secretary call Bramwell's secretary and eventually they got on the phone with each other. "You have crossed the line and will pay."

"What are you talking about Mr. Ricci?"

"I know what you're doing. You sent that animal after us. First he went for Augostino and now he comes for me. I won't stand for this, Bramwell."

"Mr. Ricci, The Reaper doesn't listen to me. He doesn't take orders from me; hell, he doesn't take orders from anyone. I warned you this would happen. I told you the other day he was going to find out who was responsible for what happened to Sal."

"Call him off. Call him off right now! I insist!"

"Mr. Ricci, you're still not listening. I can't call him off. He's like a bullet after it's been fired from a gun: all the hoping, threatening and praying in the world ain't gonna change that bullet from hitting its target."

"You sent him on us…"

'Mr. Ricci!" Bramwell interrupted him. It was strange to be talking to the most powerful crime boss in NY with such little respect. Bramwell liked it. "I didn't send him after anyone. Mr. DiFlippo is his best friend, almost like his father. I warned you the other day he was going to do what he needed to do to find out who was responsible."

"If you don't call him off, I'll declare war on the Accardo Family. I'll bring the other three families into this and we will crush you."

"Is that so? You think long and hard about that decision. We have assets everywhere. Mr. DiFlippo's been in the game a long time. A lot longer than you. He has files. He has evidence, proof. He has enough information to put you away forever. Assuming Stevens doesn't get to you first. I can make one phone call, just one, and everything you own will be frozen. All your vehicles will be flagged in every law enforcement system in America with instructions that the people inside the car are armed, wanted felons. I can even have all the power and water turned off in every building you own. You like cold showers, Ricci? Huh?"

"I don't believe you. You're bluffing. This is your last chance, Bramwell."

"Hey Ricci? Go fuck yourself. If you want to go war, I'll take you to war. You think it will be the four families against us?" Bramwell said, openly laughing at Ricci. "What? You forget about the Westsiders? They've been looking for a reason to go with one of the NY families. Once all of your assets are frozen and the cops are arresting all of your guys and a warrant is issued for your arrest, and the Westsiders are bombing and killing everything you own, how long until the other families call bullshit and bow out? Guess what? Mr. DiFlippo has files on everyone! All of their assets will be frozen! Have fun trying to fight a war against us without any money and the cops all over you. By the end of the first week, it will be over and you'll be in jail or dead. Don't forget why this is happening…"

"I've heard enough. You're full of shit, Bramwell."

"Yeah, bullshit talks and money walks, right Ricci? This is happening because someone made an aggressive move against Sal and his organization. You declare war on us, and he'll declare war on you. Have fun with that Ricci."

"You have 24 hours, Bramwell. If any of my other businesses are destroyed because of Stevens, I will declare war on you and your family." He hung up the phone without waiting for Bramwell's reply.

Ricci sat there for a minute to consider Bramwell's threat. He wasn't concerned with The Westsiders. The Irish Mafia was small and would be nothing more bothersome than a noisy fly at a picnic. He could deal with The Westsiders.

It was the other threat that gave him pause. DiFlippo had been around for a lot of years. Longer than any of the other families' bosses. He had the smallest family, but it was rumored he made the most money. He had an amazing computer guy working for him, but every family did. DiFlippo's guy was supposed to be the best, but was it true?

He had also heard that DiFlippo did keep information on the other families. It wasn't a surprise, as all families did. Information was power and you could never have enough power. He just wondered how much information DiFlippo had. Hé remembered what happened to Augostino's boss, DeMayo.

One day the government didn't have anything and the next day DeMayo was arrested, indicted, and murdered. There were always whispers that someone gave the info to the Feds that put DeMayo away but there was never any proof and no one ever took credit for doing it.

His thoughts were interrupted by his secretary telling him he had a phone call. "Mr. Moretti…"

"Mr. Ricci. Forgive me for getting right down to business, but as you're aware, we have a problem."

Kate was briefing Phillips on the flight from Rochester to New York City. She was telling him about the attack on the safe house and how Augostino was able to escape. They had several teams of people out on the lake to see if they could catch Augostino before he made it to Canada.

They also had a call out to the Canadian Royal Mounted Police and the Canadian Customs division asking for help. Before the FBI Jet could complete it's short flight to NYC, Augostino's yacht was found.

The good news was Augostino was found with his yacht. The bad news was, he was found speared to a deck chair and long dead by the time the yacht was discovered. "Speared? What does that mean?", Phillips was asking the agent reporting to him over the phone. Kate could only hear one side of the conversation, but she didn't like what she was hearing.

"Yes, I know what a scuba spear gun is. Ok....Twice? Wow! Ok, mark the coordinates of where the yacht was found, get a dive team in the water to search the area and get the thing docked somewhere. I'll have an evidence team standing by." He hung up the phone. He turned and looked at Kate and smiled.

"This is huge! Augostino is dead! Someone killed him!" Kate didn't share her boss's sense of excitement. He then filled her in on the details of how the body was found. Kate listened with clinical detachment until she heard the part about the missing ear and pinky finger.

That made her want to vomit, and she almost did. Thankfully, Phillips didn't notice as he just kept on talking. "Ok, we need to get someone back over to DiFlippo's place and see what's going on. This is obviously retaliation for kidnapping DiFlippo. We need to get some people talking to whoever is in charge now that Augostino is gone. Someone might know where the missing girl is..."

He rattled on about what needed to be done and the agents around them took notes, made suggestions and started working on Phillip's list. Kate only half listened and still felt like she was going to be sick.

She had her answer she thought. I guess I know who the real Rick Stevens is. She needed to talk to him. She would call him the second she had a free minute once they were on the ground. She only hoped he was alive to answer her phone call.

Moretti couldn't have been happier after getting off the phone with Ricci. Ricci was on board and offered two million dollars for Stevens. He expected the other three families to match his investment and said he would have his people contact them and get everything in motion.

Moretti had a big smile on his face when Conti walked into his office. "Bruno, you're amazing! My plan worked!"

"Excellent boss, there was never a doubt. I knew it would work."

"The three guys that pulled the job?"

"Taken care of. No worries. Dead men don't tell no tales, you know?"

"Very good. I can always count on you. Anything else on Augostino? Any word from him?"

"Nothing. I think Stevens might have hit one of his safe houses, but Augostino escaped. He's somewhere in the great white North, hiding. I'll reach out to Gaccione tomorrow to see if he's made contact yet."

"Tomorrow I want to send a team to Buffalo and finish off DiFlippo. No more waiting, no more messing around. I think Ricci is going to go to war with Bramwell. If we can get lucky, maybe he'll be at the hospital when we take out DiFlippo. If not, send the team by DiFlippo's estate. I want to take a run at Bramwell. If we can get him, Ricci will owe us. Owe us a lot."

"Got it. I'll pull together a crew. They're going to have to be good guys, top guys. Just so you know."

"I know Bruno, I know. I hate to lose any of them, but this is for a greater cause. Enough about work. We'll be busy enough over the next few weeks. Tonight, tonight we celebrate. Call Per Se. Have them prepare the private dining room. Invite your top two captains. Invite some women. We're going to dine at one of the most expensive restaurants in New York City, so no strippers or ding bats. I want refined, upscale women. You got it?"

"Yeah boss, I got it. I'll get this set up. We looking for a later dinner or something earlier?"

"Later. Let me know what time. I want a few guys to sweep the restaurant first. I want a few on hand to watch over the place."

"I'll take care of it boss. Don't you worry."

After the FBI landed in New York City, Kate had a voice mail waiting for her from Stevens.

"Kate…Agent Riley, its Rick. I'm sorry I missed your calls. I've been tied up all day. We need to touch base sometime today, compare notes. I have some information I want to give you. Ok, I'll talk to you soon." There was long pause, 8 seconds at least and then "I'm really sorry about last night. Truly."

She didn't know what to think. He had information? I bet he does, she thought. She paused for a second and wondered if he were still in NYC, like she was. She sent him a text saying she just got his message, had info for him, and let him know she was in NYC and, if he was still here, she would like to see him later.

She smiled. Yeah, you've been one step ahead of us until now, but we're caught up now. Maybe her implication that she knew where he was would slow him down some. He did sound sincere in his voice mail message though…

She shook her head. *KATE!* Are you kidding me? He sounded sincere? He harpooned a man to a wooden chair on a yacht! For crying out loud! Her internal argument with herself was interrupted.

"From everything that we can tell, the latest three bombings are tied to one corporation that has its corporate office in the Cayman Islands." Phillips was briefing the group. He continued "From what our researchers can find, and given the area that the explosions occurred, we are standing in..." He paused to refer to his notes, and then continued, "The Cosimo Family. Maybe we can get a meeting with Mr. Cosimo?"

"Not likely. The head of the Cosimo Family is Marcello Moretti. Vito Cosimo was the first boss of the family, back in the 1920's."

"Thank you, Kate. Maybe we can track down this Moretti then?"

The investigation was building speed but Kate wasn't hopeful they would find anything at any of the bombing sites. This seemed like a waste of time. She was getting impatient. She called the agent in charge of the Rochester investigation and asked about the witness he spoke to that survived the casino shooting and fire.

He said he e-mailed her everything he had on the incident. She asked for a description of the shooter. The witness didn't get a good look at him, not from the front anyway. He knew the shooter was a white male with black hair. He was wearing a black jacket and a baseball cap.

They were still pulling video from the surrounding businesses but, so far, they had not been able to find any promising leads. There were a lot of white guys wearing dark colored jackets and ball caps in that area of town. He promised he would call her if anything changed.

Kate knew the rest of the afternoon would be all wasted time. The investigation would move forward, but her part in it was stuck waiting. Again. She was hoping to find a witness, someone that would talk to them. She would go through the rest of the day and wait for Stevens to call. If he didn't call her soon, she was worried they would respond to more of his handy work before the day was over.

CHAPTER #19

I had killed over fifty people today and it wasn't even 6 pm yet. Most normal people were getting out of work, driving in traffic, or at home cooking dinner. I was sitting on the edge of a mattress in some fleabag hotel waiting for a phone call. Waiting for a call that would have me most certainly kill more people.

My work in New York was almost complete. I had one more person to visit and I was going to wait one more hour for my phone call and then go with plan B. The only problem was, I didn't have a plan B. Not yet.

Augostino had a lot of information and was very happy to give it to me after I subtley threatened to cut off his manhood. He didn't know where the Patrizio brothers were, but he had a few ideas. Geoff was running down those ideas for me.

After my next visit, if I didn't have any other leads, I would go with whatever idea Geoff thought had the highest probability of being right. I was thinking of other ways I could find the Patrizio brothers when my phone beeped, indicating I had a text message.

I read the message and couldn't help but smile. Kate Riley was in New York City. Interesting. She had some info and wanted to see me. That sounded dangerous to me. She knew I was behind all the attacks that occurred today. I wondered if I met with her, what she would do? Play it straight with me or take me into federal custody?

I didn't have too long to think about it when my phone rang. It was Geoff. He had some information for me. Once again, he had come through. I wrote down a few notes, and thanked Geoff. After we disconnected our call, I pulled another sheet of paper out and wrote down everything I would need.

It was time to go shopping. The clothes I was wearing wouldn't work for the next part of my plan. I had the suit I wore the night before packed in my travel bag but if everything went according to plan, I would be meeting up with Kate later and didn't want to have the same outfit on. I thought about buying a new pair of shoes, but the ones I wore last night were very comfortable so I grabbed those.

I left the hotel with my list and walked a few blocks down and a few blocks over to another flea bag motel and got into a cab. I had them take me over to Bloomingdales where I picked up a Charcoal Burberry London Milbury Suit. I picked out a white Canali Woven dress shirt and a Burberry London Burgundy Tonal Check tie to go with the suit.

I went into a changing room and put on my new outfit. I tucked the 9mm Walther P99 into the back of my pants and strapped the Tanto knife to my belt, on my left side. It was a little large, but the suit coat did a good enough job of concealing it from view. My old clothing went into the men's room trash can.

I left the department store and walked down Lexington Avenue. A few blocks up, I went into the Renaissance New York Hotel. I went into their business section and jumped on the 'net. I wouldn't have time to scout the place I was heading to as thoroughly as I preferred, so I used what information and pictures came from the World Wide Web.

I left the hotel and got into another cab. I wasn't far from my destination but I needed to get there as quick as I could. I wanted to arrive before my guest so I could at least give the place a once over with my own eyes. I had the cab drop me three blocks away and I walked the rest of the distance.

Per Se is located in the Time Warner Building. It opened

in 2004 and is one of the most expensive restaurants in NYC. It's an urban interpretation of The French Laundry in Napa Valley. The same chef owns each restaurant.

Each day, the chefs create two unique nine-course tasting menus. Reservations must be made exactly one month to the calendar date. Unless of course, you were the head of the largest criminal family in New York City, or if you had an amazing computer hacker that could get into the computer generated reservation system and add you in.

The meal I was eating was well worth the $295 price tag. The food was fantastic! Each course was just enough to leave you wanting more, but only until the next plate arrived. My only regret was that I was working and couldn't enjoy the wine the sommelier picked out for each course. I promised I would come back to this restaurant once I was done with this job.

Right then, I thought of Kate Riley. I wondered if she would join me if I asked her. I looked out over the city and realized how romantic the view was and how alone I felt. I thought back to the dinner she and I shared the previous night.

*Oh no…*I thought. I am such an idiot! The way she was dressed, the way she said no talking about work during dinner and the conversation that followed that. Oh no…That was a date! I was on my first date in over 15 years and missed it! I didn't even realize it was a date! Before I could beat myself up too bad, Moretti and his crew entered the restaurant.

Moretti had three other men with him, not counting the three bodyguards that showed up thirty-minutes ago, and five women. They were all elegantly dressed and appeared to be ready for a night out on the town. Moretti had one lady on each of his arms.

They were quickly ushered to the East Room, which is the smaller, private dining room at Per Se. The velvet drapes were closed offering Moretti and his dates privacy. That was fine with me. I had seen enough. I was here only to gather information.

I knew Moretti was coming here because I had Geoff monitoring Moretti's phones in the hopes that he would go out somewhere and leave his compound. If he was dug in surrounded by armed guards, it would be nearly impossible for me to question him.

I paid my bill and left the restaurant. I left the building and casually strolled up and down the street. I was picking out the bodyguards; there was only two outside waiting. A loose plan was starting to form in my mind.

It was after 10:00 pm and the restaurant was closing. Moretti felt good. In a day or so, people from all over the country would be calling and inquiring about the reward for Stevens. He wondered about Stevens. Was the guy really that good? Could anyone be?

Naww he concluded. There was just no way. He had just eaten a great meal, drank a lot of wonderful wine and was about to head back to the Ritz to spend the rest of the night with the two beautiful women sitting next to him.

"Ladies, excuse me." He said as he stood up. A flick of his eyes and Bruno also got up and walked with him to the restroom. "What a meal, huh Bruno?"

"It was one of the best I've ever eaten boss. No doubt."

"Take the fellas out for a good time tonight, Bruno. Call Jacky and have him bring the car around for me. I'm going to the Ritz for a nightcap with the girls. You're going to have to get another limo for you's guys."

"No problem, boss. I'll call Jacky as soon as I zip up here. Have fun tonight, boss." Bruno said with a smile.

Conti called for the car and had the driver bring it around to the front. He called the two bodyguards he had waiting outside and asked them if everything was clear. They were instructed to wait until Moretti made it in the limo safely and then they were to get their asses to the Ritz to make sure there wasn't any trouble there.

He called a friend that owned a car company and was told his limo would be there in the next 15 minutes. By the time Conti left the restroom, everyone was getting ready to leave. They all walked out of the restaurant and the building together, in one big group.

The backdoor of the limo was open and waiting for Moretti and his escorts. Jacky was already in the driver's seat and ready to go. After Moretti got into the limo, Conti closed the door and the car sped off

Moretti was opening a bottle of wine while the blond girl was rubbing his inner thigh. The dark haired one was rubbing his chest. *Jesus*, he thought, these girls were sexy! He was already starting to get aroused, and he hadn't even popped his Viagra yet!

As he was pouring the wine, the blond started to unzip his pants. Moretti couldn't help but smile in anticipation. I'm going to get a header on the way to the hotel he thought! Oh my, now the dark haired girl was joining the blond! What a great night this was going to be!

Moretti sat back, closed his eyes, sipped his wine and enjoyed what was being done to him, right up until the backdoor flew open and the blond was yanked off him and thrown outside. Moretti's first thought was thank God she wasn't using her teeth, and then he was angry. The dark haired girl had a gun pointing in her face and she quickly got out of the other side of the car.

The person holding the gun climbed in the back of the limo and shut the door. "Do me a favor, tuck that thing in your pants and zip up. You're embarrassing yourself here."

Moretti did as he was instructed to do; He smiled as he said, "Rick Stevens. We finally meet." Stevens responded by punching Moretti in the side of the head near the temple, knocking him unconscious.

My plan was simple. Find Moretti's car, kill his driver, then kidnap Moretti when he left the restaurant. In theory, it was simple anyway. I knew the car would be close, but this is the power district in NYC and there were a lot of limos. I didn't want to kill the wrong driver by mistake.

Every time I found a limo, I texted the plate number to Geoff who ran it through the Department of Motor vehicles. We knew the limo wouldn't be registered in Moretti's name so we had a list of his family members, business associates and companies he owned on hand to cross reference them with.

Six limos later and we had the correct one. The driver was parked off of Central Park in a No Parking zone. He was standing outside his car, in the well of the driver's side door, smoking. As I was walking by, I said "Those things will kill ya'".

As he was responding, I stepped into him quickly and drove my knife right into his heart. I jiggled my wrist a little and he was no longer part of this world. I dumped his body into the driver's seat, careful not to get any blood on my new suit. It was rare that I found an off the rack suit that fit me and I liked as much as this one.

I closed the door and calmly walked to the passenger side door and opened it. So far, so good. No witnesses. I reached across the seat and pulled the driver onto the large floor of the passenger side. With the tinted windows no one would see the body. The easy part was done.

I figured one of the body guards would call when it was time to pick up Moretti. I had to be there early. I couldn't get out of the car and open the door in front of Moretti or any of his people. They didn't know me, but they knew I wasn't the driver that brought them here.

So I jumped in the car and drove it to the front of the restaurant. I parked in the front like I owned the place. I could see one of the bodyguards lingering outside. He looked at the car and for a second, I thought he was going to walkover. That would have been real bad. He pulled out his phone and answered a call.

I pulled out my phone and sent Kate a text. *I'm tied up. I'm going to be later than I originally planned. I can't talk right now. I still want to see you tonight. You free 11-12-ish?* She responded quickly: *So you tease me with our first dinner which we don't eat, then ruin our second dinner and stand me up for our third?*

I smiled, but I didn't know what to respond back. I typed, *We're in NYC. They have some of the best late night restaurants. I'll be hungry at that time. Let me make it up to you. Name the place and I'll be there. One request though* . I sat back and waited. This was crazy. I'm in the middle of kidnapping the head of a mafia family and I think I'm flirting via text with an FBI agent that knows I kill people.

I looked in the rearview mirror at myself and thought of my wife and daughter. All of a sudden, I felt very alone. I felt like I was out of step with the rest of the world. The world was moving too fast and I couldn't catch up. I missed my family, but I also missed having love in my life. Loving someone, being loved in return.

My phone buzzed with Kate's message. *Ok, text me when you're finished, we'll see where we are then and figure a good place to meet.*

Request? I have one too. You first. I responded *If you're planning on arresting me, at least wait until after I've eaten. I don't want to eat federal food. Yours?*

I kept my eyes moving to make sure no one was approaching the car. Thankfully the bodyguard I could see was still on his phone and seemed to have forgotten about me. There was a valet attendant that started walking my way.

I opened the drivers side door and stepped outside, making sure to keep my back to the bodyguard. The valet walked up, apologized, and said I had to move my car. I smiled, told him who the car belonged to, gave him three $100 bills and told him to get lost. Once again, he apologized, told me to take as long as I wanted and walked away.

I got back into the car just as Kate's text buzzed my phone. *Don't blow anything else up today.* I looked at my watch, thought about the rest of my night, and thought that was very possible. The phone the driver was carrying started to ring. I picked it up and grunted out "Yeah?"

"Jacky, it's Bruno. You ok? You sound like you're taking a shit. The man is ready to go. Bring the car around. He's heading to the Ritz after this. Got it?" I wanted to keep the conversation short because I didn't know what the driver sounded like. I should have let him talk a little bit before I killed him. I responded, "Got it", and hung up.

It was all down to timing now. I watched the bodyguard. He pulled his phone away from his face, said something into it, hit a button and put it back to his face. He didn't talk, only listened. He said one or two words, hung up the phone and walked quickly down the street and got into a car, where the 2nd bodyguard was waiting.

I got out of the limo, opened the rear door, and got back in. It was a deviation from what a normal driver would do but

I was hoping the excellent meal and wine Moretti had, and his two dates, would allow him to overlook it. Luck was on my side.

After I knocked Moretti out, I used the same roll of duct tape I used on Augostino and taped him up. I would interrogate him in the back of the limo, but I needed to put some distance from where we were.

It looked like the escorts were almost to the coffee shop down the street. There was no telling who they would call. I got back behind the wheel and took off. I realized I didn't have a specific destination in mind. When I was putting this plan together, I guess I didn't plan on getting this far.

I took a drive to Union Square. A parked limo in that section of town wouldn't stand out at all. Also, people with money that lived in expensive neighborhoods tended to mind their own business.

I parked in University Place up the street from the Fifth Avenue Hotel. I got out of the front and climbed in the back. I made sure Moretti was still breathing, and then slapped him very hard several times until he came to.

He looked around, as if getting his bearings. I pulled the knife out and held it to his groin. "Don't think about yelling. If you do yell, make sure it's worth it because it will be the last thing you say before I castrate you."

He put on his hardest look and tried to stare me down. I had seen Sal give this look a lot over the years. The only difference being was that Sal's look actually was hard. Moretti's look was what a wise guy *thought* a hard look should be.

"Are you done? I'm kind of pressed for time. I have a dinner date. I'll cut right to the chase. I need to know where the Patrizio brothers are." I knew it wouldn't be that easy.

Arrogant, powerful people often struggle with coming to terms with the fact that all their power and money can't and won't help them.

I wasn't in the right location to torture someone. I didn't have the time to do it properly and I didn't have all the tools necessary to do what I wanted to do. I also wanted to keep my suit clean of blood because I was meeting Kate after this.

Moretti was still rambling on and I was getting angry. I slammed my knife through the top of his $1,000 Italian leather shoe. I clamped my hand over his mouth and twisted the knife. He yelled, but it was muffled. I pressed the knife in further, I could feel it pierce the bottom of his shoe and go into the limo's carpet.

"Ok, fast forward. You've threatened me, swore at me, called my mother a whore, etc, etc, etc. We're passed all that. We're at the part where you tell me what I want to know or, I swear to God, I will stab this knife into your other foot so hard I'll pierce the bottom of this fucking car. You will forever walk with a really bad limp because I'm not here to kill you, Moretti." I paused. I could see he was confused, trying to figure out what my game was.

"Patrizio Brothers. Where are they?" I asked him.

"Why wouldn't you kill me? You'd have to kill me, I'd hunt you forever…" I clamped my hand over his mouth and quickly pulled the knife from his left foot and savagely drove it into his right foot. I put a lot of strength and power into it.

"Wrong answer." Like I said, I drove that knife into the car's floor. "I'll answer you Moretti and then you'll answer all of my questions because I am done with this. If you fail to answer another one of my questions, I'm going to start by cutting pieces of your dick off, and Moretti, remember, I saw that pathetic little thing earlier. You can't spare much."

I leaned down and tapped the handle of my knife. "I'm not going to kill you because I don't care about you. Keeping you alive will be more of an embarrassment to you than killing you. I'm the best killer in the world, Moretti. People expect you to die when I come a calling, but leaving you alive, permanently handicapped, that shows the other families how weak and pathetic you are. I know you'll hunt me. It will be wasted money though. This is it for me. My last job. After this, I'm gone. I have more money than you can imagine, Moretti. I can buy a government to protect me. I can pay ten times whatever bounty you are offering on me."

I removed the knife and wiped off the blood on his chest. I made sure not to get any blood on me. So far, so good. "I'll set a bounty on you and I'll release every single file Sal has on you and your organization. The FBI will be all over you. Even if you manage to evade them and get out of the country, where would you go? Your assets would be frozen, all your off shore banks would be wiped clean by my hacker. In a matter of hours, everyone would know you couldn't pay the bounty on me. So tell me everything you know about the Patrizio brothers and where they are."

If my life would have gone differently, I would have made an excellent car salesman. Moretti told me everything he knew.

CHAPTER #20

Kate and I decided to meet at an all-night diner. I walked in 10 minutes later than the time I told her I would be there, but when she saw me, she still smiled. My heart did this thing where it jumped a little, sped up and slowed down all at the same time. I smiled back at her. I walked over and sat down across from her, my back to the diner's door.

"You didn't have to get all dressed up to meet me in a diner in the middle of the night, Mr. Stevens" she said as her opening line.

My smile grew as I replied "What, this old thing?" I said referring to the suit I had purchased earlier in the day. We made small talk as the waitress took our drink and food orders and left. She talked about her day, how the investigation was going and how she went from being in Miami last night to NYC this evening.

The conversation between us flowed, she did most of the talking, but she appeared like she was just talking until she worked up the nerve to say what was really on her mind. I hated that we had to talk about it, hated myself for what I had become, but pretending I hadn't said what I said last night just wouldn't work.

"Kate, about last night..." She started to say something, to interrupt, but I stopped her. "No, we need to talk about it. It's the proverbial white elephant in the room. Right now, let's not worry about it. Right now, we're just two professionals working the same case, hoping for the same end result. After we finish our meal, we'll go for a walk, or a drive and I'll tell you everything. This is just not the place to have that kind of talk."

She agreed. We ate our dinner, which was really breakfast,

as we both ordered bacon and cheddar cheese omelets and home fries, and discussed the case. She gave up everything the FBI had and what angles they were working. As I expected, I was still one step ahead of the FBI.

I thought the FBI would eventually make the connections I made and discover the information I learned, but it would be weeks or months before they did. They were already moving in the wrong direction. Which was helpful to me. I didn't need the FBI around when I was killing the Patrizio brother's and rescuing Spree.

Over coffee and a slice of coconut cream pie, I told her what I had learned. I didn't tell her how I learned the information I had, as I suspected she already knew some of it. I got to the end of the information I had and sat back to finish my slice of the pie.

"Arkansas?" she asked me doubtfully.

"Yes, Arkansas. I have my security consultant; you remember speaking to him, Allen, working on getting me as many of the details as he can come up with."

"When are you leaving?"

"Tomorrow. I have a private jet set to take me to Arkansas, I just don't know exactly where in Arkansas yet. I'm hoping by the time I get up tomorrow, Allen will have the info, or at least be able to get me close. If not, I'll fly into Little Rock, or somewhere else centrally located in the state and be ready to move when I get word on where I need to be. I wanted to leave tonight, but without a specific destination, it's kind of pointless. I think we're running out of time on finding and saving her. I am also exhausted and need some sleep."

"The task force doesn't even have a clue about Arkansas. The investigation is going in a complete opposite direction. I don't know if I can get the team to Arkansas…" I cut her off.

"I don't want the FBI in Arkansas. I want to get to Arkansas and end this. The FBI being there will only complicate things and get Spree killed." I could see Kate bristle at my implication that the FBI was a large, bureaucratic entity that lumbered along at its own pace and did more harm than good. I held up my hand and apologized.

"What I mean is, I think we're out of time. If it's just me, I can move at my own pace, without the restraint of any rules. You have to admit, Kate, I've done more to advance your investigation by myself then your entire task force." Before she could respond, I continued.

"Here is one of my problems with inviting the FBI along. The FBI can be effective, given the right circumstances. I know the problem with the FBI. The problem is easy. The FBI cares more about following the letter of the law, following the process, than it cares about getting results."

"I'm not sure I would agree with you…"

"I don't expect you to. Just think about it. Think about the investigations you do, the task forces you've been involved with, the agents in charge of everything that you've worked for and with. First and foremost, they worry about their own ass, if they're covered. The way they cover their ass is by following the letter of the law, crossing all the "t"s and dotting all the "i's." I could see I was getting through to her. I knew Kate was very intelligent, probably more so than I was. She would think about what I said, process it and come to her own conclusions.

"I work better alone. Like I said, without having to color within the lines. I boil it all down and make things real simple. I leave the emotion out of it. In my world Kate, emotion is useless. It will complicate your thinking and get you killed. I understand two things: Action and reaction. Cause and effect. The success or the failure of the job, or mission, is all on me. If it all goes to shit, I don't hide behind a team of lawyers and make excuses and point fingers."

"What if you run into something you can't handle? What if you need help?"

"I'll deal with it…"

"Please. Stop the macho bullshit for a minute Rick, and think about this. If I went with you, I could help you." Before she was finished talking, I was already shaking my head no.

"No. There is no way. That's not going to happen."

Kate's eyes were such a vivid shade of green. Her temper was up and this was a warning sign. "Why not?" she asked in an angry huff.

"I'll explain it to you in the next conversation we have. When we leave this place." Without taking her eyes off of me she called out, rather loudly, "CHECK PLEASE!"

We left the diner and started walking down the street. I was reminded of our walk from the previous night. Did that really happen last night? Between then and now, so much had occurred. So many people were killed. I shook my head. I killed so many people. I did, and for what? To save one life? What was my motivation? Was I more concerned with saving Spree or killing the Patrizio brothers?

"Are you going to talk to me now Rick, or are we going to walk all the way to Arkansas together?"

"I'm going to tell you everything about me, Kate. Everything I've done. Everything that has brought me to this point in my life. I'll tell you everything I plan to do and after that, you'll understand why I don't want the FBI around."

As we walked, I started talking. I went as far back as high school. I told her about my parents' deaths, being raised by my Aunt and Uncle, feeling lost after graduation. I told her about joining the Army, the purpose I felt. The training I went through, the things I did in the name of my country.

I told her about that jungle in South America. The jungle that changed my life. As I was telling her what we did, what I did there, in the back of my mind, I wondered privately if I had ever left that jungle? Would I ever be able to leave it?

I told her about going to school to be a pastor and about meeting my wife. I told her of the love we shared. The life we had started, the plans we had made. I told her how it ended on a Sunday evening in July, many years ago. How my life ended that day as well.

We continued to walk. While I was telling her this part of my story, she walked closer to me and grabbed my arm. She didn't let go. It was one of the nicest, most thoughtful things anyone has ever done for me. Something inside of me, changed right then.

I tried to explain the depth of loss I felt, the loneliness. The anger, the bitterness, all the hatred. The betrayal I felt from God. I told her about having lunch with Sal and what he gave me. I told her how I prayed all night over what to do. How I searched and searched for the correct answer, but the Heavens remained silent.

I tried to explain the rage I was feeling inside. This growing fire that was quickly consuming me, burning me from the inside out. I whispered how I killed the person that killed my wife and daughter. I whispered it to her, because I was ashamed at what I had done. Ashamed at how weak I was and how disappointed my wife and daughter feel about what I had become.

I got choked up and stopped talking. We continued on in silence. Kate didn't say anything; she just walked along side me, still holding my arm. After a few minutes, I found my voice again and continued.

I explained how I went from that first murder to what I am and who I was today. I told her about all the deaths I caused just today. With every word I said, I kept waiting for a negative response from Kate, but it didn't come. She never said a word, she never interrupted me and she never let go of my arm.

I had run out of things to say. I had told my story to an FBI agent. I didn't gloss over anything; I didn't try to paint myself in a different or better light. I am what I have become. There is no sugar coating the harsh reality of what I am. I had stopped talking and we had stopped walking. She faced me, and we looked into each other's eyes.

I don't know what she saw in mine, but I saw a myriad of different emotions in hers: sorrow, pity, regret, and helplessness to name a few. I expected to see anger and disappointment, but I didn't. I was speechless.

She hugged me and held me tight. I held her back. I closed my eyes, breathing the scent of her in. My heart was beating out of my chest. I was feeling a bunch of different emotions I hadn't felt in a long time, in years. I held onto her and didn't want to let her go. I didn't want whatever magical spell that was holding us together to be broke.

She tilted her head up from my neck and softly, gently kissed my cheek. At first I thought I imagined it. Did I? After kissing my cheek, she didn't turn her head away. She kept her lips against my face, pointed towards my mouth. I kept my eyes closed, moved my right hand from the back of her shoulders and cupped her face, and bent down and kissed her.

At first, we kissed softly, only using our lips. As our desire grew, our kisses became more passionate, more sensual. I don't know how much time went by, but we eventually stopped kissing and were left just holding each other.

Neither one of us had spoken yet and my mind was racing. I hadn't kissed a girl in 15 years. I hadn't felt whatever the hell it was I was feeling since I was with my wife. I couldn't help but be amazed by our many contrasts: I was taller and thicker than Kate, older and damaged where she was young and beautiful. I was bitter and full of hate where she was optimistic and hopeful. I was a killer, where she had dedicated her life to helping people.

I didn't know where this night would lead us. I didn't know if this was the start of something wonderful that would ultimately save me, or if this was just a moment to be shared by two lonely people. I didn't care. For the first time in fifteen years, I felt something! Something other than hate or misery or disappointment. I would hold onto this night, whatever happened, for as long as I could.

We never stopped holding each other. Not while we were walking, not while we were in the cab, and not while we were in the elevator heading up to her room. Sometimes we kissed; sometimes we just enjoyed the physical contact of being with each other.

When we got back to Kate's room, our desire to be with each other consumed us completely. The hotel room door was barely closed, and we were in each other's arms kissing frantically. Kate tilted her head back and I lightly bit her neck. She moaned softly into my ear and I felt her entire body tremble with anticipation.

I continued to lick and kiss her neck, slowly sliding my hands down the backside of her amazing body. In the gap between her shirt and her jeans, I felt her bare skin. I kissed a spot under her ear and slid one of my hands up the back of her shirt, feeling her skin. Her skin was soft, hot and electric.

I glided my hands down farther feeling the muscles in her

small, but sensual backside flex as I picked her up. She wrapped her legs around me, and I carried her to the bed.

Later, after we were finished enjoying each other, I put my arm around her, and Kate put her head on my chest. I delicately stroked her head as I breathed in the scent of her hair. We were both overwhelmed by the amount of pleasure we had just felt and shared. I was on the verge of falling asleep when Kate got up, grabbed my hand in hers and said, "I'm pretty sure there's a Jacuzzi tub in my bathroom."

CHAPTER #21

Primo was glad he had taken the extra day to celebrate with the two hookers and relax. He was in a great mood as he pulled out of the rental car lot. He would be in Arkansas the following afternoon and he couldn't wait to get his hands on DiFlippo's granddaughter.

He had spoken to his brother earlier that morning. His brother and Russo had driven into Missouri and ended up going to a few clubs. They ended up hooking up with some ladies that wanted to party and everyone had a good time.

Russo had gotten a bit rough with his date, but she was into that sort of thing and enjoyed it. Bull told Primo he thought Russo was in love. The two brothers laughed and then hung up. Ignoring the No Smoking sticker on the rental car's dashboard, Primo cut the end of a cigar and lit it.

Tomorrow, he would be in Arkansas. He decided to sell DiFlippo's granddaughter for drugs. The day after he arrived, he would meet up with the buyers for Spree. One day after that, the three of them would be in New Orleans. He thought they would spend a few days in the Big Easy before leaving the country. A smile played across Primo's face as he thought of Roman Russo wandering down Bourbon Street.

After our bath, we ended up in each other's arms again in bed. Our kissing led to a second round of enjoying each other completely. The second time was just as good, if not better, than the first time, only not as rushed.

I woke up in the morning to an empty bed. In the background, I could hear the shower running. I stared at the ceiling and thought about my life, my family and God. I wanted to feel guilty for what I had done the previous night but I didn't.

There was definitely a special bond, a connection between Kate and me. Right then, I knew I could walk away from everything I was, everything I did just to be with her.

I was thinking about having a normal life with Kate when I fell back asleep. I woke up again to her walking into the room wrapped in a robe. Her hair was still wet and freshly combed, but she wasn't wearing any makeup. The belt of the robe was tied loosely around her waist and I thought that I had never seen anyone as beautiful as her.

She walked over and kissed me on my lips, "Hi" she said.

"Hi" I said back. She looked at me and smiled and I smiled back at her. She started telling me about the meeting she had with her boss and the task force this morning. She said once that was done, she would tell her boss she was following up on a lead in Arkansas. She would let him know it was a long shot, but still something that needed to be done.

I told her I would have a private jet waiting to take us to Arkansas. I just needed to make a few phone calls to work out the details. I jumped in the shower and thought about what I would need in Arkansas.

While I was in the shower, I heard the phone in the other room ring. A few minutes later, Kate came into the bathroom.

"That was my boss on the phone. Marcello Moretti's body was found about an hour ago, but you already knew he would be found." I didn't say anything. I could tell by the tone of her voice she was irritated.

I had told her last night that I took Moretti out. I just didn't give her any of the details, or how or where I left his body. I rinsed the shampoo from my hair and waited. I didn't have to wait long.

"You could have warned me Rick. This is going to be a

circus. The press is already there. My task force meeting is canceled and I have to go spend the next few hours at a crime scene, that I already know who is responsible for."

"I have a few errands I need to run before we leave for Arkansas. Take as long as you need. I won't leave without you."

"You're damn right you won't leave without me. In front of his house, Rick? I mean, are we going to find any physical evidence that ties this to you? My entire career is in jeopardy because I should be arresting you instead of making love with you."

After I had gotten everything I needed from Moretti, I decided I wanted to make an example out of him. I stopped at a gas station and picked up a tow rope and a can of soda. I drove over to Moretti's house. He lived in an affluent neighborhood out in the suburbs. I tied one end of the tow rope around the can of soda and threw it over the street light that was right in front of Moretti's house.

I pulled Moretti out of the trunk and tied the other end of the rope around his neck. I used a black magic marker and wrote one word on his forehead in big, block letters. I ripped off the duct tape from his mouth and pinched his nose shut. When he opened his mouth to breath, I reached in with a pair of needle nose pliers I picked up at the same gas station and grabbed a hold of his tongue.

I pulled his tongue out of his mouth as far as it would go and then used my knife to cut it off. I tucked his tongue on his shirt pocket and tied the other end of the rope to the spare tire in the trunk. I shut the lid of the trunk and got back in the car.

In my rearview mirror, I could see Moretti thrashing around on the ground in pain. He knew where he was and was trying to call out for help. I put the car in drive and took off slowly. I wanted to make sure the tow rope didn't snap. Moretti was dragged along the ground for a few dozen feet and then lifted off the ground. I drove until Moretti's head was about a foot underneath the street light and then stopped. I put the car in park, got out, and walked away.

I peeked my head out of the shower and looked at her. "Making love? Is that what you call it Kate?" I said, playfully.

In spite of herself, she smiled and said "Yes, but I'm still pissed at you. You could have given me a heads up here."

"You're right, I'm sorry. I did that for a reason. When you get down to the scene, you'll understand why. This is going to confuse your task force and send them off in the wrong direction so I can finish this. Trust me, you'll see."

Kate leaned over and kissed me good-bye and left to finish getting dressed. By the time I finished my shower, she was gone. I got dressed and left the hotel in search of coffee, breakfast, new clothes and supplies for Arkansas.

Heading to the most recent crime scene, Kate kept thinking about last night. There was a deep connection between the two of them. She had never felt anything like this before in her entire life.

The cynic inside of her said Rick was using her. Using her for information about the investigation, keeping her close so he could accomplish what he wanted to and then he would either disappear or kill her. This worried her a little.

She thought back to when he opened up to her and told her about his life. The sincerity in his voice, and the pain in his eyes. No way. There was no way he was playing games with her. This was the real deal. She would risk her career and her life to end up with him.

As expected, the crime scene was a complete mess. It appeared that the police had the entire block of houses surrounded with yellow crime scene tape. After badging her way onto the crime scene, she met up with Phillips.

He was excited and could barely contain himself. Another mafia boss was murdered and the story was already national news. Tom Phillips was growing and living in each fresh news cycle. His name was becoming a household word. They talked about what the crime scene meant and which direction the task force should head in.

It was apparent to Kate that finding Spree was no longer Phillip's focus. Not with bombings, mass shootings and dead kingpins littering the streets of NY. Kate listened patiently and suggested she take the lead on finding Spree while he focused his efforts on the rest of it.

A big smile spread across his face and he readily agreed. Moretti was removed from the street light by the time Kate got to the crime scene. She didn't understand what Stevens had meant when he said the task force would go off in the wrong direction.

Phillips was handing out orders and preparing for a press conference. Kate told him about a lead in Arkansas she needed to follow up on. He half listened before telling her to do what she thought was best but keep him in the loop. He didn't even ask how she planned on getting to Arkansas.

Before leaving the crime scene, she stopped by the coroners van and asked to see the body. She was reading the coroners initial report, taking note of the stab and puncture wounds Moretti had suffered. As she got to the part about his tongue being found in his pocket, the coroner unzipped the body bag and she saw what Stevens was talking about.

He was absolutely right. The task force would waste a lot of time and money running down this new, false angle. In the center of Moretti's forehead, in big, black letters was three letters. If you were in the mafia, they were the worst three letters that could ever be associated with you. Stevens had printed the letters R-A-T on Moretti's forehead.

I jumped in the backseat of a cab and told the driver where I wanted to go. I pulled out my phone and called Geoff. When he picked up, I said, "Tell me some good news."

"Man, I was waiting for you to call. I have a lot to tell you. You've asked me for a bunch of stuff over the last few days, and I think I have most of the answers for you. What do you want first?"

"Tell me about Arkansas"

"Ok, I don't know where the Patrizio brothers are staying, but I do know who they are meeting. Because of the info you gave me last night, I was able to crack this thing wide open. The people the Patrizio brothers are meeting are cousins. Cletus Dixon and Jethro Hicks"

"No shit, Geoff? Those are their real names?"

"No shit. I know it's like a bad joke. Don't let the names fool you. From the research that I've done, these are some bad dudes. They're into all kinds of illegal stuff and associated with the white supremacist group, Supreme Southern Confederates, or SSC. Rick, they're going to sell Spree to these guys."

"Just wonderful…."

"Yeah. You need to stop it before it happens, Rick."

"Don't worry, I will. Get me a plane ready and tell me where these guys are located."

After getting the rest of the details from Geoff, I thanked him and thought about how much harder everything had just become. Before I could get too lost in thought, the cab arrived at my destination.

After paying the driver extra to wait for me, I walked into the giant outdoor store. I got a shopping cart and started to fill it with everything that I would need. I sent a text message to Kate asking her what her shoe and clothing sizes were. She responded with, "Why?"

I didn't want to explain everything to her through text, so I sent back "I need to know. Shopping right now. For Arkansas. I'll explain on the plane." She gave me her sizes and I thanked her.

I bought us each two pairs of hiking boots, several pairs of shorts and pants, shirts, light jackets, climbing rope, water bottles, knives and bullets. Lots of bullets. I wanted to buy a shot gun or two, but buying a weapon, any weapon, in NY is too much of a hassle. I figured I would hit up a pawn shop once I got to Arkansas to finish buying the weapons I wanted.

I also bought two duffle bags to pack everything into. I didn't know how many bags Kate had with her, but we were flying privately so it didn't matter. Geoff had sent me a text message letting me know the plane would be ready in 45 minutes and would wait at the executive terminal at JFK until I arrived.

I sent Kate a message telling her to meet me at the terminal at JFK and asked for an ETA. She texted me back 60-90 minutes. Perfect. Our timing was lining up. I had just enough time to pick up a six pack of root beer and a large garlic pizza pie from Totonno's Pizzeria Napoletana and get to the airport. I jumped in my waiting cab and asked the driver, "Are you hungry?"

CHAPTER #22

Kate arrived at the airport 10 minutes before I did. She looked a little annoyed at having to wait on me, until she saw I was carrying lunch. She approached me, kissed me on my lips and helped me carry the bags through the terminal to our private plane. We boarded the plane and ate our lunch.

After lunch, we talked for a few minutes and then we each closed our eyes and slept. Two hours later, we landed in Arkansas. I had reserved us a four wheel drive sport utility vehicle. We picked it up and left the airport.

Geoff was able to get into the phone company's system and track the incoming and outgoing calls for Dixon and Hicks. It was easy to figure out which number belonged to the Patrizio's: it was the phone number with the New York State area code of 716.

Geoff took it a step further and ran through the calls from the NY cell phone and discovered there was one number that continued to call it: another cell phone from NY. Well, hello there, Patrizio brothers.

I asked Geoff if he could have all of the phones tapped so we could hear what was being said. He said he couldn't do that. I asked Kate if she could do that, but of course, the slow moving federal government would need a bus load of lawyers, probable cause, a friendly judge and several days to make it all happen.

Geoff said he had an idea, and he wasn't sure if it would work or not. He told me he would call me back after he checked a few things out. We had the addresses for Dixon and Hicks, but we needed an address for the Patrizio brothers.

Geoff had reserved us a room at a hotel that was located in Pinnacle Hills, off of the freeway and near a large, outdoor mall. He said the reservation was in Kate's name and had already paid for the entire week. While Kate was getting the room and I grabbed a baggage cart and wheeled it out to the truck. I loaded the two duffle bags I packed onto the cart and Kate's carry-on bag and suit case.

By the time I wheeled them inside, she had the keys to our room. She was also carrying a large, white envelope with her name on it. "What's that?" I asked her.

"I don't know. It was waiting for me at the desk when I checked in."   I told her not to worry. The only person that knew we were here was Geoff. I figured it would be some information I requested from him earlier.

"Who is Geoff?" she asked me.

Shit. I forgot I had given her the fake Allen name. I smiled sheepishly and explained that Geoff was really Allen and gave her the Reader's Digest version of how and why I used different names for him. She was annoyed that I had lied to her and made me promise to never lie to her again. Ever.

We took the elevator to the top floor and walked to the end of the hallway. Kate had a big smile on her face as she opened the door. "He got us the Jacuzzi suite!" She said excitedly.

I smiled back at her. The room was huge. There was a large front area that had several couches, a dining room table and a small kitchenette, minus the stove. There were two bathrooms and the large bedroom over-looked the freeway and the mall. In the corner of the bedroom was a large Jacuzzi tub. I smiled, remembering our bath from the night before.

Kate opened the envelope and peeked inside. "What does Geoff do again?" She asked me.

Remembering the promise I made to her four in a half minutes ago, I said "He's an information broker….Never mind. He's the best computer hacker in the country. Why? What's in the envelope?"

"There is an Arkansas driver's license with your picture on it, but not your name and several credit cards in the name on the license."

"Excellent. That was great thinking on his part. Now I can walk into any pawn shop and buy any weapons I want. I'm sure the identity he picked is able to pass the Brady Background Check."

"Ok, just stop for a second. You've done this before? I mean, you routinely do things like this?"

"Yes. It kind of goes with the job."

"I know, it's just I'm still getting used to having a hit man for a boyfriend, it kind of goes against everything I do and stand for."

"I understand. Listen, this is it. I was thinking, this is my last job. Once I rescue Spree and kill the people responsible for this, I'm done Kate. I'm done."

"Really?"

"Yes, really. I know we haven't talked about last night yet, but I felt something, and I know you felt it too. There's this thing, this..."

"Connection..."

"Yes! This connection between us. I can't ignore that. I can't walk away from that not knowing what could have happened. I don't know if you and I can have a future together, I don't know if you can set aside the things I've done, but I want to try."

"I want to try too Rick. I've felt that connection with you since we met. I don't know how we'll make it work, but I want to try."

We hugged each other and then kissed. I started

unpacking the clothing I purchased and hung it up. I was smart enough to also buy underwear, t-shirts and socks for myself, and really smart enough to *not* buy them for Kate.

"I'm going to run out and get a few things I think we'll need. I didn't buy you any personals, you know, tee-shirts and stuff, so if you want to keep the truck and take it to the mall, I'll catch a cab."

"You take the truck. Drop me off at the mall and I'll shop. After you get what you need, call me and come get me."

"The WHITE South will rise again!" Cletus Dixon shouted to the 12 other members of the Supreme Southern Confederates. Two of the members were rail thin and chain smoked, and the other ten were all overweight. The biggest in the group, Grady Holliday was over four hundred pounds. He had to have Jethro Hicks remove the front seat from his car and modify his back seat so he could fit all of his girth in the vehicle and still be able to drive.

He was dumb as a box of rocks, which, coming from Hicks, was really saying something. He was as strong as an ox, and loyal, and that's really all the SSC leaders cared about. Dixon was the leader and Hicks was his right hand man. SSC had over 55 active members spread out throughout Northwest Arkansas.

All of the members sported tattoos that identified them as members of a white pride gang: Iron crosses, Nazi symbols, SS lightning bolts, pictures of Viking warlords and confederate flags. Everyone in the SSC had to have their gang's logo tattooed on their body in a visible place. It was in their by-laws, not that many of the members of SSC could read.

The SSC gang logo was a confederate flag but superimposed in the center of the flag was a circle and inside that circle were two SS lightning bolts. Tattooed above and below the flag were the words "The White South Will Rise Again."

Most of the members held down blue collar jobs in addition to the illegal activities they worked on the side. The 12 members that were at the meeting tonight were SSC's cooks. They all lived in the same trailer park in an unincorporated part of Benton County and they used five of the ten trailers they owned to cook methamphetamine, also known as crack, ice, glass, crystal, meth, speed, geep, geeter, go fast, and redneck cocaine.

From where they were located, they could move the meth into either Missouri or Oklahoma with a simple, short car or motorcycle ride. This 12 man operation was one of the largest methamphetamine makers in this part of the United States.

One of the many illegal side businesses Hicks and Dixon were involved with was human trafficking and prostitution. They would import teen-age runaway girls from other areas of the country, get them addicted to meth, and then force them out on the street to support their habit.

Sadly, there was never a shortage of girls. From where Dixon and Hicks lived, within 6 hours they could be in Dallas Texas or most of the larger cities in Oklahoma and Missouri. Not to mention Little Rock. No, there was never a shortage of unhappy, runaway girls.

Even more sadly, for as much supply as there was, the demand was always more. There was never a shortage of depraved men that would pay to have sex with a teenage girl. The internet had made getting the supply to the demanders much easier.

Dixon's brother, God rest his white soul, served time with a guy in Moretti's operation. They had a lot in common and got to be close friends. When both men were released, they stayed in touch with each other. Dixon's older brother started making monthly runs of meth to NY to sell to Moretti's guy.

On one of these runs, outside of St Louis, a black state trooper attempted to arrest Dixon's brother. There was no way Dixon's brother was going to be arrested by someone from such an inferior race and a fight ensued.

The trooper was the same age as Dixon's brother but that was where the similarities ended. The trooper regularly ran several miles a day and kept himself in excellent physical condition. He was a vegan, and didn't drink alcohol or smoke. Dixon's brother fit the mold of the typical SSC gang member: He chain smoked, never exercised, and ate a diet that consisted of fast food and beer.

It was almost comical when the larger, out of shape guy grabbed the trooper and attempted to punch him in the face. The trooper reacted immediately trapping the larger man's hand to his chest and then striking the larger man in the face first, breaking his nose. The trooper pivoted his legs and swung his hips and tossed the larger man over his back and onto the side of the highway.

The larger man had been in a lot of fights and slow as he was getting to his feet, he still got up. He smiled through his broken nose as blood covered his face. He reached behind him and pulled out a hunting knife.

The trooper drew his 40 caliber Smith & Wesson M&P 40 and instructed Dixon's brother to drop the knife. The last words Dixon's brother said in this world were "Fuck you, Nigger" and he stepped towards the trooper. Only three and a half feet separated the trooper and Dixon's brother and at that distance the trooper had no problems putting a three round burst in a circle that measured less than half an inch directly over Dixon's brother's heart.

Since that day, Dixon was in charge of the SSC. The SSC still supplied Moretti's organization with methamphetamine, but Dixon wasn't the one making the deliveries. When Moretti's number two guy put them in contact with a couple of Wop's that had a girl they kidnapped and wanted to sell, he and Hicks were interested.

Once they had seen pictures of Speranza DiFlippo, Dixon and Hicks were very interested. She was exotic looking. She had long, raven black hair, deep, dark oversized brown eyes and a small, trim body with over-sized breasts for such a small frame.

They agreed that she would be a keeper and not sent out to the street. They would use and abuse her as they saw fit. They would share her as their own personal sex slave. They had been in contact with the 'Dago Brothers' as they referred to them and couldn't wait to make the buy. They were supposed to get her the following day or so.

The meeting was breaking up and Dixon was opening another can of beer when the relative silence was cut by the opening chords of Lynard Skynard's "Sweet Home Alabama". Dixon had a phone call.

"Yeah?"

"Hello, is Mr. Dixon available?"

"Mr. Dixon's my daddy. He ain't been available for about 10 years, not since some darkie stabbed him in Tucker."

"Jethro?"

"Who wants to know?"

"It's Patrick. I'm calling about the delivery. We wanted to let you know that the merchandise is going to be slightly used, broken in. You know?"

"That ain't gonna cut it, son. The deal is for unused merchandise, in pristine order. We have plans for that there merchandise in the condition it's in."

"The deal has changed. Take it or leave it or better yet, go fuck yourself."

"Fuck you, Yankee. You're pretty damn brave over the phone, ain't you? My daddy always said never trust a man from the North. Listen up fuck-stick, y'all pretty brave sitting in that cabin up on top of that holler in Bella Vista. That's right; I know where y'all are and where my merchandise is being kept. I got eyes on you right now. You and that big Yankee. Maybe I send some of my gang over there right now to collect the merchandise, what you think about that boy?"

Patrick was in a bind. They were trading the girl for a bunch of meth. Pounds of it actually. They wanted the meth for the next part of their plan. With the amount of money Primo was able to get from DiFlippo, they could easily afford to purchase the meth, but they didn't have a buyer and finding a buyer on such short notice that could provide them the amount of product they needed would take time.

"My brother really wanted to sample the merchandise before we moved it to you." He said weakly.

"I give a fuck about your brother now? You know what? Have him call me; that way we can work it out, adult to adult." He said and disconnected the phone. These damn I-talians, Dixon thought, complete pains in the ass.

I dropped Kate off at the mall and drove to a pawn shop in Bentonville. As I expected, the back counter was full of pistols and the half of the back wall was full of rifles and shot guns. I loved the South!

I purchased a slightly used AR-15 semi-automatic rifle. It was a Bushmaster and the weapon was decked out for full tactical use: L3 EoTech Red Dot Site, arm strap, and three 30 round magazines. I purchased 10 boxes of .223 ammo for the weapon. As the clerk was ringing me up, I noticed several cross-bows hanging on the wall.

I asked the clerk a few questions, and he was very eager to assist me. He pulled one off the wall and went over in excellent detail on how to use it.

"What do people do with it?" I asked

"You can hunt with it. I got a six point last year with mine, and it's not as nice a model as this one is." I just smiled. Perfect.

After passing the mandatory Brady background check, I left the store with a new assault rifle, ammo, a crossbow and twenty razor tipped arrows. I had also picked up a fully tactical Mossburg 20 gauge shot gun. The weapon was all black; it had an extended pistol grip, a slide handle on the pump, a vented barrel with a flashlight mounted below and five boxes of shells to go with it. I had spent just over $2,200 in the store and it only took me most of 20 minutes. Did I say I love the South?

I left the pawn shop and called Kate. She said she would be ready by the time I got there to pick her up. I was surprised that I could drop her off at a mall and within 35 minutes, she had completed all of her shopping.

After putting her bags in the backseat, she got in the passenger side, leaned over and kissed me and said, "I'm starving. Let's find somewhere to eat." I thought she had an excellent idea because I was famished also.

"Are you in the mood for anything particular?" I asked her?

"I don't care. No pizza. That pizza we ate on the plane was amazing, but I am pizza-d out. Something with meat would be good." As she was saying this we drove past a sign for a restaurant called 'Tusk & Trotter American Brassier'. Kate pointed to the sign and said "Tusk & Trotter. Sounds like meat. Take me there, please." And she smiled.

I typed the name into the GPS and was happy to see we were only about four miles away from the restaurant. I told her about my trip to the pawn shop and the items I had purchased. I told her I was disappointed that I couldn't get us bullet proof vests. She told me she was disappointed I only got her a 20 gauge shotgun and not a 12 gauge shotgun. I was falling in love.

We made a right off of Walton Blvd onto Central Avenue. We took Central Ave into the heart of downtown Bentonville, the town square. The town square was exactly that: a square park in the middle of downtown Bentonville.

The square was beautifully landscaped and there was a fountain and a statue in the center of the square. The statue was a Confederate Memorial honoring James H. Berry. The square was surrounded by independently owned stores and restaurants. Walton's five and dime and the Wal-Mart museum were the main attractions down there. We drove through the square and, when the GPS told us to turn right, we turned right onto A Street. At the end of the block was our destination: Tusk & Trotter.

The restaurant was located on the corner of the street. It was in a beautiful brown brick building that had a deep, rich brick-reddish sign and large gold lettering. The ambiance inside was as beautiful as the building was on the outside.

The restaurant was done up in dark woods and had a very open flow and feel. On one wall, they had a large chalk board thanking the local farmers and community for supplying them with the food they prepared in the kitchen. The other wall had a large butcher's picture of a pig on the wall showing the proper name for each cut of the animal.

There was a large open passage way that led from the

dining room into the bar. The bar was stunning. I had been to a lot of bars in my time but this was one of the nicest I had seen. My eyes immediately scanned the whiskey & bourbon section and I was thrilled when I saw the round bottle with the light tan label and the buffalo staring back at me. They had Buffalo Trace Kentucky Bourbon Whiskey.

We were immediately greeted and asked if we would like to sit in the dining room or the bar. We decided to sit at one of the high top tables in the bar. The menu was amazing. I talked to the waitress and discovered the restaurant had a different menu for lunch, they had a special happy hour menu they called the "Tusk at Dusk" menu; there was a different menu for Sunday brunch; Sunday dinner had a different menu and of course, there was a different menu for dessert.

"What do you think?" I asked Kate.

"This is a great menu. I've got it narrowed down to 8 or 9 things I want to try."

"I know. Where else are you going to find blackened red fish, duck confit and fried chicken and waffles all on the same menu?"

"I know. I literally want to try one of every entrée they have. I said I wanted meat, but the truffled shellfish risotto just sounds too delicious to pass up." It did sound delicious. Lobster, tiger shrimp, scallops, roasted garlic, saffron, radish, wild mushrooms, fresh herbs and white truffle oil mixed in with an in-house, handmade risotto.

"Why don't we do this? I'll order the 12 oz New York Strip and you get the Shellfish Risotto and we'll share?"

"Stevens, I was wrong about you. You do know how to sweet talk a lady," Kate said smiling. I smiled back at her. For just a moment, I forgot that I was a killer, Kate was an FBI agent, and we were here to probably kill a bunch of white supremacists and rescue a kidnapped girl. For just a moment, we were just two people out on a date, enjoying each other's company.

The waitress came to take our order. In addition to ordering our dinners, Kate ordered an appetizer called Pork Belly Cheese Sticks and a glass of wine. When I was asked what I wanted to drink, I chose a glass of water and a glass of Buffalo Trace on the rocks. I never drink alcohol when I am on a job, but tonight, I wasn't on a job. Tonight, I was on a date, enjoying life.

The pork belly cheese sticks were incredible. They had homemade pesto, mozzarella & house cured pork belly served on house made focaccia bread and drizzled with a balsamic reduction. After eating the appetizer, I decided I would buy a place in Bentonville, Arkansas just so I had a reason to come back to this restaurant. That's how good it was.

While we ate our appetizer and drank our drinks, we talked about everything except why we were in Arkansas. When our dinner came, she was telling me stories about her and her family growing up. She absolutely glowed when she talked about her family. It touched me on so many levels.

Impossible as it may seem, our dinner was even better than the appetizer we shared. We both enjoyed each other's dinner and the time we spent together. We were both full when the waitress removed our plates. Kate was working her way through her second glass of wine and I was thinking about ordering another Buffalo Trace when our server brought over the dessert menu.

Kate politely declined dessert, but I asked to see the menu. The dessert menu consisted of seven items, and I wanted to try them all. Kate looked at the menu and together we narrowed it down to the fresh lemon cream tart and the triple orange tort. We couldn't decide between the two, so we ordered both desserts.

Not surprisingly, both desserts were fantastic. After paying the tab, we headed out to the rental car. Driving back to the hotel, my cell phone rang. I looked at the display and did something I hadn't even thought of doing in many years: I silenced my phone and didn't answer Geoff's call.

We barely made it into our hotel room and we were once again in each other's arms, consumed by desire.

CHAPTER #23

Dixon and Hicks wanted some assurances about the girl they were buying before they paid for her. They didn't want to talk to the half-wit brother. They wanted to talk to the man in charge, Primo. Face to face.

Dixon and Hicks went back and forth with Primo on where and when to meet. They both finally and reluctantly agreed to meet in an abandoned farmhouse in rural Northern Benton County. Primo agreed to go alone without his brother or Russo. Dixon and Hicks agreed to show up alone as well.

Primo wasn't worried about facing Dixon and Hicks alone. He had faced off against more than one adversary on many occasions and always walked away. He wasn't worried about two redneck hillbillies.

Dixon and Hicks arrived 15 minutes later than they were supposed to. They sat in their Ford or Chevy pick-up truck, Primo couldn't tell what make or model it was, for another two minutes before opening the doors to get out. The first bullet hit the driver, Hicks, right in the throat. The second hit him under his right eye as he was falling backwards.

Before Dixon had a chance to react, two bullets hit him in his upper chest and the third went through his mouth, shattering the few remaining teeth he had. His John Deer ball cap landed next to his lifeless body in the dirt.

I had been sitting in the empty farmhouse for the past six hours waiting for them to arrive. I was in an abandoned second floor bedroom, with the rising sun to my back, facing the weed covered driveway waiting for Dixon and Hicks.

The phone call I refused to take the night before was from Geoff. In an excited voice I could barely understand, he left me a message saying to check my e-mail and then call him back. The next morning when I finally called him back I discovered why he was so excited.

He started explaining how he was able to use the addresses from Dixon and Hicks to search the cell phone company data bases until he found the correct cell phone carrier. From that, he hacked into their main computer system and 'nosed around' as he said.

He was able to find all the call logs and text messages, but he wanted to take it one step further and hear the actual phone calls. This is where his voice rose with excitement. He said he first hacked into several of the phone company's satellites to see what data he could get from them.

He was excited because he had never hacked into a satellite before and was really surprised at how easy it was. At this point, Geoff was Geoff, and became sidetracked on why we were talking and started explaining and comparing how hacking into a satellite was similar to hacking into a company's main computer system.

A few encouraging words by me later and he was back on track. The phone company satellite gave him the capability to listen to the actual phone calls that were routed through it. I didn't exactly understand the technology end of it, but I understood enough to realize how huge this could be.

He said he then wrote a program to track and notify him of when certain phone numbers were being used through that satellite. He added Dixon and Hicks's phone numbers. He sent me a file and I listened to Dixon's conversation with Patrick Patrizio. Geoff had the brilliant idea that I call Dixon back and pretend to be Primo.

I liked where Geoff was going, but I was worried that after I had called Dixon and pretended to be Primo, Primo or Patrick would call Dixon back. Geoff told me not to worry because he would make it so that if any of the known cell numbers the Patrizio brothers or Russo had called Dixon or Hicks, the call would be re-routed through the satellite to a voicemail system he had set up on his computer.

As long as the Patrizio brothers used the phones we knew about, we wouldn't have to worry. If Primo stopped at a gas station in Missouri and called from a pay phone, Geoff said we would be screwed, but he would continue to monitor Dixon and Hick's cell phone and, if that happened, he would disconnect the call.

So I called Dixon and pretended to be Primo. I acted very pissed off at his request that I couldn't rape and abuse the girl. We went back and forth and before I could suggest a meeting to talk this out man to man, Dixon said he wanted to meet to talk it out man to man. Perfect.

Geoff was listening in on the phone call and sending me instant messages through the chat room we were in together on-line. I wasn't familiar with Benton County and was trusting Geoff to be able to find the perfect place for our meeting.

I don't know how he did it, but he found an abandoned farmhouse in the middle of nowhere. I figured Dixon would refuse that location but he agreed. He said he knew exactly where it was and he would be there.

Kate and I talked about the meeting we were going to go to. I told her I wanted to be at the meeting place at least six hours before the scheduled time. She asked me what I would do until the meeting started.

I told her I would wait. She asked me what she was supposed to do. I told her she was supposed to wait as well. She didn't like my answer. She asked if she could sleep. I said probably not. The farmhouse had been vacant for a while so there wasn't any furniture. If there was, it would probably be mold and bug infested. I also wanted her to keep an eye on the back of the house while I covered the front of the house.

Kate said while we were waiting for six hours we could talk. We could spend the time getting to know each other more. She must have recognized the panicked, deer-in-the-headlights look I gave her because she smiled, and told me she would spend most of the time reading on her kindle. She said she had just downloaded the newest Michael Connelly thriller and couldn't wait to start reading it.

After firing my shots, I realized I had crossed a line killing Dixon and Hicks in front of Kate. Not only was she a living witness that knew me, she was also a cop and she was violating the very oath she swore to uphold by not arresting me.

I kept sweeping the area, looking for other members of Dixon and Hick's gang. After what seemed like a very long eight minutes, I handed the Ar-15 off to Kate, told her to cover me, and went to retrieve the bodies.

I loaded Dixon and Hicks into the back of the pick-up truck they arrived in. I picked up Dixon's John Deere ball cap and tossed it into the back of the truck. I drove the truck 50 yards into the backyard and stopped next to the abandoned well.

I searched each body, taking only the things that I thought I would need. Then I dropped Dixon and Hicks' bodies into the empty well shaft. The forgotten hole in the earth swallowed up both bodies. I was about to drop Dixon's green and yellow ball cap into the well after him but I decided to keep it. By the time I pulled the truck around to the front of the house, Kate had our rental car packed and ready to go.

It was almost time for them to say good-bye and move

on. Russo could sense these things. He was excited because before they moved on, he would finally have a turn with the girl. He couldn't wait to have her alone, all to himself.

Just the thought of the things he would do, the pain he would cause her made him aroused. He didn't know if she was really asleep or just faking it but he didn't care either way. Her beautiful, pale, naked, body made him feel yearnings deep within his loins that nothing else but her could ever satisfy.

He would give up his share of the money in trade for her. He would make the offer to Primo when he got there. God forbid, but if something happened to Primo along the way, if he were to get arrested or die in a car wreck or something, Russo would kill Patrick and take the girl and disappear.

He had a little nest egg built up and a cabin in Northern Canada. That would work for him, he thought, at least for a while. He wasn't sure where Patrick was and didn't care. He wanted to feel her, to touch her. She was so beautiful. He wanted to consume her beauty. He made sure the door was locked and approached the sleeping girl.

Spree pretended to be asleep. She could feel the big one looking at her. She could smell his unwashed body and his desire for her. She would rather die than have that animal touch her. When the time came that he forced herself on him, she would fight him with everything she had. She would be ferocious, she would try to gouge out his eyes, tear his face apart. She would hope to infuriate him enough that in his anger he would kill her.

His scent got stronger, and she knew he was approaching her. She willed herself to remain calm, to keep her breathing even and steady. She felt his hand touch her calf, and slowly slide up her leg, to her inner thigh, and then across her backside. She felt like she was going to vomit.

She prepared herself to fight until she was dead. She was waiting for the right moment to spring, to launch her attack on the beast that fondled her, when there was a knock at the door. "What the hell? Open the damn door, Russo!"

The fondling stopped and his stink retreated a little. She heard the lock turn and then the door open. "What the fuck ya doing in here? Why is this door locked?" Patrick demanded.

"Sorry Patsy, I was just enjoying the scenery. I wanted some alone time you know? Hey, I'm following the rules, I'm waiting my turn. I promise."

"Zip up your pants and come up stairs. Primo will be here in 10 minutes."

CHAPTER #24

I lay on the bed in our hotel room with my eyes closed. I wasn't sleeping, I was waiting. I was not a stranger to killing people and hiding their bodies, but Kate was. I didn't know if she had ever taken a life before and didn't know how she would react to what had just occurred.

The ride back to the hotel was off. She wasn't her talkative self: she was more reserved. She walked into the room after taking a shower. Without opening my eyes I asked her "Have you ever killed anyone before, Kate?" She stopped doing whatever it was she was doing and paused before answering me.

"No, Rick. I haven't."

"I know you've never experienced anything like what we did today. I'm wondering how you feel about it?" She was silent for over a minute before she answered me.

"I feel kind of torn, actually. My father is a cop and I grew up my entire life wanting to be a cop. I've lived by a certain set of rules my entire life and I'm not sure how I feel right now. On one hand, I'm thinking I should handcuff you right now for at least two murders, which I witnessed, and then call Phillips and hand over the rest of the investigation…" She paused again.

"But…"

"But, there is a kidnapped girl out there and you're our best chance of getting her back alive. The people you killed Rick, they were bad guys. They were going to buy or trade for a kidnapped girl. They're in charge of a hate gang that does God knows what. You saved the taxpayers a ton of money by just making them disappear…"

"But…" I asked again

"But it's a slippery slope. Where do you draw the line? Have you ever heard the F.B.I. oath of office?"

"No, I never have."

"I memorized it. I knew this as a kid. I always wanted to be an F.B.I. agent. I remember mentioning it to my daddy when we were fishing. I was about 8 or 9 years old and he said to me, 'FBI? I thought you wanted to be a *real* cop?" She said, with a distant smile on her face. She was silent for a bit, lost in the memory of a long ago fishing trip with her father. Then…

"I, Kate Riley, will support and defend the Constitution of the United States against all enemies, foreign and domestic; that I will bear true faith and allegiance to the same; that I take this obligation freely, without any mental reservation or purpose of evasion; and that I will well and faithfully discharge the duties of the office on which I am about to enter. So help me God."

She was quiet again. I continued to lie still, without moving. I could tell she was wrestling with a decision. It was a decision she would have to come to by herself, freely, without my input or advice. She let out a heavy sigh.

"Some people would say I violated that oath today. Some people would say I was just as much responsible for the deaths you caused today. Some people would consider me a worse person than you for standing by and allowing you to do what you did. You know what Rick? Screw them. Maybe I violated the letter of the law but I damn sure didn't violate the spirit of the law. The most important thing is getting that girl back and making sure the sick people that did this never, ever, do it again."

"Kate, you realize what's going to happen when Geoff calls me back with the location of where the phone calls originated, right? You know I'm going to kill every single person that is there and responsible for this. If you're not comfortable with that, I understand if you don't go with me. Like today, there will be no warnings, no calls for surrender, no identifying ourselves as the F.B.I."

"Rick, I know."

"Kate, I don't care if there is one person in that house or one hundred; I'm going in under a black flag. I'm going in to eradicate every single one of them and I won't stop until they're all dead or I am."

When Primo finally pulled up to the house from the long, winding driveway, he was happy to see his brother and Russo come outside to greet him. Everyone had big smiles on their faces and the three men all hugged.

The brothers went into the house while Russo stayed behind to grab Primo's bags from the car. Russo was preoccupied on making his pitch to Primo about trading his part of the money for the girl. He was thinking that if Primo didn't agree to his proposal, Russo could kill both brothers and just take the girl.

He was deep in thought when the ratty old pickup truck pulled up the winding road and stopped behind Primo's car. Three large men piled out of the cab of the truck, and all of them were carrying guns.

Primo unlocked the door to Spree's room. He went into the room, but did not close the door. Spree was afraid. She had never seen this person before and she was worried that this was the end for her.

She didn't want to die: she was afraid of dying but she would fight right up until the last breath rushed out of her body. Fighting and dying were a much better outcome than what these men had in store for her.

"Speranza DiFlippo. It's nice to finally meet you. I knew your grandfather. We went way back to the old days. Long before your time."

"Then if you know him like you say you do, you know you're as good as dead."

"I did not say I know him, I said I *knew* him…"Primo replied. He started flexing his hands, opening and closing them. "I beat the life out of his old body with these hands, then I set him on fire, and I am certain he is still burning right now in Hell." A small white lie, but she would never know the truth.

Her reaction was unexpected. First, it shocked Primo. Second, it frightened him. She looked into his eyes, almost as if she could see into his soul, and then smiled. There was no warmth in the smile, only vengeance. Before he could react, she said,

"Are you a religious man? I'm guessing you aren't. I'm pretty certain there is a whole lot you don't know about, and religion is just the tip of the iceberg…" Primo found his voice.

"I have no use for meaningless things like religion. I've figured it out, seen through the lies. Young lady, do you want to know the truth about religion? Want to know its secret? I'll share it with you."

"This ought to be good. Please, tell me this secret only you know." She said, mockingly. This one had fire, Primo thought. She was definitely DiFlippo's bloodline.

"You mock me, but see if what I say doesn't ring true. Religion is simple. Religion is an opiate for the masses. It's a tool created by the people in charge to control the multitudes through fear and guilt. If it gives you comfort to believe a magical man lives in the sky judging our good and bad deeds and offering everlasting life then, by all means, take whatever comfort from that which you can. The sad truth is, religion is nothing more than a tool the few in charge use to control the many that are not in charge."

"That's your secret? Ok. Like that wasn't something I've heard a million times already. You stare at me with a smug look on your face and a cocky smile because you think you've won. You really don't have a clue, do you?"

"A clue about what? I've been on this earth a lot longer than you have, seen a lot more than you ever will, survived a lot longer than you could ever hope to survive and I'm the one without a clue? Who's the one naked, and chained to a wall? Whose about to get gang raped until they're dead?" Primo said, cockily.

He was sure his reference to the gang rape would elicit some sort of response but, again, her reaction shocked and scared him. She smiled, sadly this time, and shook her head.

"There's a bible verse you should become familiar with. It's from Matthew, 13:39. Depending on which bible you read it from, the translation can differ. My favorite translation is from the New Living Testament."

"Let me guess: this verse is about forgiveness, right?" Something about turning the other cheek or forgive me for I don't know what I am doing? Is that it?"

She shook her head. "No. Not even close. The verse goes *'The enemy who planted the weeds among the wheat is the devil. The harvest is the end of the world, and the reapers are the angels'*. If you knew my grandfather as well as you said you did, you would know we're an Old Testament kind of family." Before Primo could form a response, Patrick rushed into the room.

"Hey, I need you up stairs right now. We have a big problem." Patrick left the room as quickly as he entered. Primo turned to follow his brother out of the room, and the last thing he heard from the girl was

"The Reaper is here. It's the end of your world, mother-fucker. It's the end of all of you."

The three men from the dusty pick-up truck immediately separated from each other, making them harder to hit since they weren't all bunched together. The person that got out of the driver's side of the vehicle spoke first. He raised the pistol he was holding and pointed it right at Russo's face.

"You Primo?" He said, in a thick, slow, southern drawl. Russo stood there for a second and then slowly put the bags down. He was trying to figure out if he could draw his own pistol and take out the three new visitors before they got him. Whichever way he looked at it, he was the one dieing.

He raised his hands slowly, making sure to keep them away from his body. "No, not me. I'm just the hired help. He's inside." He pointed towards the front porch with one of his raised hands.

The man Russo had spoken to and one of the other men walked up on the front porch and into the house without knocking. The third person stayed behind and kept a sawed off pistol grip shotgun pointed at Russo.

"Nice weather we're having." Russo tried.

"Fuck you, Yankee. Yaw'l gonna pay for what ya done to Cletus." Russo decided it would be best to wait the situation out in silence. If an opportunity to make a play was available, he would take it. If not, he would wait and see what happened.

Patrick was opening the fridge to get out three beers when the two men walked into the house. Patrick was half in and out of the refrigerator and the first guy through the door rushed him, slamming his body into the fridge's door. Both of Patrick's hands were trapped in the refrigerator.

The two men were face to face and Patrick could smell the other man's unwashed scent. It was a mixture of manure, old grass and chewing tobacco. The man asked him, "You Primo, boy?" Patrick was frightened. All he could do was shake his head. "Know where he's at? I know he's here."

"In the basement. He's in the basement."

"Do me a favor. Run on down there and have him come up. We have some talkin' to do. Be smart boy, don't be reaching for no weapon or nothing. We just here to talk. Don't do nothing to change all that, ya hear?"

Patrick left the kitchen in a hurry to get Primo. He walked in on him and the girl in the middle of a conversation. He didn't know what they were talking about, but he could tell his brother was troubled.

"Hey, I need you upstairs right now. We have a big problem." Without waiting for his brother's response, Patrick turned and headed back the way he came. Primo heard what Spree said about the end of his world and The Reaper being here now.

He had heard stories about a hit man that was a ghost. He was quietly referred to as The Reaper but Primo had never put much stock into what he heard. There were always stories about an untouchable hit man that could get into and out of any locked building or room, undetected and murder someone and then disappear, like smoke.

He always thought the stories were false. As he walked into the kitchen to see the two rednecks standing there holding guns, a rush of relief passed over him. He didn't realize he had been holding his breath. Primo smiled and extended his hand to shake the closest person's hand.

"Mr. Dixon, I presume?" The redneck he was talking to ignored his hand and said

"You Primo?"

"Yes, I am it's nice to…" Before he could finish his sentence, the redneck exploded in a rush of movement and had Primo face down on the floor of the kitchen with the blade of a buck knife pressed to his neck. The other redneck leveled his pistol at Patrick's face and smiled and shook his head, indicating for Patrick not to get involved. Patrick just stood there.

"I'm gonna ask this one time. If you lie to me boy, I swear to God, I will bleed you out all over this kitchen floor. You git me? Where's my brother at?"

Primo was confused. What was this hillbilly talking about? His brother? How the hell should he know where his brother was? "I think there is a misunderstanding." Primo gasped.

"Only misunderstanding we have is you don't think I'll do it. I ain't playin' here, boy. I'll cut your damn head off and make your pussy ass brother walk around the yard with it."

"Mr. Dixon, Cletus, I really…"

"Cletus? I ain't Cletus! What the hell you tryin' to pull here boy?" Primo was really confused. If Cletus Dixon wasn't holding a knife to his throat, then who was?

"Who are you? I'm supposed to meet with Cletus Dixon tomorrow about a business arrangement we have been working on." The man sat back and removed the knife from Primo's throat.

"I'm Jessie Dixon, Cletus's younger brother. He told me he was meeting you today at some farmhouse somewhere. It was supposed to be at 11:00 o'clock this morning. He left for the meeting and then never returned. So I want to know where the fuck he is."

"Good question. I just got here, literally five minutes

before you walked in this house. I've been on the road driving. As a matter of fact, I was in Missouri at 11 this morning. That was the last place I stopped to get gas. I still have the receipt from the gas station in my wallet."

Primo felt the man's hands go to his pocket and remove the wallet. A few seconds later the man dropped Primo's wallet and stood up. "Well, sum bitch. What happened to my brother then?"

There were four people in the house and two people outside. I could tell the situation was tense. I didn't know what the issue was with the two groups and didn't care. Geoff had come through for me yet again and pointed me directly to this house.

If Spree was anywhere, it was going to be here. I was prepared to kill and die. I was wearing all black: BDU pants and shirt, tactical gear and webbing, knee and elbow pads. I was carrying two pistols, my combat knife and had the shot gun on a sling on my back.

Kate was similarly dressed but she was 100 yards away from me. She was carrying her own pistol and the carbine rifle. Once the shooting started, she would take out the vehicles in front of the house eliminating that avenue of escape. She would then provide cover for me and shoot anyone trying to leave the house.

I was looking through the scope of the crossbow I had purchased and was sighting in on the man's heart that was holding the gun. I had zeroed out the scope and gotten comfortable with the crossbow earlier in the day at the farmhouse. I felt comfortable hitting a target up to 100 yards with the crossbow.

I was within 25 yards of my target and my crossbow was loaded with Grim Reaper Razor Tip Broadheads. I took a deep breath in, holding it. I gently applied pressure to the trigger, breathing out as I did so.

The arrow exited the crossbow and, in a blur of motion, entered my target's heart. The arrow struck the man with such violent force that he was thrown to the ground, almost as if all of his bones had turned to liquid at once.

I loaded another arrow into the Barnett Ghost 400 crossbow and pointed it towards my second target, who was almost to the front door of the house. I aimed as best as I could and I squeezed the trigger.

The arrow moved at over 400 feet per second and punctured my target. I didn't know where it hit him, or if it was fatal or not. I heard a scream and saw blood on the doorframe. My target had made it inside the house. He was wounded and now everyone else in the house would know they were under attack.

Kate must have come to the same conclusion because as I started to make my way towards the house, she started firing the carbine. Kate was an excellent shot with the rifle and soon all of the cars were resting on four flat tires. Kate also sent a few rounds into the engine blocks of each vehicle.

With the cars being taken out, I knew Kate was heading to her second position, on the back corner of the house. She would be able to cover the back and one side of the house. It would be my responsibility to cover the front and the other side of the house.

I could see movement through the living room window and fired another arrow through the glass. I set the crossbow down and shouldered the shot gun. I had the gun loaded with deer slugs. I approached the front door. There was a trail of blood from the injured man. I pointed the barrel of the gun at the door handle and pulled the trigger.

Russo came through the front door like a freight train. He was yelling and bleeding and looked very pissed off. Everyone in the kitchen stared at him for a second in disbelief. They could all see the arrow sticking out of his left shoulder. Patrick was the first to find his voice.

"What the hell? Indians?" Everyone looked at Patrick.

"Ain't no damn Injuns in Arkansas using arrows to stick people. What the darn Hell is happening outside?"

"I'll take a look" Vaughn Johnson, the man that came in the house with Dixon, said. He went to the window in the kitchen and started to reach for the drapes to draw them back. An arrow burst through the glass, surprising everyone. Then everyone heard gunfire.

"We're under attack! Someone is taking out the vehicles!" The sound of everyone checking their weapons could be heard. Russo sat on the floor in the corner of the kitchen, whimpering in pain.

"Should I go check on the girl?", Patrick asked.

"You stay here and fight with us! She's fine. She's chained up in a locked room." Primo responded. Russo was the closest person sitting near the kitchen door. "Roman, reach over and throw the deadbolt."

Roman reached over and was turning the deadbolt to the 'locked' position when the lock and Russo's hand exploded into pieces.

Kate waited until she heard the roar of the shotgun and then made her move. She crossed the open yard as fast as her feet could carry her. She kept expecting to feel the impact of a bullet but she made it to the side of the house safely.

So far, Rick's plan was working. He was supposed to draw the brunt of the gun fire from the front of the house, allowing her to gain access to the basement to rescue Spree.

She approached the cellar doors that were built into the ground cautiously. Just as she expected, there was a solid, steel padlock securing the doors. She swung the carbine to her back and drew her .45 and took aim.

She paused before pulling the trigger and could hear lots of gunfire coming from the front of the house. She felt confident that no one would hear her firing her pistol. Her aim was true, and the padlock disintegrated. She pulled open the doors and descended into darkness.

After pulling the trigger on the shotgun, I jumped off the porch and lay directly against the concrete base of the house. I made myself as small as possible, and as I expected, the front door was shot to pieces from the people inside the house.

I thought I heard a scream as I was jumping off the porch but the shotgun was so loud I couldn't be sure. So far, so good I thought to myself. I hoped Kate was having as much luck as I was.

The house was set up so when you entered through the front door, you were in the kitchen. There was a door leading to the basement and the living room from the kitchen. The window I had sent the arrow through earlier was elevated, so I scooted on my back away from the house and leveled the shot gun at the window.

I had reloaded the weapon and had six shots. I pulled the trigger and pumped the gun as fast as I could. I sent all six shots through the walls of the house around the kitchen window. I was hoping to hit someone, but the real goal here was to keep them occupied so Kate could get in and get Spree out.

Once the gun was empty, I rolled back into the relative protection of the house and crawled around to the far side. I heard more yelling and more gunfire from where I just departed. I took a deep breath and reloaded the shot gun.

I smiled and admitted that I was having fun. I was doing what I was meant to do in this life: kill and destroy. In the middle of a gun battle with at least five other armed men, I was a man at peace.

Russo screamed as loud as he ever had when his hand was reduced to a bloody, pulpy, stump. He rolled over on the floor, cradling his injured arm and screamed. Primo was the first to react and he did so by emptying his gun into the front door.

If anyone was going to breach that door, they would be cut down in a hail of gun fire. Before he was finished emptying his gun, everyone else in the kitchen had joined him. The front door was reduced to splinters in no time at all

Vaughn was up on one knee reloading his pistol when the first slug blasted through the wall. It hit him in the side of the face or head, reducing it to sheen of fine, pink mist. Everyone else hit the floor as five more slugs tore through the house.

Patrick was lying on his back and started firing back through the wall where the slugs had come from. Primo was proud of his brother and joined in. Dixon finished reloading his gun and fired a few rounds as well.

He made eye contact with Primo and said, "We gotta go Bubba. We sittin' ducks in here." Primo motioned to head through the house, towards the back patio. From there, if they could get to the garage, Primo knew his brother had a vehicle in there they could use to escape.

He crawled over to his brother who was reloading his weapon. "We have to get out of here. We're going to secure the back door and patio. That's how we'll get out. Go to the basement and get the girl. Meet us at the back patio. We'll use her as a shield to get to the garage so we can get out of here."

Patrick nodded his head as relief washed over him. He felt he would be safest in the basement, underground. Dixon and Primo started making their way through the house to the back patio as Patrick crawled over to the basement door and opened it.

Russo continued to hold his mangled hand as he bled out onto the floor. He gently rocked himself and cried as his body started going into shock. Dixon and Primo never once glanced his way as they left the kitchen.

Kate didn't want to turn on any lights in the basement. There was enough ambient light coming through the windows that she could make out where she was going and shapes around the room.

The basement was largely unoccupied other than a washing machine and dryer. In the far corner, there was a room and a closed door. Kate started making her way towards the room when she heard the sound of someone coming down the stairs to her right.

There was nowhere for her to hide, so she just lay down on the floor and trained the muzzle of the AR-15 on the bottom of the steps. A man entered the basement carrying a pistol and headed towards the room.

Kate wasn't sure if the man was going to enter the room and execute the hostage or use her as a shield. She remembered Rick saying that everyone in this house was going to die today. Kate thought about the internal affairs investigation and the Office of Professional Responsibility investigation she would have to endure and knew if she shot a man in the back she would lose her job.

"Hey asshole…" Kate said in a normal, even tone. As

expected, the man spun around towards the sound of her voice. Before he could comprehend what was said, three .223 rounds from the AR-15 tore into Patrick's chest, ripping his heart to shreds and killing him instantly. Kate smiled and approached the room.

The door was locked but a swift front kick popped the door open. Inside the room, she found a naked Spree chained to the wall. Spree looked confused for a second and then said, "You're not Mr. Stevens."

"No, I'm with the FBI. I'm here to take you home."

"There are men, bad men here…"

"I know. We're taking care of them. Rick, Mr. Stevens, is with me."

"Rick's with the FBI?" Spree asked, incredulously.

"Honey, it's a long story. Let's get you out of here and then I'll explain everything."

They were either going to come out the front door or the back door, onto the patio. I knew that escaping from the basement was out of the question because Kate had gone that way and would kill anyone that came that way.

I figured everyone in the house had enough of being in the kitchen and would make their way to the patio exit. It was also the closest exit to the garage.

I went around the side of the house that would allow me to keep an eye on the patio door and the basement exit. Kate and I were doing this mission without the luxury of communication devices and I really wanted to see her.

I was watching the backdoor and the basement when Kate popped up from the basement, sweeping the barrel of the carbine across the landscape. I smiled when our eyes met and she smiled. She gave me the 'thumbs-up' signal and exited the basement and came my way.

Spree was nearly naked, wearing only a bloody shirt that was way too big for her. She looked tired, but not beaten or shell shocked. She was definitely a DiFlippo. They made their way to me and knelt down. Kate kissed me on my cheek.

Before I could say anything, Spree said, "You're Mr. Stevens?"

I was perplexed because I had only met Spree one time, and that was when she was a little girl of five years old. "Yeah, call me Rick. You remember me Spree?"

She shook her head. "No, I'm sorry I don't. I knew you would come to help me though. You're the reaper."

"What? How do you know this?"

"My grandfather told me. When I was a little girl, I spent the night at his house. I had a nightmare and he stayed with me until I fell back asleep. He said I didn't have to ever be afraid because he would protect me. He said if he wasn't around to protect me, my parents would be. I asked him what happened if neither one was around to protect me. He told me not to worry because you would."

"Mr. Stevens, I knew what my grandfather did. He kept a website, a private website that had your contact information on it. Sometimes there would be a phone number, sometimes just an e-mail address, or a bulletin board to sign onto and a code word. He also gave the e-mail address and phone number for some computer guy in California and told me he would always know how to get a hold of you."

"One Christmas eve, we were in NY visiting my grandfather and he and my dad had drunk too much Prosecco. We had watched that old Dickens' movie, A Christmas Carol, the one with the three ghosts?" Kate and I both nodded, indicating we knew which movie she was talking about.

"The third ghost, The Ghost of Christmas Yet to

Come, scared me. I thought that ghost was the grim reaper. My grandfather laughed. He told me not to fear the grim reaper because he was a friend of his. I remember looking at my grandfather wide-eyed when he told me you were The Reaper, Mr. Stevens. Ever since then, knowing I had my grandfather, father and you to protect me, I haven't been afraid of anything. I knew you would come and save me. I knew it."

I didn't know what to say. Sal had never told me any of this. He had never told me I was the one that would protect his granddaughter should anything happen to him. I was speechless; choked up. I felt honored Sal had chosen me. I felt righteous that I was able to rescue Spree and get her back to him safely.

"Ok, listen Spree, Kate's going to take you through the woods to our vehicle. She's going to get you out of here, to safety."

"What about you? Are you coming with us?" She asked.

"Me? No, I'm going to finish reaping."

"Your brother ain't gonna make it back up here. I'm telling you, we need to git while the gittin's good." Primo was refusing to make the dash to the garage to get the car so they could leave. He wanted to wait for his brother and the girl.

"We have to wait. He'll be here. There is no other way out of the basement. The cellar doors are locked from the outside. He has to come back up here."

"Not unless someone from the outside *unlocked* them there cellar doors and killed your brother. Do what you want man, but I'm leaving." Primo thought Dixon was right. There was no other reason why Patrick shouldn't be back with the girl already. It was time to move.

We decided the quickest and safest way for Kate and Spree to leave was by cutting across the lawn to the back of the garage. The garage would provide cover and was also the shortest distance to our rental car.

The plan was for Kate to take Spree to the nearest hospital and call in reinforcements. By the time anyone got here, I would be gone. I would call Kate and explain the final body count and where everyone was, so she would be able to write up her report. She would walk away a hero.

While Kate and Spree made the run for the garage, I was supposed to send six rounds from the shot gun through the back door, keeping everyone inside down. I started to move into position when Kate said, "Hey Stevens, be safe. I'll see you on the other side." She bent down to kiss me.

I turned my head for a second so I could kiss her on the lips. I took my eyes off the back door for less than two seconds and everything changed. As I was turning my head to kiss Kate, The back door popped open and Primo stepped outside. He saw me before I saw him and leveled his pistol at me.

"RICK!" Kate yelled and pushed me out of the way. I heard gun shots and watched as Kate fell to the ground, bleeding. I had dropped the shot gun when Kate pushed me out of the way. I quickly pulled my pistols and turned toward where the gun shot erupted from. I did not have a target.

I saw the backside of a man enter the garage and a second man rush around behind the garage. I emptied my magazine into the garage door. I dropped the pistol and drew my other gun. I started advancing towards the garage when Spree called out to me 'Rick, she's hurt bad. Rick! HELP!"

The front of the garage burst open as a car drove straight through the door. I fired at the car but my rounds missed the driver. The road leading off the hill we were on was winding. If I hurried and cut through the woods I could make it to the street below in front of the car. I knew I could send enough rounds through the front of the car to at least stop the driver, if not kill him.

I also knew Kate had been shot and was bleeding. She needed immediate medical assistance or she would die. I had a decision to make. I could cut through the woods and kill the person responsible for all of this or I could stay where I was and administer medical attention to Kate until paramedics arrived. I turned towards the woods.

CHAPTER #25

Primo was taking Dixon's advice and leaving. As he was making his way to the garage, he saw Diflippo's guy and the FBI agent come around the far corner of the house. These two. These were the ones that were trying to ruin his plan.

Primo didn't hesitate; he raised his gun and fired off a few shots. Without looking at the results of his firing, he continued his dash towards the garage. He got inside the garage and got the vehicle started. Knowing that seconds could be the difference between getting away and being killed. Primo didn't wait for the garage door to open up.

He hit the gas and drove straight through the garage door. All he had to do was make it to the end of the hill and he would be home free. It was less than a half mile, but the road twisted back on itself. If someone were still pursuing him, they could cut through the woods and maybe come out in front of him. It would be close

Kate lay in her hospital bed recovering from two gunshot wounds to her upper left chest. The media had already crowned her a hero and the FBI was pumping and riding that for all it was worth. After all, the kidnapped girl had been recovered and several of the kidnappers had been brought to justice, all without the cost of an actual trial.

As far as the bureau was concerned, it was the ultimate win-win situation. They rescued the kidnapped girl, brought the perpetrators to justice and even had an injured, hero agent; or rather, an injured, hero *female* agent with a flawless record to parade in front of the media.

Kate hadn't seen Rick in two days, since the day of the gun battle and rescue. She didn't know where he was or what he was doing, but knew she would see him again. She had to.

What they had was special, real. She hoped it was sooner rather than later though. She missed him.

There was really no choice. I had to do what I could to save Kate. I couldn't save Julie or Faith, but I had the opportunity to save Kate. If I were to find any redemption, it would be with Kate. We don't get many second chances in life, so when one is presented to us, we have to learn to grasp it.

Sure the driver would get away. I was comfortable with him escaping. It would only be for a short while. I pulled out my phone and dialed 911. I gave the address and said a cop had been shot and needed immediate medical assistance. I didn't have any quick clot with me, but I did have the next best thing: tampons.

Kate had two bullet wounds to her upper left chest. She was unconscious, but still alive. I knew each bullet had missed her heart or she would already be dead. I pulled out two tampons from my pants pocket and inserted them into each wound and pulled the strings.

As gently as I could, I rolled Kate over. I breathed a sigh of relief as I found the two exit wounds. I pulled out two more tampons and repeated the process. I asked Spree to sit at her feet and used her lap to prop up Kate's legs. I ran into the house and retrieved a smelly blanket off one of the beds and covered Kate with it.

While I was in the house, I came across two bodies in the kitchen. One was dead and the other one was in shock. He was shaking and bleeding out all over the kitchen floor. He made eye contact with me and said, "Help me..." So I helped him. I put a .40 caliber round through the front of his face, ending his life.

After covering Kate with the blanket I felt for her pulse. It was there, strong, and I knew she would make it. I looked to the sky, dipped my head in submission and mouthed the words 'Thank you'.

I pulled Spree aside and explained exactly what she should say to the police when they arrived. I went over the story she was supposed to tell them several times until I felt comfortable that she had it. When I heard the first police car making its way up the winding road towards the house, I disappeared into the forest and retrieved our rental car and left the area.

I checked out of the hotel we were in and found a different one and used an alias to check in. I called Geoff and told him where we were. I told him I needed minute by minute updates on Kate and her condition.

Geoff hacked into the hospitals computer system and fed me the reports as soon as they were added to their system. My heart leapt with joy when I discovered she would live and be ok. She was awake when I walked into her room. In order to get by the guard at the door, I was dressed in hospital scrubs and I was carrying a basket of needles and tubes.

"More bloodwork." I said to the guard as I approached. He just nodded and waved me in.

"How are we feeling today, Ms. Riley?" I asked.

I grabbed her hand and fought back the tears that threatened to fall from my eyes. I knew she was alive and well, but knowing and actually seeing are much different things. I was so overcome by emotion that I couldn't speak.

"I'm doing great now, *doctor*." She replied and smiled. Then, "We have to talk. There have been some developments."

"Kate, I'm glad you're going to be ok. I don't know what to say. You saved my life. Thank you."

She smiled "You repaid the favor by saving mine. You always carry tampons with you? You might just win boyfriend of the year award. A man secure enough with himself that he can go into a store and buy feminine hygiene products. Very impressive, Stevens."

I just smiled. I found out later that the tampons I used ended up saving Kate's life. Without them, she would have lost too much blood and died before reaching the hospital. I was all choked up and found speaking hard.

"Rick, I have to ask you something. It's a *work-related* question. Were you involved in the shooting of a federal witness in Texas a few days before we met?"

Of all the things Kate could say, this one came out of left field. I was surprised. I smiled sheepishly, and said "I may have been in Texas the week before we met, on business. Why were the US Marshalls covering a federal witness??"

"Apparently, there is a fugitive the Marshalls are very interested in getting their hands on, and they thought if this guy knew where this Collucci was being hidden, he would make a play to kill him."

"What does this have to do with me, Kate?" She ignored my question.

"What are you going to do now, Rick?"

"I'm going to finish this Kate. Two people that were involved in this got away and I'm going to hunt them down and kill them."

"Can't you just walk away Rick? Can't you just leave it alone and walk away? For me?"

"Kate, I will walk away, but before I do, I have to finish this. I can't walk away with a job unfinished. You would never walk away from an unfinished job, would you?"

Again, she ignored my question. "I met with Phillips

this morning. There is a ten million dollar reward on your head Rick. Three crime families have put out on the wire that anyone that brings your head to the commission will be rewarded with ten million dollars." I was speechless. I didn't know where this was going. Kate continued

"Everyone will be hunting you, Rick. Everyone. Can't you just walk away?

"Kate, DiFlippo's not dead. He' still in a coma, but the prognosis is good. The doctors believe he'll come out of it. The reason he was attacked was because everyone thought I was dead. I have to finish this to protect him. I have to finish this for me, Kate. I've never left a job unfinished. When this is over, when this is all done, I want to be with you Kate, if you'll have me."

"Rick, every person in the criminal underworld will be hunting for you. Do you understand that? Someone fed your information to the U.S Marshall's service. They are quietly searching for you too. The other guy that got away? He was one of the people's brother's we killed at the farmhouse. He's now in charge of that white supremacist group. He's spreading through the white supremacist groups that anyone that brings him your head will get a reward. Rick, everyone is looking to kill you."

"So be it. Let them hunt. I'll also be hunting. I have Geoff watching the money that was stolen from DiFlippo. I'll find the other person involved in this and finish it. I don't care who is hunting me. I can't be with you until this over. Kate, do you want to be with me?"

"I do Rick, I do. I'm afraid you'll be killed before we can be together. I'm afraid that once we are together, you'll be bored or another issue will come up and you'll continue working for DiFlippo. If I wait for you Rick, will you be able to walk away from everything to be with me?"

"I know how lucky I am to have you in my life and my future. Let me finish this so we can be together."

"I love you Rick. Please don't get yourself killed."

I told Kate I loved her, because I did. I kissed her on the cheek, then the lips and left the hospital. I had a price on my head and was the most hunted man in America. It didn't matter. I had a job to finish so I could be with Kate. That was all that mattered to me now, being with Kate.

When my family was taken from me, I was lost. I loved my family so much I killed for them. Kate loved me so much; she was willing to die for me. That revelation alone brought me to my knees. I would finish this last job and then walk away. I didn't know what I would do with the rest of my life, and I didn't care. As long as I had Kate by my side, I knew I would be fine.

I pulled out of the hospital's parking lot and picked up my cell phone. I scrolled through my contact list and found the number I was looking for. I punched the phone number, and listened as the phone on the other end of the line rang. I thought about what I had to do as I waited for the call to be connected.

ACKNOWEDGMENTS

First, I'd like to thank all the great people at Buffalo Trace Bourbon Whiskey for allowing me to use their image on the cover for this book. I asked them to be my sponsor because they really are my favorite bourbon! THANK YOU!

Writing a book is a journey with many stops along the way. I am thankful & grateful for all the support I have gotten during that journey.

I have to give a special heartfelt THANK YOU to my wonderful Aunt Shirley Zastrow for editing this book. I can't thank you enough for all of your help and direction. Any errors that remain, and there are always errors, are mine and mine alone.

I have to also thank my parents, Larry & Gayle DiRienzo. Thank you Mom for doing the first rewrite of this novel for me. Thank you Dad for giving a read through and offering suggestions. This book wouldn't have been as good without your help.

I have to thank Chef Rob Nelson & all the great people at Tusk & Trotter American Brasserie. Thank you for allowing me to host the release Party of The Fisherman and agreeing to host release party of The Reaper.

Speaking of Tusk & Trotter, the cover of this book was taken at their awesome restaurant. Thank you De Anna Dray for getting up WAY TOO early on a Saturday morning to kill a few hours to help me out. I sincerely appreciate all if your help & patience!

As always, my biggest thank you goes out to you, my readers. You all are really the best. Seriously. You all make writing worth it. Thank you for your kind words of support, inspiration and criticism. I am humbled by the interest everyone has shown in The Fisherman & Rick Stevens.

You're the reason why this 2nd novel is here. I had only planned on writing one novel with Rick Stevens. He's a great character, and one we all can identify with on some level. We've all lost our faith in something at one time or another.

I was surprised at all the questions from everyone on what was going to happen next with him. At the time, I thought "Nothing" as I was already off and writing about a new set of characters based in Las Vegas.

I was happy to let everyone interpret the ending of The Fisherman for themselves. Did Rick Stevens find redemption or not? The truth was, I didn't know.

All of the questions I kept getting asked made me start thinking…Did Stevens have more to share? Was there more to his story? I poured a glass of Buffalo Trace over three cubes of ice and opened a blank page on my laptop.

Here is part #2 of what I *think* will be a three part series. You never know with Stevens though. I hope you enjoy reading this as much as I enjoyed writing it.

Mark DiRienzo – November 2013

ABOUT THE AUTHOR

Mark D. DiRienzo was born & raised in Niagara Falls, New York. Shortly after his 22nd birthday, he moved to Las Vegas, Nevada. During his eight years in Las Vegas, he embarked on many adventures and worked in many industries.

He specialized in security, law enforcement, investigations, casino surveillance, and corrections. He was fortunate enough to work for several companies that paid him to travel the Western Half of the United States.

He now calls Northwest Arkansas home. When he is not running a team of insurance investigators, he can be found watching his son's soccer games or hanging out with is super awesome Wife, Danielle. They share their house with a happy, rambunctious boxer pup named Charlie.

If you would like to contact him, please do. You can visit him on Facebook at Mark D. DiRienzo-Books. He maintains his own Facebook page and responds to all messages. For a more traditional approach, drop him a line:

Mark D. DiRienzo
PO BOX 2762
Bentonville AR 72712

He can also be found on Amazon.com or at his own E-Store at: www.createspace.com/3626400